Volk

The
Sitter

Also by R. L. Stine
Published by Ballantine Books

EYE CANDY

The Sitter

R. L. Stine

BALLANTINE BOOKS • NEW YORK

A Ballantine Book
Published by The Random House Publishing Group

Copyright © 2003 by R. L. Stine
Excerpt from *Eye Candy* Copyright © 2004 by R. L. Stine

All rights reserved under International and Pan-American Copyright Conventions. Published in the United States by Ballantine Books, an imprint of The Random House Publishing Group, a division of Random House, Inc., New York, and simultaneously in Canada by Random House of Canada Limited, Toronto.

Ballantine and colophon are registered trademarks of Random House, Inc.

www.ballantinebooks.com

ISBN 0-345-47654-9

Manufactured in the United States of America

First Trade Paperback Edition: July 2003
First Mass Market Edition: October 2004

OPM 9 8 7 6 5 4 3 2 1

For Matt Stine,
my twenty-something adviser and new
reader

The
Sitter

Prologue

We stepped into the shade of the pine trees. My sandals slid over the thick blanket of needles on the ground. The air always grows colder as we pass the guest house.

I glanced at the dark windows, caked with too much dust to reflect the light. The sour odor of the mold-crusted shingles made me hold my breath.

What an ugly place. I tried not to think about the stories I'd heard about the guest house. I knew they couldn't be true.

Why don't Chip and Abby just tear it down? Why let it stand here, rotting?

Beyond the guest house stood a rolling, grassy sand dune. Beyond the dune—the glorious ocean beach.

"Thirsty," Heather said. "Thirsty." She rode on my shoulders, legs wrapped around my neck. Her hands tugged my hair.

"Heather, sweetie, please let go of my ponytail," I said softly.

"Thirsty."

"Sweetie, wait till we get to the beach. We're almost there. We always have our juice boxes at the beach—remember?"

"Thirsty. Thirsty."

Two-year-olds know a lot of words. But none of them is *wait*.

She suddenly changed her tune. "Play? Play in the little house?"

"No, we don't want to play in that dirty old house," I said. "We want to go to the beach, right?"

Brandon's hand slid out of mine. He moved behind me and grabbed the bag of beach toys with both hands. I staggered back as he began to tug it.

"Brandon—what are you doing? Stop! You're going to pull me over."

He ignored me and pulled again, harder. "Brandon, please stop, honey. You're going to pull my head off! The bag is wrapped around my neck!"

I dropped the umbrella and blanket. Reached up both hands, grabbed Heather by the waist, and lowered her to the ground.

"Pick me up! Pick me up!"

I ignored her and turned to Brandon. "What are you doing? What do you want?" I dipped my shoulder and allowed him to pull the bag off my neck. "There you go. Now what?"

He dropped to the ground and bent over it, struggling with both hands to pull it open.

"Brandon, honey, don't you want to go to the beach? We want to have fun at the beach, don't we?"

His dark eyes narrowed in concentration. He has a narrow, intense face, and his big, round eyes and tensed lips always make him look worried or afraid.

He worked at the bag until he managed to rip it open. He held it upside down and shook it hard, sending the plastic shovels and buckets and cups and sand molds spilling onto the ground.

"Brandon, this is *so* not helpful," I said. I made a grab for the mesh bag, now empty, but Brandon tossed it onto a clump of tall grass.

He grabbed a shovel, the biggest one, and took off, running awkwardly in his blue flip-flops, back toward the guest house. His baggy swimsuit, black with a yellow Nike swoosh on one leg, had slid down on his slim frame and threatened to fall off as he ran.

"Brandon, honey—stay away from there!" What on earth was he thinking?

Raising both arms to me, Heather let out a wail. "*My* shovel! *Mine*. Give *back*!"

I let out a frustrated sigh and ran after Brandon. He dropped onto his knees in a clump of weeds and began digging furiously in a patch of soft, sandy ground.

"Uh, Brandon? Hel-lo?"

The curly, dark hair bounced on his head as he worked. His breath escaped in shallow wheezes, almost groans.

The sand flew. He didn't raise his eyes.

"Brandon, Heather and I want to go to the beach." I bent down and tried to take the plastic shovel from him. But he jerked it away and spun his back to me. He lowered the plastic shovel, both hands wrapped around the handle now, and then tossed up a shower of sand.

I crossed my arms and stood beside him, watching him work. Sweat rolled down his pale forehead. He was breathing through his open mouth—"Unh . . . unh . . . unh . . ."—grunting with each shovel stroke.

And then a soft *thud*. The edge of the plastic shovel hit something. And Brandon jumped, eyes suddenly wide, and jabbed the shovel in again. Another *thud*, louder this time.

"What is it? What's down there? Buried treasure?" I asked, leaning over the shallow hole. "Maybe you've found a pirate's chest filled with gold! Wouldn't that be cool?"

Brandon ignored me.

He lowered the shovel with both hands, scraping sand away, shoving it furiously from the hole. "Unh . . . unh . . ." Sand flew over the weeds, over my sandals.

"Unh . . . Unh . . . unh . . ."

And then I saw something curl up from the hole, as if reaching from beneath the ground. Something slender and white and curved and . . .

The cloud pulled away from the sun. Bright white light flooded over us. So bright, I squinted behind my sunglasses and stared at what Brandon had unearthed. So white and bleached out in the sunlight, like an over-exposed snapshot.

But still clear. Still chillingly clear.

I couldn't help it. I had to scream. So many horrors . . . Since I arrived here, I'd faced so many horrors. And now this . . .

My chest started to heave. I couldn't breathe.

But, whoa. No way I could let go. Not with Brandon and Heather there.

I had to be the grown-up. I had to protect them somehow. So I swallowed hard, swallowed my cry. Swallowed again, my throat dry as sand.

I dropped to my knees. I slid an arm around Brandon's slender waist and gazed down.

A rib cage, poking up from the yellow sand, glowing in the white light, shimmering and unreal. Bones buried in such a shallow grave behind the guest house.

I felt Brandon tremble. Jumping to my feet, I hoisted

him up and spun him away. But he twisted his body, kept his eyes down, kept his eyes on the curled, white bones.

Still silent. Still breathing so fast, I could feel his hummingbird heartbeats.

Who is buried here? How did he know about it?

Are the stories about the guest house true?

Still holding him, I lowered my face to Brandon's ear. "Brandon, honey, are you okay?" I whispered.

He didn't answer.

And behind me, sounding so far away, miles and miles away, I heard Heather's chant: "Mommy's bones! Mommy's bones!"

PART ONE

PART ONE

1

What are you drinking?" I shouted.

My friend Teresa stared back at me. We had moved to the bar in the corner of the club, but it wasn't much quieter over here.

"*What are you drinking?*"

She squinted at me. "Huh?"

"*What . . . are . . . you . . . drinking?*" I screamed over the music.

"Oh." Teresa held up her glass. The ice cubes jangled in a dark liquid, darker and thicker than Coke. "It's Red Bull and Jägermeister. Here. Try it, El."

She shoved the glass into my hand. I took a sip, swallowed, and felt my face shrivel up. "It's disgusting. That's the worst thing I ever tasted."

She smiled. "I know." She took back the glass and raised it, toasting me.

The place was called Beach Club, even though it was nowhere near a beach. We were on Second Avenue on the East Side of Manhattan. It was our favorite club, our subterranean hideaway where we escaped nearly every weekend.

My name is Ellie Saks, and I'm twenty-four years old. Why do I need a subterranean hideaway? Don't ask.

A long metal stairway, dark and kind of creaky, like a subway entrance, led down to the club. And when we got to the bottom, our heels clicking on the rickety metal steps, we found ourselves in this amazing place, all silver and chrome and lights and mirrors.

Rows of silver tables and booths stretched along both walls, with the dance floor between them. Couples jammed the wide dance floor. Red and white lights pulsed in time to the throbbing dance music.

An enormous ceiling mirror reflected the dancers and the lights. Following Teresa to the curving chrome bar in the back, I had stared up at the upside-down dancers and thought it might be fun to be up there with them, graceful and oblivious, safe from the chaos below.

The bar was full, but two tall, long-haired girls in embroidered red halter tops and short shorts stood up just as we arrived, and we grabbed their high-backed stools. I ordered my usual glass of chardonnay. Then I made the mistake of tasting Teresa's drink.

I kept swallowing, trying to get rid of the taste. "It tastes like . . . bubble gum and Robitussin."

Teresa tilted the glass to her mouth and took a long drink. "Hey, you got it. Cough medicine. Yeah." She laughed.

She has a high, hoarse laugh, sort of like a little boy's. She doesn't look like a little boy, though. She's tall and a little plump, with sexy big green eyes, and piles of long, coppery curls streaked with blond, hair that she's always playing with, tossing from side to side.

"Everyone's drinking it. Know who introduced me to it? Ellie, remember Paulo? The guy in the mail room?"

I set my glass of chardonnay down on the bar. "You went out with Paulo?"

Teresa nodded, grinning.

"Does he speak English?" I asked.

"I'm not sure. The bar he took me to was as noisy as this one. I couldn't really hear a word he said. Then we went back to his place. On Avenue A, I think. But he didn't talk much."

I shook my head. "Teresa, why did you go out with him?"

She coiled and uncoiled a thick lock of hair. "I wanted to see the *rest* of his tattoos."

We both laughed.

I turned the stem of the wineglass between my fingers. "And? Go on. Tell. *Did* you see them?"

She nodded. "Yes. But it didn't work out. When I read one that he had down there—you know, *down there*—I had to leave."

"Excuse me? What did it say?"

"*M-O-M.*"

I shouldn't have taken a drink. White wine went spewing out my nose. I was sputtering and choking and laughing, all at the same time.

The guy next to me turned around. "Are you okay?"

My eyes had teared up, but I could still see that this guy was drop-dead gorgeous. Sort of a young Brad Pitt, with a curl of streaky brown hair falling casually over his forehead and a stubble of beard over his boyish cheeks.

"I'll probably survive," I said, wiping my nose with

my hand. I reached for a cocktail napkin on the bar and knocked the wineglass over.

But he caught it before it spilled.

"Wow. Good hands," I said.

His blue eyes flashed. "I'd better have. I'm going to be a surgeon in another two years." He slid the wineglass back to me.

Okay.

Teresa and I had been hanging out at this club for months. And yet, somehow this was the first time a movie-star surgeon-to-be had said hello to me. Maybe things were looking up.

He leaned closer, bringing his face close to mine, so close I got a strong whiff of his Gio cologne. He breathed into my ear, "Maybe I could operate on *you* tonight."

I knew Teresa was watching this whole exchange intently. I could feel her breath on the back of my neck.

I slid away from the Love Doctor. "Could I offer you some advice?"

His eyes narrowed. "Advice? You mean, don't ever say that line again?"

I nodded.

We both laughed. He clinked his Heineken bottle against my wineglass. "One-to-nothing, you," he said. He didn't take his blue eyes from mine. He didn't even blink. "You're kinda pretty."

I smiled. "So are you."

He didn't react to that at all. I guess he hears it a lot.

"You'll have to cut me some slack tonight," he said. "I spent the whole day with cadavers."

I took a sip of chardonnay. "Is that your second-best pickup line?"

I know. I should have been nicer to him. I could feel

Teresa's disapproval, feel her eyes burning through the back of my blouse. She'd been trying her best to find me a new boyfriend, and here I was, letting her down.

I took a sip of wine and decided to show some interest. "Which med school do you go to?" I asked.

He emptied his beer bottle, set it down, and then grinned at me. Perfect teeth, of course. "I'm taking a home-study course."

I laughed. "You're getting funnier."

"Actually, NYU," he said. He signaled the bartender for another Heineken and ordered another glass of wine for me. He stuck out his hand for me to shake. "I'm Bernie."

Bernie? With that face? How can he be a Bernie?

"Ellie," I said. His hand was cold from the beer bottle.

I took a long sip of wine. Someone bumped me from behind. I heard Teresa groan. A hand grabbed my shoulder. "Ellie, hey. Here you are."

I let go of Bernie's hand and spun around. And stared into a familiar face, its red cheeks glistening with sweat, eyes cloudy, furry eyebrows moving up and down rapidly, as if alive.

"Clay? What are *you* doing here?"

"Looking for you, naturally."

"Whoa, listen—"

Teresa stuck her face between us. "I don't think she wants to see you."

Clay blinked several times, as if clearing his head. He frowned at Teresa. "Who are you?"

He swayed a little, still holding on to my shoulder.

Clay's friends call him Bear because—well, he looks like a bear. He's stocky and broad-chested, with muscular arms and legs, covered with dark brown hair. He has a round, boyish face, with red cheeks you want to pinch. Wiry brown hair on his head, cut short like fur, and round gray eyes under thick brown eyebrows.

I used to think of him as a cute teddy bear, but I don't now. After I told him I didn't want to go out with him anymore, Clay stopped being cute.

He started calling me night and day, following me, showing up at my apartment in the middle of the night, totally wasted and strung out, sending flowers and gifts, flooding me with e-mails, begging, pleading.

It took me a long while to realize he was stalking me. I mean, it's not exactly something that happens to you all the time.

And then when I finally figured it out, I didn't know how to deal with him. You see, I never meant for it to get serious.

Clay was one of the first guys I met when I moved to New York. He took me out to restaurants and to Knicks games at the Garden, jazz clubs in the Village. It was great to be living in New York City and have someone to be with on weekends.

He was an intense kind of guy. But I never stopped to realize how serious he was becoming. And then when I knew I had to get out of it, I tried to explain it all to him. I tried to be nice. I didn't want to hurt him.

I just wanted him to be gone.

And now he had his arms around me, and I tumbled off the bar stool. He was holding on to me, grinning, his eyes glassy, unfocused. "Just one dance, Ellie."

"Clay, you're totally wasted, aren't you," I said, struggling to loosen his hold.

"Maybe. I guess I'm a little fucked up. Hey, I have some little pills we could share."

"Excuse me?"

He pulled me with both hands. He was very strong. His shirt was open. I could see sweat glistening on his carpet of chest hair. "Maybe we could talk. You know. Just . . . talk."

"On the dance floor? Clay, I can't hear a thing."

We stumbled into other dancers. His face grew even redder under the pulsing lights, like a bomb about to explode.

The music repeated:

Y'all ready for this?
Y'all ready for this?

No, I'm not ready for this. I didn't want to dance with Clay. I didn't want him to pull me away, his eyes so crazy, his whole body so desperate, sweating like that.

I gazed up at the dancers in the ceiling mirror. I wanted to be up there with them.

"Maybe we could talk, Ellie."

"No. Really—"

"Just fucking talk."

I turned back to the bar and saw that Teresa had slid onto my stool. She had her hand on Bernie's, she was tossing her hair back and forth, and they were talking and laughing together.

Good luck, Teresa. Why should tonight be a total waste for *both* of us?

"Stop pulling me, Clay. I don't want to dance."

I don't think he heard me over the throbbing music. He pressed his hot face against my cheek. "I've got some X, Ellie. Do you want it? Let's take it, huh? I've got Ecstasy. We could take it together and have a good talk."

"Clay, you know I'm not into that," I said sharply. "You know I don't do that stuff. Why are you always trying—?"

In the middle of the dance floor, but we weren't dancing, and Teresa seemed a million miles away. Poor Clay. He's not a bad guy, really. He could be someone's teddy bear. He could. But why does he care so much about me? We saw each other for less than a year, and it wasn't even an exclusive thing. So why does he care so much?

I feel sorry for him now. Is that why I let him pull me out of the club? Or is it the wine? Did I have three glasses or four?

Up the stairs and out onto Second Avenue and into a taxi. He's squeezing my hand so tight, like he's never going to let go.

"We said good-bye, remember?"

Doesn't he hear a word I say?

"We'll have a good talk, Ellie. We were always so open and honest with each other."

We were?

He's so sad. I've made him so sad.

And now we're walking up the steps to the brownstone where he lives, bumping each other, leaning on each other. "Just one last time," he's whispering.

And we're in his stuffy, cluttered one-bedroom apartment on the second floor. I'm staring at the travel posters on the wall, British Rail posters, trains arriving at cold-looking, stony beach towns. Why does he like these posters?

I let him pull me to his bedroom. Yes, I let him. My head still throbs from the club music. The floor tilts as he leads me.

Y'all ready for this?
Y'all ready for this?

He's undressing me. "Clay—please . . ."

He's undressing me so feverishly with those clumsy bear paws.

I'm letting him. Yes, I know. I should fight or scream or something. But I'm letting him.

My glittery top. My short black skirt. He's pawing at my skirt, tugging it down as he leans over me, pushing me onto the unmade bed.

"One last time," he whispers, his breath so hot and wet in my ear. His dark eyes spinning. "Ellie, please . . . one last time."

No. This is wrong, Clay. No. Stop.

Did I say the words? Or did I only think them?

His hand between my legs. Then he pulls down my black underpants. "One last time."

No. Don't.

I'm only thinking the words.

I'm letting him . . . letting him. My underpants are around my ankles. And he's on top of me now. And now he's in me. Now . . . now . . . now . . . now . . .

What is he saying?

He's talking rapidly, talking, moving on top of me, and talking the whole time. But I can't hear the words. I can't hear his voice.

And once again, I see the blond boy in his place.

Once again, I see the blond boy moving on top of me, not Clay. The adorable blond boy, so light and fair, like a fine, pale deer.

Not Clay. No, not heavy, bearish Clay.

The blond boy is here again, and Clay disappears.

And I'm sliding, sliding, sliding into a kind of dream-world. Only I don't slide all the way because I know what I'm doing. . . .

I know the blond boy isn't making love to me.

I know the blond boy is a ghost.

But I don't care. I want him there. After all these years, I still want him.

After all these years.

And now Clay is finished. I hear him groan and see him lifting himself off me.

Why do I let him take advantage of me? My under-pants still knotted around one ankle. I don't want to be here.

I let him . . . I let him . . .

He slides beside me. Presses his hot mouth against my cheek.

I take a deep breath. I don't know if I can breathe in here. "Clay . . . this is the last time," I whisper.

His lips are against my ear. "You can't get away from me, Ellie."

"No, Clay. Listen—"

"You fucking can't get away. I won't let you."

But I'm already gone.

Did I say the words? Or did I just think them?

2

The next morning—a windy, gray Saturday in late May. I called my mom.

I call my mom once a week, and she always acts surprised to hear from me. Like it's been a year or two since we spoke.

First we do the weather report. "It's kind of blustery here in New York, Mom. Not like summer yet. I think it's going to rain. How is it in Madison?"

Cold, of course. It's always cold in Madison. Well, except for those few months when it's swelteringly hot, and the humidity off the lake practically knocks you over.

Then I ask about my cat, Lucky. I miss Lucky so much. I've had him since I was twelve, but I had to leave him behind when I moved to New York. "How is Lucky, Mom?"

"He's okay. How should he be?"

Then I get the report on Wendy, my successful, hardworking, married, nearly rich, fucking yuppie of an older sister, whose stupid, sacred shadow I walk in. And don't you ever let me forget it, Mom.

"Wendy and Noah bought a BMW, an adorable little convertible. I hate to tell you what it costs."

Oh, go ahead and tell me, Mom. You know you're *dying* to.

Then she asks me what I'm doing, and her voice changes—it suddenly sounds as if she just stepped in dog poop. "Ellie, dear, what's new? Are you still temping at that stockbroker's?"

"Well, I'm still temping, Mom. But the stockbroker thing ended. So I'm going to be starting somewhere new."

"I thought you had a friend there. That young woman you mentioned. Teresa something. She was going to find you a real job there."

"Teresa's only a secretary, Mom. She really doesn't have enough pull to get me a job."

"Oh, I see. I didn't realize you were working at such a low level. And I guess you couldn't get a real job on your own?"

"Uh . . . well . . . I enjoy temping, Mom. Really. And I . . . I'm still trying to work things out."

"Still hung up in the past? You're really saying this to me? What year is this? Did I fall into a time warp? Are we living some kind of science-fiction movie where I'm doomed to live the same scene over and over?"

"Mom. Come on. I didn't call to argue."

"What's past is past."

"Mom—"

"Why don't you get a tattoo like all the other crazy people your age? You could tattoo that on your forehead: *What's past is past.* You ran off to New York to forget it all, am I right?"

"I didn't run off. I made a decision, and I moved here. Give me a break, Mom. I'm trying."

"You're trying? You're trying my patience, that's what you're trying."

"Ha ha. You're such a comedian, Mom."

"Then how come I talk to you and I want to cry?"

"Please. I'm really trying to get over the past. I need a real change. You know. A fresh start."

"Ellie, you're twenty-four. You're going to run out of fresh starts soon."

"Thanks for the encouragement, Mom."

"Listen to me—"

"Mom, I'm sorry. Got to go. I have another call."

Sometimes I say that just to get off the phone. But this time, I really did have another call.

"Ellie, I didn't get to tell you about your dad's root canal. Three hours in the chair. You wouldn't believe the pain that poor man—"

"Mom, please. It's beeping. I have to take this call. Bye."

I clicked her off, but I knew her raspy, two-packs-a-day voice would ring in my ears for the next hour or two.

"Hello?"

"Hey, babe. It's me. Clay. I was thinking maybe we could get together tonight."

3

The next Saturday, Teresa called and said to come over and we'd do lunch or something. I hadn't seen her since that night at Beach Club.

What would I say if she asked me what happened with Clay? Could I tell her the truth? No way. Too embarrassing.

I pulled on a pair of pale blue chinos and a navy polo shirt and swept my hair into place with my hand. Then I stepped outside into a warm, sparkly day—June first, and summer was just about here!—and began to walk up West End Avenue.

In a windowsill, some late daffodils swung gently in the soft, warm breeze. Someone had planted red and purple tulips around the trees that lined the avenue. Two blond-haired boys zipped past me on their silver Razor scooters, jackets flying behind them.

How could I know that this was the day that all the horror would begin?

Teresa lives on West Eightieth Street, just a few doors down from the legendary H & H Bagels store. H & H has its ovens going twenty-four hours a day, and the wonderful aroma of baking bagels floats up the block—and into Teresa's windows. She says she'll never move.

She shares a three-bedroom apartment with two other women in an old building with a marble lobby and an elevator that creaks and groans and barely makes it to the eighth floor. Teresa and her roommates have covered the walls of the apartment with movie posters and furnished the place with things from IKEA, a few old chairs found on the street, and a massive, brown leather couch that sits in the middle of the living room. No one is sure how it got there.

The kitchen is about the size of a phone booth—no kidding. They have to go in there one at a time or they might get stuck. But like a lot of the older West Side apartments, the ceilings are high, the windows are tall, and the rest of the rooms are big and comfortable.

Sarah, one of Teresa's roommates, answered the door. "Just heading out for a run," she said, slipping past me. "Teresa's in her room."

I found Teresa sitting sideways on her bed, legs crossed, leaning against the wall. She wore a green-and-white-striped tank top over faded denim jeans. She had her hair piled up, a green bandanna tied around it. She had no makeup on, which made her face very pale, her green eyes even more prominent than usual.

She raised the Mary Higgins Clark book from her lap. "Ellie—hi. Have you read this one?"

"Nope. I haven't read any mysteries since Nancy Drew."

Teresa snickered. "You used to read those things? They were so old-fashioned and dorky."

"I know. But I didn't care. I read a whole bunch of them. I loved them. I loved solving the mystery before Nancy did. But my mom made me stop reading them. She said I had to start reading *real* books."

"Well, this is a really good mystery," Teresa said. "I'm almost done, and I can't figure out who the stalker is."

Of course that made me think of Clay.

"Hey, I miss you at work," Teresa said, pulling me from my thoughts. "I got used to seeing you every day. You know. Having lunch together and everything. Did the agency send you to another job?"

I shook my head. "No. I'm still waiting by the phone."

"I asked Mrs. Snow if she had anything for you. Full-time. But she said there's a hiring freeze."

"Teresa, that's so nice of you."

She shrugged. "Hey, we're pals, right?"

Teresa and I had met at Charles Schwab the previous December. I was temping for the woman who had the cubicle next to Teresa's. Teresa and I started talking over the cubicle wall—we hadn't even seen each other yet—and pretty soon we were laughing and gossiping and having a great time.

I was so glad to make a new friend, a real friend. My first year in the big city, and it was hard to get to know people. Most people I met seemed to be racing from place to place, too busy to make new friends.

Of course, I had hooked up with Clay. But that wasn't like having a friend. Not anymore, anyway.

I spun the chair away from her dressing table and sat down. I found myself staring at Teresa's giant poster of Johnny Depp.

"Why didn't I notice that before?" I asked.

"It's new." She grinned. "You like?"

I studied it. He had his slick, black hair plastered straight back, and he stared out with deep, dark, sad eyes. "Teresa, why Johnny Depp?"

"Because he's not human," she said, staring at it with

me. "He's a Martian or something. See his face? It's perfect."

I opened my mouth to say something, but she didn't give me a chance.

"No. Really. I mean, it's perfect. Look at *that* side; then look at *that* side. You see? It's symmetrical. Both sides are the same. He's the only human in the universe who has a perfectly symmetrical face."

I nodded. "I see you've made a real study of this."

"Ellie, how many times in life do you see total perfection?"

"Speaking of that," I said, "what happened between you and Bernie last Friday night?"

She turned away slowly from Johnny Depp. "Bernie? Oh. You mean the Swingin' Surgeon? He wasn't interested in me. He lost interest after you left. I guess he likes you Winona Ryder types."

"Excuse me? Winona Ryder? What the hell does that mean?"

"Well, you know. You're kinda waifish, El. You've got the big round eyes and the straight black hair, and the . . . uh . . . tiny body."

Waifish?

"Besides, Bernie was engaged or something," Teresa said.

She folded down the page in the book and tossed it onto the bed table. Then she picked up a pack of Parliament Lights, slid a cigarette into her mouth, and lit it with a plastic lighter.

"Hey, what happened with Clay that night? Did you have trouble getting rid of him?" she asked.

"Uh . . . a little," I said.

"Talk about clueless," Teresa said, sending a cloud

of smoke into Johnny Depp's perfect face. "What happened?"

"Well, we talked for a while," I said. "But I don't know if I got through to him or not."

And that was about as close to the truth as I could bear to admit.

Blinking away Teresa's cigarette smoke, I saw pictures of that night, of Clay's apartment, of Clay . . .

I let him.

I let him.

"He . . . he's still haunting me," I said. "He's still stalking me. He won't leave me alone."

I picked up a Magic 8 Ball from Teresa's vanity. I turned it upside down. It answered, REPLY HAZY, TRY AGAIN before I even asked it a question.

Teresa took a long drag on her cigarette, her eyes narrowed, studying me. She let the smoke out slowly. "You should call the police, Ellie."

I sat up and shook my head. "I just want to get away from here for a while," I said. "You know. Get away from Clay. Get out of the city. Did I tell you that my sublet is up the end of May?"

"That's in two weeks."

"Tell me about it. In two weeks, I have to pack up and—"

"You could move in here for a week or so. You could sleep on the couch, I guess."

"Thanks. You're great."

"Whoa. Wait." Teresa jumped up, stubbed the cigarette on the bed table's ashtray, and turned, suddenly excited. "Here's one thing you could do that would be fun. You could join our summer share in the Hamptons. I think there are still some places open. That would be awesome!"

I shook the Magic 8 Ball. Once again, it said, REPLY HAZY, TRY AGAIN. Maybe it was in a rut—like me.

"I can't," I told Teresa. "I can't afford a summer share in the Hamptons. Besides, that's only weekends, right? Where would I live during the week? On the beach? I'm nearly broke. I can't keep temping. I have to find a real job."

Teresa took the Magic 8 Ball from my hand. She started pacing back and forth over the patchy, brown rug, tossing the plastic ball from hand to hand.

"Oh, I know," she said, stopping and dropping down beside a small bookcase beside the window. "Hold on. I think I still have them."

I stood up and crossed the room to her. On the windowsill, two pigeons were parading back and forth, strutting, cooing, bumping each other.

"Have what?" I asked.

She pulled out a stack of newspapers. "From the Hamptons. I used them to find my summer share. Maybe we can find you a job out there, Ellie. Wouldn't that be cool?"

"I don't understand," I said. "If I get a job in the Hamptons—"

"We'll find you a cheap place to live," Teresa said. "Then we can hang out together all summer. Partying on the beach every weekend? Endless guys? Endless sun? It'll be excellent—just like in those beach movies, only real life."

She took the first newspaper, the *Southampton Press*, and handed it to me. "Check it out. The job ads are in the back."

The paper was bigger than the *New York Times*. It

took me a while to find the right section. I saw listings for a couple of sales jobs in Southampton boutiques. It didn't sound so appealing to me, but Teresa made me call.

Both jobs were already filled.

"This isn't working," I said, folding up the newspaper.

Teresa tossed the plastic ball at me. I made a fumbling catch before it sailed into the wall. "What's wrong with you, El? You give up after only two calls?"

"The whole idea is crazy," I protested. "I don't think—"

"Give me that." She grabbed the newspaper. "I'll read the ads. You just dial the numbers."

After six or seven more unsuccessful attempts, I called a store in Watermill called Country Modes. A woman with a hoarse, scratchy voice answered. "Country Modes. How may I direct your call?"

I don't want you to direct my call, I thought. I just want to speak to you.

"I saw your ad in the newspaper," I said. "Are you still hiring?"

"Yes, we are, dear."

After so many loser calls, the answer took me by surprise. "You . . . have a job?"

"Yes, we do."

I flashed Teresa a thumbs-up. "I'm interested," I said. "I'm looking for a full-time job. What do I have to do?"

"Just come in and fill out an application."

"That's all? It's a sales job?"

"Yes, dear. Do you have any sales experience?"

"Oh, sure," I lied.

"Well, when can you start? Miss . . . uh—?"

"Saks. Ellie Saks. I guess I can start right away. I mean, in a week or two."

"That's very good. I'm writing down your name. My name is Sheila. Come in, fill out the form, bring some ID, I'll do a very short interview, just to get to know you a little, and then we can talk about your salary."

"Well, thank you very much, Sheila," I said. "Are you open tomorrow? Sunday?"

"Yes, we are, dear. See you tomorrow."

I was grinning when I hung up the phone. "You were right. It was easy!"

Teresa and I slapped high fives.

"You want to go tomorrow?" Teresa asked. "I'll go with you. I'm in a new share house this summer, and I haven't even seen it yet. I'll drop you off in Watermill and go check it out. We can spend the day. I'll show you the beach and everything."

"Excellent! Thanks," I said.

"Party summer!" Teresa cried.

"Party summer!" we both chanted.

I picked up the Magic 8 Ball. "Are we going to have a great summer?" I asked. I shook it hard.

The words came up: REPLY HAZY, TRY AGAIN.

4

Teresa explained to me that the bus that travels from Manhattan to the Hamptons is called the Hampton Jitney. It makes several stops up and down the east side of the city. Then it makes its way across Long Island to the Hamptons. For a bus, it's very luxurious and comfortable, and they give everyone water and a snack. Real first class.

"This is the world-famous Long Island Expressway," Teresa announced, pointing out the window. "It's not bad today because there's no beach traffic—but wait till summer!"

I gazed out the window. I'd never been to Long Island before. We were at exit 38, and it looked pretty suburban. Trees lined the highway. Beyond them, I could see stores and small redbrick row houses.

The two women in the seat in front of us were talking loudly about a Botox party they'd attended. A man in a pin-striped suit sat in the seat across from us, tapping away on his laptop computer and muttering to himself.

I squeezed Teresa's hand. "Thanks for coming with me," I said. "You've been so nice to me. You're always helping me."

She shrugged. "I don't know. I guess that's my thing.

I had four younger brothers. You know, a big Italian family. I took care of them all. They called me Mommy Number Two. Really."

I laughed. "Well, thanks, Mommy Number Two."

Teresa raised her knees to the back of the seat in front of her. "Well, I rented a car in Southampton. So while you're having your job interview, I'm going to check out the share house. Then I'll come back and pick you up."

The woman in front of us said, "The Botox needle slipped, and now she can't open her eyes and she can't move her mouth."

"Omigod," her friend exclaimed. "That is so ironic."

"Are you nervous?" Teresa asked. "About the job interview?"

I shrugged. "Not really. It sounds like a done deal."

Teresa coiled a thick strand of hair around her hand. "A sales job in one of those trendy boutiques could be fun. Bet you'll meet some interesting people."

"Probably," I said, keeping my eyes out the window. "I need a real job. Something steady with regular hours, you know." I turned to Teresa. "I need some kind of success. I mean, I really have to show myself something. I mean . . . well . . . I don't really know what I mean."

I sighed. Teresa was studying me.

"I've kinda wasted the past few years," I said.

She waited for me to explain. But I didn't. "Let's talk about you," I said. "Did you really live your whole life in Brooklyn?"

She told me about growing up in a crowded apartment in the Bensonhurst area of Brooklyn with her parents and her four younger brothers. The rest of her big, noisy Italian family—cousins, grandparents, aunts, and uncles—all lived within a few blocks of each other.

"Every dinner was a festival," Teresa said. "I don't think my mother ever stopped stirring the big pot of tomato sauce on the stove!"

Growing up in such a crowd was fun for her, but it was hard to get noticed, hard to find her own identity. When Teresa announced that she planned to move across the river to Manhattan, her family reacted with shock. How could she even dream of leaving home before she was married?

"It probably seems like no big deal to someone from Wisconsin," Teresa said. "But crossing the East River was the hardest move of my life. My family is just so old-fashioned. I'm the first one to make the move. And here I am, working for a famous brokerage house on Park Avenue, living on the Upper West Side."

"That's so great," I said. "Such a nice story."

I thought of my mother—pretending she wanted me to stay, but so eager for me to leave Wisconsin, to leave home, to make a new start somewhere and take my sadness with me.

"And I'm not going to stay a secretary forever," Teresa said. "I'm saving my money. I'm going to get an MBA at Columbia. After that . . . well . . . we'll see."

The bus had turned off the expressway. We were on a narrower road now, rolling past wide, grassy fields interrupted by thick stands of pine trees.

Teresa took a long drink from her bottle of water. "I've been doing all the talking," she said. "Now it's your turn, Ellie."

I took a deep breath. "Well—"

My cell phone rang. I pulled it out of my bag and squinted at the caller ID. "Oh, no. It's Clay."

Teresa reached for my phone. "Don't answer it."

Too late. I'd already pushed the button. "Hi, Clay," I said, moaning the words. "What do you want?"

"Hi, babe. I just wondered when you're coming back."

"Huh?"

"When you're coming back to the city. I thought—"

"Clay, you know I don't want to see you. You know I'm not going to change my mind."

One of the Botox women turned around to stare at me. I guess I was talking pretty loudly. I sank back in the seat and lowered my voice. "Good-bye, Clay. I mean it. Good-bye."

I clicked off the phone. I glared at it for a moment as if it were to blame. My heart was pounding. I shoved the phone back into my bag.

"You should change your cell-phone number," Teresa said. "Maybe he'd take the hint."

"He doesn't take hints," I said bitterly. "He'd still find me."

"But it would make it harder for him," she said. She tossed back her hair. "Forget about Clay. Let's talk about all the new guys we're going to meet this summer."

She crossed her fingers. "I just know this is the summer I meet a really great guy. Someone I can really care about." She sighed. "I'm going to be twenty-six, Ellie. I'm really ready. Ready to meet the right guy. Maybe even settle down."

"Well, good luck," I said. "Maybe—"

"Maybe you'll meet someone, too. Then you really can forget about Clay."

"I wish. But how can I forget about him?" I asked, my throat tightening. I felt myself getting angry. "What makes you think he'll stay away? What makes you think he'll ever give up? I'm sick of him. Sick of all his bullshit and self-pity. He's out of control. He—"

"Ellie, please. We can deal with this."

"I feel like he's a hunter," I said. "He's a hunter and I'm the deer he's stalking. I feel like—"

The bus jolted hard.

Startled shouts all around. The squeal of tires.

Teresa and I flew hard into the seat in front of us. My shoulder hit, and pain shot up my arm. Across the aisle, I saw the man's laptop go sailing to the floor.

The bus windshield went dark. A heavy blackness, as if night had fallen.

A hard thud, and the bus bounced again.

"We hit someone!" a man shrieked.

And then I couldn't help myself. I couldn't stop it. I opened my mouth and let out a shrill scream of horror.

A scream from deep inside me. Not from today. A scream from years ago . . . A scream I'd been holding in for seven years.

5

I realized Teresa had hold of my shoulders. She tried to shake me. "Ellie, please. Stop! Stop screaming! Please stop. Ellie—!"

"It's only a deer!" I heard someone shout.

"Only a deer," Teresa repeated, holding on to me, her face close to mine, her green eyes wide with surprise, with confusion. "Only a deer. Please stop!"

Am I still screaming?

"Ellie, stop! Stop! It was only a deer."

The scream faded in my mouth. My throat ached. Something much deeper inside throbbed and hurt. Yes, the pain was still there.

I knew people were looking at me. I pretended I didn't see them. I turned back to Teresa. "I'm sorry," I whispered.

Teresa loosened her hold on my shoulders.

"I'm the frightened deer," I whispered, my throat raw and dry. "I was just saying it . . . how I'm like a deer. And now the deer is dead. Dead in the road. Oh, Teresa, this is such bad luck. Don't you see? It's really bad luck."

"Ellie, take a deep breath," Teresa said. "It's no such thing. The bus hit a deer, that's all. It's not like it's some kind of omen. You don't believe in that kind of stuff, do you?"

I took a deep breath and held it. I heard police sirens outside the window. The driver had climbed out of the bus. Some people were hurrying out to look at the dead deer.

I could see it. It had been thrown into tall grass beside the bus. It was just a fawn. It lay on its side. Its neck had snapped. White shoulder bones poked through the fur. The round black eyes were frozen wide in fright. And blood . . . I saw an ocean of blood.

Teresa held on to my hand. "Why did you scream like that? Ellie, it's like you were in a total panic. I couldn't get you to stop."

"I'm sorry. . . ."

How could I begin to describe it all? What should I tell her? Teresa was my friend, a good new friend. But how could I begin to tell her?

"I'm sorry," I repeated. "I was in a horrible crash. In high school. Ever since then, I—well . . . It was just so awful."

She let go of my hand. "Oh, my God. A car crash? How bad? What happened?"

"Yes, bad," I whispered, staring down at the floor. "It was a really bad crash. We went over an embankment. I—I was killed."

A long silence. Teresa stared hard at me, her face twisted with confusion. The bus had emptied. We were the only ones still in our seats.

"Killed?" Teresa finally choked out. "You?"

I swallowed. "Huh? Me? No. Oh . . . wow. Did I say that?"

Why did I say that? Why did I say that I was killed?

What kind of a slip was that? Did I really wish that I had been killed alongside Will?

No.

Of course not.

"Someone else was killed, Teresa," I said, steadying my voice, finally starting to breathe normally. "A guy. I mean, my boyfriend. His name was Will. My high school boyfriend. What a weird slip. I guess seeing the dead deer—"

"You know, there are a million deer in the Hamptons," Teresa said softly. "They're everywhere. And they're always getting hit by cars."

"Yes?" I didn't quite get her point.

"You were talking about feeling like a frightened deer. And then the bus hit a deer. But what I'm saying is, it happens all the time. It was not an omen, Ellie. It was just a coincidence."

I gazed out the window. The sun faded behind a cloud. Darkness rolled over the bus. "Yeah," I whispered. "Of course. Just a coincidence . . ."

6

Will's house was always neat and spotless. The floors sparkled. You could see your reflection. Everything clean and dusted and in its place.

I felt so intimidated whenever I stepped into his house. I always took my Doc Martens off at the door and walked in stocking feet. I knew Mrs. Davis, Will's mother, didn't approve of me. For one thing, I had crazy, purple-streaked hair, and I just let it flow wild and un-brushed behind my shoulders. And I dressed in baggy, loose-fitting outfits like everyone else at Menota North High.

Maybe it was just me. But I always felt that Will's mom was staring at me, watching what I touched, wait-ing for me to leave so she could wipe my fingerprints off the furniture.

I'm not making this up. I once saw her eat a Popsicle with a fork and knife. Who the hell does that?

It was a February afternoon. The temperature about two hundred below in Madison, not counting the wind-chill and the stiff gusts off the lake. Snow blowing and shifting in the wind, drifts to my knees.

Will led me to his house after school. I had a hooded

sweatshirt under my parka and two sweaters under that, and I was still shivering, too frozen to speak.

He gives me a quick, frozen-lipped kiss. He thinks it's funny. Two polar bears bumping noses.

And then we're inside his house, shoving the kitchen door closed behind us. My boots are dripping on the glowing kitchen linoleum—tough break, Mrs. Davis!— and I toss my wet parka down and start rubbing my arms, furiously rubbing the cold away.

Will puts on the kettle for instant coffee.

His mother is at work, and his sister is in an after-school program. So Will and I have the house to ourselves for a few hours in the afternoons.

We sometimes hurry up to his bathroom on the second floor where we open the window, no matter how cold it is outside. And we smoke pot. Yes, Mrs. Davis, the world is not a neat place. You cannot keep control of everything—not even your family—by keeping everything neat and clean.

It just doesn't work that way.

Will keeps the pot in the back of his sock drawer, and his mother has never found it. He buys it from a friend of his cousin's at the junior college. We smoke a joint, or maybe two, quickly, passing it back and forth, our heads at the bathroom window, the wind fluttering our hair.

What if she came home while we were smoking it? Or what if she smelled it?

Giggling, kissing, blinking to focus our eyes, we spray a lot of room freshener afterwards and leave the window open until the odor is gone.

You need something after school, you know. And instant coffee just doesn't do it.

But today we don't hurry upstairs. We wait in the per-

fect kitchen with its glowing stove and refrigerator, the
brass sun clock over the sink, the gleaming knives in
perfect order in the rack above the counter, the hand-
painted tiles of chickens and ducks on the wall above the
stove. We wait for the kettle to whistle. Will goes to the
stack of mail on the kitchen counter.

I study him while he flips through the magazines and
catalogs. I find myself looking at him a lot. Somehow,
even though it's been three months, I can't believe we're
going together.

I mean, he was going with another girl—for a long
time, I think—and he left her for me.

All through high school, I hung out with a lot of guys.
I was in the popular crowd; I don't really know why. But
you just find yourself in a group in high school, and
there you are. That's your place for the next four years.

But I was never really serious about any guy, except
for Will. And I had to be serious about him, right, because he left someone for me.

It felt kinda grown-up. And totally flattering. And I
knew kids at school talked about us all the time.

And so I find myself looking at Will a lot. He has a
real Wisconsin face. His family has been here since the
fur trappers, I guess. His face is round with a broad
forehead. Not a baby face, and not really a high school
face. An open, likable face. His blue eyes crinkle up
when he smiles, and he even has a single dimple high on
his right cheek.

He has thick, white-blond hair, which comes down
over his collar. Of course, his mother complains that it's
too long and messy. I know he spends a lot of time on
his hair, brushing it this way and that over the part on
the left, making it look as if it hasn't been brushed. He'd

be embarrassed if anyone else knew he fussed over himself like that.

Will was one of the first guys at Menota High to have his ear pierced. He has a tiny, silver ring in his ear. He took a lot of teasing at first, and some of the teachers were appalled, and then all the guys started doing it.

And now I watch him sifting through the mail, and I'm pouring the boiling water into our cups, the steam rising, warm against my still-frozen face. And I'm starting to feel a little better. "Think your car will start?" I ask.

He raises his blue eyes from the mail. "My car? Why?"

"Maybe we could go see *Clueless* tonight."

He frowned at me. "*Clueless*? It's like a dumb California teen movie, right?"

"Cindy says it's awesome. She says it's not dumb. Some other kids told me it was good, too. I thought maybe . . ."

I could see he wasn't listening to me. He was staring at a gray envelope in his hand.

"I don't believe this," he whispered.

He tore open the envelope. Unfolded the letter inside. His eyes narrowed as he read it. He tore at his hair, making it stand high on his head. Then he let out an excited cry.

"Will? What is it?"

"I don't believe it! I don't believe it!" He started jumping up and down, holding the letter above his head.

"Will—?"

He leaped over to me, threw his arms around me, hugged me hard. His face was red with excitement. When he hugged me, I could feel his pounding heart through his sweatshirt.

I never forgot that moment.

The heart pounding against my chest. Feeling another person's heart. Will's heart.

Such a fragile thing.

Could I ever forget what that felt like?

Especially after he died. That tiny heartbeat. It was like something he left for me.

"I got it," he said, letting go and waving the letter in my face. "I got it, Ellie. Early admission to Princeton!"

"Wow!" I let out a scream. I grabbed his head and kissed him. "Wow!"

And immediately, I was thinking—I'm staying here in Madison, starting at the university, and he'll be off at Princeton. That's in New Jersey, right? A long way from here.

How do I feel about that?

Will must have read my face. Because he came over and put his arms around me—strong, athletic arms because he was a basketball forward and he likes to work out—comforting me.

"We'll see each other a lot," he said. "No problem, right? We can visit each other at school. And there are a lot of breaks. You know. Winter break, spring break."

"Yeah, sure," I muttered. I liked having him hold me like that, and I liked the way he reassured me. But I kept thinking . . . thinking . . . thinking. . . . You can't stop your mind. It just keeps going.

How do I feel about that?

"I'll come home for every holiday," Will said. "It won't be bad. We'll see each other a lot, Ellie. And we won't go out with anyone else."

Whoa.

How do I feel about *that*?

Will and I had been together only for three or four months. Was I really willing to make that commitment?

Yes, I cared about him. Sure, I did. I liked the strong, sure way he walked. And his smile. The way he tossed his head sometimes and trotted like Mrs. Havers's greyhound down the block. And the way he held me as if he owned me. And the way his hair felt so soft and babylike between my fingers.

"Four years is nothing," he said. He pressed his lips close to my ear. "Then we'll be together forever, Ellie."

We will?

Forever?

We're up in his room now. He closed the door. He's holding me, kissing me. He wants to make love. He wants to seal the bargain.

He keeps some condoms in his sock drawer, under the Ziploc bag of pot.

Yes, we've made love a couple times before. But this is different, he says. This is special. This is a pledge. A pledge of our love.

He's so happy. He's so excited.

Shouldn't I be happy, too?

Shouldn't I be overcome with emotion right now? Instead, I'm thinking, what if his mother comes home early? What if his sister comes home? Shouldn't we pull the shades?

What if I meet another guy I like?

That's what I'm thinking when I should be thinking of Will.

I'm pulling off my jeans, and I should be thinking of Will.

I'm pulling down my tights and not bothering with my two sweaters.

No time. He's in a hurry to celebrate. To seal our bargain.

I'm climbing into his single bed under the Michael Jordan Bulls poster, and I should be thinking of Will.

So happy. Early admission. But we'll stay together.

Yes. Together forever.

Why am I so surprised?

Why can't I feel more? Shouldn't I feel more right now?

And then we're making love.

I'm letting him.

I'm *letting* him.

He swings me on top with those powerful arms, and I'm moving over him, and we're both moaning in a steady rhythm, eyes shut.

I'm moving . . . moaning . . . moving on top of him . . . so wet . . . not neat . . .

And I shouldn't be thinking at all.

But I'm glancing back at the bedroom door. And I'm thinking about dinner. I was supposed to get home early and help out. And I'm thinking about Lucky. Did I remember to buy cat food? And about a boy named Gary who offered to help me with my Politics paper . . .

Oh . . . oh . . . oh, yes . . .

I'm moaning and I'm feeling guilty. And I don't think we'll stay together when we're apart.

Oh . . . oh, yes . . .

I feel so bad about it. Because I care about him. He's holding my head, holding me so firmly, as if he's captured me.

Will?

Will? Where are you?

If only I had held on, too. . . .

7

By the time we reached Southampton, the clouds had given way to bright sunshine. I took a deep breath as I followed Teresa off the bus. I thought I could smell the ocean nearby.

Teresa immediately pulled out a pack of Parliament Lights and lit one. "All this fresh air can kill you," she joked. I waited for her to get her nicotine fix. Then we went inside.

We were at a long, low, redbrick building called The Omni. It seemed to be a bus station, gym, and restaurant combined. Teresa rented a car and drove into Southampton, a cute little town, all red brick and white, with rows of shops on either side of the tree-lined main street.

She turned off Main Street and onto another street of shops called Jobs Lane. "There's your store," she said, pointing. "Jump out, El. After your interview, walk around town a bit. I'll pick you up on the corner—in front of the old library—in half an hour."

"Thanks, Teresa." I glanced back to make sure no one was coming and then hopped out of the car. Country Modes was in a low, white clapboard building with a tall display window covering the front.

Three lanky teenage girls had stopped to gaze at the

window display. I peered over their shoulders. It didn't look too countryish to me. Five or six mannequins wearing string bikinis.

A bell rang over the glass door as I stepped into the store—a long, narrow store with a glass display counter in front and shelves of clothes on both sides, stretching to the back.

Dance music rang out from a small shelf stereo behind the front counter. Two middle-aged women were picking through tie-dyed beach cover-ups near the back.

The woman behind the counter was tall and very thin. She had raven-black hair pulled tight behind her head, lots of blue and black eye makeup, and a red lipsticked mouth so bright that it seemed to float on her pale face.

I cleared my throat. "Hello."

She glanced up from the local newspaper she had spread over the counter.

"Are you Sheila?" I asked.

She frowned. "No. I'm Shirley."

"Well, hi," I chirped. I was determined to make a good impression on my new employer. I had worn my only business suit, a gray Ralph Lauren that I'd spent at least two weeks' temping money on. "I spoke to Sheila yesterday. About the job here."

Her eyes seemed to disappear behind the black rings of mascara. "Job?"

I nodded. "Sales clerk? Full-time? She said I just needed to come in for a short interview and fill out a form."

"Oh. Yeah. We filled that job."

My throat tightened. "Excuse me?"

"We filled all the summer jobs. Some girls came in yesterday."

"But I don't understand. Sheila said if I came in—"

"Sheila doesn't work on Sunday. You know. Standing so long, it's hard on her back."

A young woman stepped out of the dressing room, carrying two black tankinis in her hand. "I'll take these two," she called to Shirley. "They're perfect."

She wore a pale violet tank top tucked into white tennis shorts. She had a purple bandanna wrapped around her head. She was already very tanned, even though it was still May. Probably from one of those tanning places, I figured.

I turned back to Shirley. "So there are no jobs?" I asked, unable to hide my disappointment.

She shook her head. "All filled. Have you tried the shoe store next to Nancy and Company?"

"Uh . . . no."

I turned and saw the woman in the purple bandanna staring at me, studying my face. She didn't look away, even when I stared back at her.

Finally, she blinked. She wrapped her hand around my shoulder, as if testing if I were real. "Did you say you were looking for a job?"

I swallowed. "Yes, they told me yesterday—"

"Do you know anything about kids?" she asked, still studying me. "I mean, have you ever baby-sat? Would you consider a nanny job?"

"Well . . . yes. I love kids," I said. "I was a camp counselor back home. And I tutored kids after school."

"It's a live-in job," the woman said. "Taking care of two little kids. Our nanny left last week, and we're desperate. Would that be a problem for you? Living in? I'll pay you really well."

My mind whirred. Since I was losing my apartment in

less than two weeks, the idea of a job *and* a place to live sounded all right with me!

"It sounds kind of exciting," I said. "I'd love to talk to you about it."

"Can you come to the house after lunch? Around one or so?" She didn't wait for me to answer. She took a Country Modes business card from the holder on the counter and scribbled her name and address on the back.

"Here. Sorry to sound so ditzy," she said. "I didn't even ask your name."

"It's Ellie. Ellie Saks."

Her eyes widened. "Like Saks Fifth Avenue?"

"Not related," I said.

"Well, I'm Abby Harper." She gave my hand a quick, hard shake. "See you at one? I'm sure you'll be wonderful, Ellie. Chip and I really are frantic. We have kind of a . . . difficult situation, you see." She bit her bottom lip. "Yes. Very difficult," she whispered.

"Uh . . . How do you mean?" I asked.

But she didn't answer. She squinted at me one more time, as if memorizing my face. Then she grabbed her package from Shirley and hurried out the door.

A few minutes later, Teresa pulled up, and I climbed into the car. I told her the whole story in one long whoosh, without taking a breath. I showed her the address on the card.

"Wow. Flying Point Road in Watermill. You may have lucked out, El. It's probably one of those glitzy houses right on the beach. This could be an awesome summer!"

Yes. Awesome summer, I thought. But as we headed out to get some lunch, a few things tugged at my mind.

Didn't Abby Harper seem a bit too eager to hire me?

And why did she say it was a difficult situation?
Stop it, Ellie. You always do this.
Just stop.
It's two little kids to take care of.
How bad could it be?

8

Teresa and I had lunch at an old-fashioned soda-fountain-type place called the Sip 'n Soda.

It was filled with laughing, noisy high school kids and about a million little kids with their moms. We had greasy cheeseburgers and shared some fries, and we talked the whole time, but my mind was on the job interview. What would Abby Harper's kids be like? What would she ask me about? Would I get the job?

After lunch, Teresa drove me to their house. We passed a cluster of car dealerships—a big Mercedes place, BMW, Range Rover.

"The Hamptons are the Mercedes capital of the world," Teresa said. "In town once, I saw six of them parked side by side, all of them black. Mercedes is like the Chevy of the Hamptons."

We were moving past an ocean inlet now, with flat blue water and a narrow sand beach. Several cars were parked there. About a dozen people in wetsuits were taking Windsurfers out onto the water.

"They're always here," Teresa said. "They don't care if it's cold or not. This is their beach. We're on Flying Point Road. The seashore is right up there." She pointed.

"You're a hell of a tour guide," I said. We had the windows rolled down. The sea air smelled salty and fresh.

"I should be. I've been in a share house out here for the past three summers. Want to see the ocean?"

I glanced at my watch. Nearly one o'clock. "Better not. I'm going to be late."

Teresa made a sharp left turn. "The house should be up here. See the houses on the right? They're all facing the ocean. Can you imagine what they cost?"

I stared out the window. "Millions?"

"No one ever sells them," Teresa said. "Would *you* sell a house right on the ocean?"

As we drove, the houses became farther apart, and the sandy dunes grew higher. Teresa slowed down to read the address numbers on the mailboxes.

I saw several seagulls flocked together, swooping high in the blue sky. I wondered if gulls were good luck or bad. But then I thought about the dead deer back on the side of the highway and decided I'd had enough omens for the day.

Give it a rest, Ellie. Make your own luck.

Teresa's voice broke through my thoughts. "Wow. Check out their house!"

She pulled into a curving asphalt drive. We drove past a front yard of tall grass and reeds, waving up from the sandy ground. A cluster of trees stood near the house.

The house rose up like a battleship—all white wood and glass. I saw a three-car garage, a black SUV, a red Porsche, and a tricycle at the top of the drive; a tall hedge of rhododendrons not quite ready to bloom; a light-wood deck stretching along one side—and glass windows stretching to the red tile roof. Like the beach houses you see in movies!

Sunlight glared off the tall windows, making it look as if the house were ablaze. Behind the house, I glimpsed a tall, grassy dune. As Teresa stopped the car, I could hear the ocean in back.

"Wow. You lucked out," Teresa said. "This place is to die for."

"Teresa, I don't have the job yet."

I don't think she heard me. She was too busy gawking. "The back of the house is probably *all* glass. It must be an awesome view. This is *so* not to be believed. I can't wait for you to invite me over."

I pushed open the passenger door. "Well . . . wish me luck."

"Luck." She flashed me two thumbs up. "I'm off to the spa in Sag Harbor. Call me on your cell when you're finished."

I watched her pull away. Her tires slid in the sand on the road. Then I turned back to the house. I could see a little face watching me from an upstairs window. Boy? Girl? I couldn't tell. The face was a ghostly image behind the sun's glare.

I followed the flagstone walk, then climbed the white steps to the double front doors. Big clay pots of purple impatiens stood on either side of the door. I could hear music inside the house. Reggae music.

I took a deep breath.

Go, Ellie.

This could be a new start. A whole new life. New people. A summer of fun. Maybe a new guy . . .

I hope the Harpers are nice. I hope they like me.

I hope this job doesn't suck.

I pressed the brass doorbell.

9

A man opened the door. He was tall and trim, probably in his early thirties. He had short, wavy brown hair over a tanned, square face, a nose that had probably been broken a few times, a stubble of whiskers, and round brown eyes set close to his nose.

He wore a loose-fitting blue polo shirt, untucked, over wrinkled khaki shorts. He was barefoot.

He looks familiar, I thought. Have I seen him before? I quickly dismissed the idea.

"Hi. Are you Ellie? I'm Chip Harper." His breath smelled of gin. And as he ushered me in, I saw that he had a drink in his hand.

"Nice to meet you," I said. He switched his drink to his left hand, and we shook hands.

I gazed into the living room. The blond-wood floors were beautiful. I saw a high, cathedral ceiling stretching over a white balcony.

Chip Harper raised his glass and smiled. "I know it's early. I'm having one for the road. I'm heading back to the city."

"You . . . go back and forth?" I asked.

Somewhere in the house someone turned off the reggae music.

"Yeah, I'm an I-banker. You know. Investment banker, so I have to be in the city. I come out for long weekends. But I'm coming out to stay for a while in June. You know. My vacation."

He took a sip of the drink, ice cubes clinking, then motioned to the black SUV in the driveway. "You need a ride back to the city? You can come with me."

"No. Thanks. I have a friend. I'm going back with her."

He flashed that slightly crooked smile again. His brown eyes sort of took me in, checking out my suit. I straightened my skirt and followed him to the living room.

My eyes swept over the room. Two white leather couches facing each other, a couple of wicker chairs, a fireplace with black wrought-iron fire tools on one side, a tall window facing the front, colorful pillows spread out along a cushioned window seat.

A collection of fashion magazines was stacked on a low glass coffee table. Beside it, a Martha Stewart gardening book. Several paperback mysteries were strewn on the table.

"Hey, Abby? Where are you?" Chip shouted. His voice echoed off the high, white walls. He turned to me. "I think she's upstairs with the kids. Our bedroom and the baby's room is down here." He pointed to a hall at the back. "But the other bedrooms are upstairs. Your bedroom, too."

Your bedroom. As if he already had given me the job.

I gazed up at the cathedral ceiling. The balcony ran the length of the second floor, and I could see the upstairs rooms along it. An enormous antique quilt, red and blue stars on streaming patterns of yellow, hung over the side of the balcony. "It's a beautiful house," I said.

He nodded and took another long sip of his drink. "Yes, it is. I wish I could spend more time out here. Abby and the kids have been staying out here since the beginning of May. But I have to go back and forth to the city. I can't wait till the end of June . . . my vacation," he repeated.

I realized he was studying me again. "Are you from here?" he asked.

"No. I'm from Wisconsin, actually. Madison. We don't have much ocean in Wisconsin."

He snickered. Then he shouted again. "Hey, Abby. Where are you? The new sitter is here."

Abby appeared on the balcony. She leaned over the side and waved to me. "Hi, Ellie. I'll be right down."

I watched her come down the stairs. I hadn't really seen her clearly in the store. For one thing, she had that bandanna around her head. And when she started talking about a job, I was too startled to see anything!

She was drop-dead gorgeous. I mean like a fashion model or something. She had her black hair cut short, parted in the middle, very shiny, very stylish.

She had dark brown eyes, high cheekbones, and that awesome tan, real or not. She wore a brightly colored flowery beach cover-up over a key lime one-piece bathing suit. Coral-colored plastic bracelets jangled on her wrist as she walked.

She flashed me a warm smile and took my hand in both of hers. "Ellie, hi. Thanks for coming out. As I told you in town, Chip and I are really desperate to hire a new nanny."

She eased herself down on one of the white leather

couches and motioned for me to sit beside her. "I see Chip has helped himself. Can I get you anything to drink? A Diet Coke or something?"

"No. No thanks. I'm fine."

She glanced up at her husband. "What are you drinking?"

"Gin and tonic. Want one?"

She glanced at the silver clock on the end table. "It's one o'clock in the afternoon."

Chip laughed. "Are you scolding me? I need one for the road." He sat down across from us in a wicker chair and rattled the ice in his glass. He grinned at me. "I'm not an alcoholic—I just *love* to drink!" He laughed.

Abby shook her head. "Chip, no one ever laughs at that joke. No one else thinks it's funny."

"It's funny," he muttered. He winked at me. "You think it's funny, *don't* you, Ellie?"

I cleared my throat. I didn't reply.

Abby took my hand. "So, Ellie, tell me all about yourself. Do you really want this job?"

"Well . . . yes," I said. And then I started my sales pitch, the pitch I had been rehearsing all through lunch. I'm very good with kids, and kids always love me yada yada yada . . .

Abby listened intently, her dark eyes never leaving mine. She played with her plastic bracelets as I talked. "What are you doing now?" she asked. "Do you have to give notice somewhere?"

"No. I'm only temping. I moved to New York last year, and I've been temping since I got here."

"She's from Wisconsin," Chip chimed in. "I don't think she's ever seen the ocean before!"

"Well, actually, I have. My aunt used to have a house

on the Jersey shore, so my family visited her several summers."

"That's not like the Hamptons," Chip said, shaking his head. "That's like, 'Let's go hang out at the tattoo parlor and drink a couple of Budweisers.' "

"Don't listen to Mr. Snob," Abby said playfully. "A few years ago, he'd have been *thrilled* with the Jersey shore."

Chip rubbed his stubble of beard and muttered something into his glass.

"Ellie, where did you go to college?" Abby asked.

Should I lie?

Should I tell the truth?

Yes. They seem really nice. Maybe the truth.

I mean, part of the truth. Only part.

"I didn't go to college," I said softly. "I was accepted at a bunch of colleges. But I had to go to work. My father got sick, and I had to help support my family."

Okay. That part is a lie.

I mean, I really was all set to go to school at the university in Madison.

And then Will—

The thing with Will—

It changed everything. And I could barely face the world, barely drag myself out of bed each morning.

It took so long to get on with my life. So many years . . .

So many long, miserable, blank years.

"Tell me about the kids," I said. "There are two of them, right?"

Abby nodded. "Yes, Heather turned two last week. She's wonderful."

Chip snickered. "She'll keep you busy. You'll spend a lot of time chasing after her."

"And then there's Brandon," Abby said. She let go of her bracelets and shifted her position on the couch. "We have kind of a difficult situation here."

Uh-oh.

"Uh . . . How do you mean?" I asked.

"Well . . ." She hesitated. "How should I put this? Brandon is four, and up till a few weeks ago, he was fine. But . . . a few weeks ago . . . well . . . he stopped talking."

Abby stopped there. I think she was waiting for me to react. But I kept my face thoughtful, intent, and didn't say a word.

"He just went silent. We don't know why, Ellie. Not a clue." She brushed a tear from her eye with the back of her hand. "I'm sorry. I don't want to get emotional. But . . . it's been hard."

Chip stood up and moved over to us. He squeezed Abby's shoulder lovingly. "We have a psychiatrist here three times a week," he said. "Dr. Kleiner. He's been working with Brandon. Trying to figure out what upset the poor little guy."

"But he hasn't made much progress," Abby said, her voice breaking. She raised her dark eyes to mine. "Brandon has to be looked after constantly. I don't want him left alone."

"Okay," I said. "I understand."

"Hey, I think you should meet the kids," Chip said. "They're upstairs. I'll go bring 'em down." He set down his glass and trotted to the stairs, his bare feet thudding against the shiny wood floor.

Abby smiled reassuringly at me. "I think you'll really like them," she whispered.

I pushed myself to the edge of the couch. It was so soft, I found it impossible to sit up straight.

I could hear Chip upstairs. "Come on down, kids. I want you to meet someone."

"Carry me!" said a little voice that had to be Heather. Then footsteps came clumping down the stairs.

This is a horror story, remember.

You know that, right? That this is a horror story I'm telling you.

Well, here come the two kids.

And there's poor, innocent me, sitting there on the edge of the couch, waiting. Clueless as can be.

And this is where the horror begins.

10

Chip carried Heather on his shoulders. She held on to his ears and bounced as he walked.

Brandon hung behind his father, as if trying to hide. He was a pale, slight boy, small for four, with serious, dark eyes, wild, curly, black hair that I immediately wanted to run my hand through, and a pointed, elfish nose.

"Hi, guys!" I said.

They both ignored me.

"This is Ellie, your new nanny," Abby told them.

Chip set Heather down on the floor in front of me. She was wearing a bright yellow sundress over her diaper. She had fine, blond hair, a bright red butterfly barrette pinned at the top of her head. She had a round face and looked exactly like a tiny blond version of Chip.

"Well, you're a real cutie! You and I are going to have a lot of fun all summer," I said. I started to pick her up—and she burst into tears.

Bad start.

Abby took the sobbing baby from me and held her. "Heather, what's wrong?"

Chip laughed. "Ellie, you're hired. You have a way with kids!"

"Stop it, Chip," Abby snapped. "You're not funny." She turned to me. "You have to ignore his sense of humor. Everyone else does."

Chip picked up his drink and finished it—ice cubes, too.

Heather instantly stopped crying. She put her finger in her mother's nose and laughed.

"Heather is a little shy with new people," Abby explained to me. "After a few days, she'll be poking her finger in your nose, too."

We both laughed.

All the while, Brandon stared at us blankly. He had his hands tucked into the pockets of his baggy shorts. He kept biting the inside of his mouth.

It didn't take a genius to tell that the poor kid was miserable.

What does that to a four-year-old kid? What happened to Brandon Harper?

"Hi, Brandon. I'm Ellie," I said, bending down to be closer to him. "Do you like to go to the beach?"

Nothing.

I took his hand. It was ice cold. "Brandon, you know, where I come from—in Wisconsin—there are no ocean beaches. Do you believe that? No ocean at all. So I can't wait to go to the beach. I want to spend hours and hours at the ocean. After I move in here, do you think you could take me to the beach and show me how to play there?"

He just stared at me with those joyless eyes. Ancient eyes on a little boy's face.

Did it creep me out? Yes. But at least this job would be a challenge. It wouldn't be a boring baby-sitting job. Maybe I'd be the one to get through to this troubled boy.

Yes. Think on the bright side for once, Ellie. The job will be a *challenge*. This was my new, positive personality at work. After so many years of aimlessness and unhappiness, I was going to change my attitude—and change my life.

"You and I are going to be good friends," I told Brandon, letting go of his cold hand.

"Brandon will *love* to show you the beach," Abby said. "He likes to build big castles and forts there."

"Me build, too," Heather chimed in.

"Oh, I know what would be good," Abby said. "Brandon, take Ellie up to your room and show her the new present your dad brought you."

"A present?" I said. "I'd love to see it, Brandon."

He shrugged and jammed his hands back in his pockets.

"Go ahead," Chip said, giving the boy a gentle shove. "Show Ellie what I brought you. Go!" He didn't hide his impatience.

Brandon stared at me.

"I'd love to see your room," I said.

Finally, he turned and started walking to the stairs. I glimpsed Abby and Chip nodding to each other, pleased that their son was cooperating.

Score one for me.

I followed Brandon up the stairs. The wooden steps were steep and slippery, highly polished. He used the banister to pull himself up.

The long hall at the top had several doorways to the left. I peered over the balcony and saw Chip and Abby conferring, Abby talking in a hushed tone, Chip nodding his head.

I guessed they were deciding about me.

Brandon's room was the second door. It was bright and spacious, and the white rug on the floor was cluttered with action figures, games, picture books, wooden puzzles, and a lot of toys I didn't recognize.

"Wow! What an awesome room!" I said. "I love that horse poster over your bed, Brandon. Do you like horses?"

No response.

He disappeared into the closet. I heard a *cheep cheep*. He came out cradling a tiny yellow baby chick in his hands. He carried it over to me and held it up so I could see it.

"How adorable," I said. "A baby chick. Where do you keep it? In a cage?"

He nodded.

"Can I pet it?" I reached out a finger and stroked the chick's fuzzy back. "So soft."

Gauzy white curtains fluttered at the half-open window. I crossed the room. "Brandon, can you see the ocean from your window?"

Nothing. Nada.

I stepped up to the window and pushed the curtains aside. "Wow! Amazing!"

The window faced the back of the house. I could see a small, sandy yard, a sloping dune with a row of pine trees at the top. Half-hidden behind the trees was a small, shingled structure. A storage shed. Or maybe a guest house.

And then, beyond the little house, another dune. And then, a wide, sandy beach—deserted as far as I could see—and the tossing blue ocean.

"Brandon, you can see the ocean from your room. It's gorgeous! And you can hear it. What a wonderful sound. And you can *smell* it! Isn't that exciting? To live so close to the ocean? Isn't that awesome?"

No reply, of course.

I turned and took a few steps back to where he was standing in the center of the room. "Brandon? Is something wrong? Why do you have that weird look on your face?"

Then I lowered my gaze.

And stared at the wet, yellow fuzz in Brandon's fist.

"You—you squeezed it—"

Slowly, Brandon uncurled his fingers. The chick's lifeless head flopped over the side of his hand, like the limp finger of a glove. The chick's little body was a pulpy, yellow mess.

"You squeezed too hard, Brandon." My voice escaped in a choked whisper. "Didn't you realize? You squeezed it too hard."

His face remained blank. His intense eyes locked on mine. And then, slowly, very slowly, he lowered his gaze. And stared at the mangled chick.

Then he tilted his head back and started to laugh.

11

How can I describe what it felt like to see Ellie after all this time?

How can I describe the shock? The disbelief that she could return to my life this way?

Of course, I had to hide my feelings. And I did a good job of it. I pulled down a mask and kept it in place.

But behind the mask, I was seething, churning.

How could this happen?

It's as if my thoughts had come true.

I've been thinking about her a lot. Thinking about how much I hate her. Thinking about what she did to me.

No, I haven't been able to lose the anger. I've carried it with me all these years. I've spent my life—my whole damn life—angry and unhappy, thanks to that bitch. That skinny, lying bitch.

She's ruined so much of my life. Ruined so many nights. Ruined so many years.

And there she was, walking into the house.

Stepping right out of my nightmares and back into my life.

Sitting in my living room in that expensive suit, so prim and pretty, as if I don't know what she's really like.

There she was, sitting in my living room, talking to my kids. So eager. So fucking eager.

Looking right at me. Smiling at me.

Looking right into the face of the person who hates her the most in the world.

Doesn't she even remember me?

That's what pissed me off more than anything. That's what made me want to strangle her in front of everyone.

Has she forgotten?

Has she?

Has she forgotten what she did to me? How she killed me?

Well, I haven't forgotten.

I acted so calm, so polite, so friendly to her.

And, of course, I had to hire her.

Yes, I kept the mask in place. I kept myself hidden from view.

How could she not know me?

How could she not remember?

I was so nice. "Yes, Ellie, you have the job. Yes, Ellie, please start as soon as you can. Yes, Ellie. Yes."

And all the time, questions kept going through my head.

Could I fuck her up really bad?

Could I kill her?

Could I?

I might be angry enough.

I just might.

PART TWO

12

Hey, Teresa. I just finished unpacking. My room is small, but it's really nice."

"Which side of the house are you on? Can you see the ocean?"

"It is *so* not to be believed. I'm upstairs, right? I can see over the little guest house to the beach. It's an incredible view. And it smells so good. I feel like I'm on a boat."

"I'm so jealous. They had more cutbacks at the office. Do you believe it—now I'm reporting to two people. I've got like double the work. And no raise or anything."

"You should quit and come out here and live on the beach, Teresa."

"Oh, sure. And what about my career?"

"Hey, sorry. I was just joking."

"Ha. So was I. My career is a joke. I'm going nowhere fast."

"Hey, don't sound so down. This is our party summer, remember? When are you coming out?"

"I'll be out this weekend, Ellie. Maybe you can give me a tour of the fabulous beach house. What are you doing today?"

"First thing I've got to do is go shopping. I don't have a thing. I don't even own a bathing suit."

"Where are you going to shop? Are they letting you drive their car?"

"They lent me my own—do you believe it? It's a little white Taurus, very cute. It's for me to use and to drive the kids around in."

"Oh, yeah. I forgot there were kids involved. How's it going?"

"Well, you know. I just got here yesterday. The little girl is adorable, but very demanding. I guess all two-year-olds are. The little boy is . . . well, weird. He just stares at me with this blank look on his face. He never talks."

"Weird is right. Listen, go into Easthampton. There's a shop called Scoop. You'll love it. Great bathing suits. Everything you need to be a Hamptons person."

"Teresa, I'm laughing. Do I want to be a Hamptons person?"

"Of course. Listen to me. Scoop. They've got the best jeans there. You know. Seven. The ones that make any woman's booty look like J. Lo's. Great tops, too. Lots of tie-dyed stuff. Everyone is tie-dyed this summer. And they have silver chain belts to go with your jeans."

"Where would I be without you? But I'm not going that way. I have to go to Southampton and pick up some things for Abby."

"She's the wife? How is she? Nice?"

"Yes. She's been wonderful to me. She told me there's a department store there. It's called . . . uh . . . I wrote it down. . . . Hildreth's. She said I could probably buy a cat bed there."

"A cat bed? They won't give you a *real* bed?"

"Ha ha. That's what I wanted to talk to you about, Teresa. I need a favor."

"And it involves a cat bed?"

"Well . . . yeah. The Harpers are letting me bring my old cat, Lucky, out here. Remember? I told you about Lucky?"

"Only every time I talk to you."

"I miss him *so much.* Mom sent him to my cousin Marsha in Connecticut. If Marsha brings Lucky to you in the city in a week or so, can you bring him out to me?"

"Does he bite?"

"No, of course he doesn't bite. He's a sweet old cat. You'll love him to death."

"Well, sure. No problem. Give your cousin my address. Tell her just to call first. Then drop him off after work."

"Cool. Thanks, Teresa. You're terrific. You know, I'm also going into Southampton for another reason. I'm going to change my cell-phone number."

"Oh, wow. Clay again?"

"You guessed it. He called me twice last night. He's really starting to piss me off. Listen to this. He called my mother and got my address out here."

"Oh, good. Thanks, Mom."

"Well, it's not her fault. She doesn't know what's going on. But I—"

"Why did you go out with Clay in the first place, Ellie? Pardon me for asking, but have you *always* had such rotten taste in men? I mean, *hel-lo.* He's a fucking tax accountant."

"You want to know the *real* reason? This is the honest truth, Teresa. Why I went out with Clay. He can juggle."

"Excuse me?"

"He can juggle. He's a tax accountant who can juggle. Don't you see?"

"No."

"He had something special. He wasn't ordinary. At least, that's what I thought. He . . . I don't know how to say it. He had another dimension."

"A juggling dimension?"

"Will you give me a break? You're so not funny. It's what I always wanted, Teresa. Instead of just being me. 'There's Ellie. What you see is what you get.' My sister, Wendy, was always off being a superstar. And there I was, just being me. I always wanted another dimension, too. I wanted to be *me* who also did something else, something surprising, something terrific."

"Wow. This is getting heavy. It still doesn't explain Clay."

"He was so much fun when we first started going together. And he was cute. Really. Like a big teddy bear. But now—"

"Bears can be dangerous, Ellie. Don't you watch the Discovery Channel?"

"Well, I'm going to change my number in town. And—"

"And if he follows you to the Hamptons, you've got to tell the police."

"I made it really clear to him on the phone last night. I really don't think he'll follow me out here."

"You sure?"

"Yeah. Definitely. I'm sure," I said. And I wondered if

I sounded as phony on her end of the line as I did on my own.

"You just have to remember that the bay is to the north and the ocean is south. There's only one main highway that cuts through—twenty-seven. So you can't really get lost. If you hit water, turn around, and you'll end up back on twenty-seven."

I knew Abby meant to be helpful, but the instructions didn't make a whole lot of sense to me. I guess I must have looked confused, because she put her hand on my shoulder and said, "I'm really sorry, Ellie. I wish I could go with you and show you around. But I have to drop the kids off and take the Porsche in to be serviced and—"

"No problem," I said, waving the map. "As long as I've got this, I'll be fine. I'm a good map reader. Really. When my family went on long car trips, I was always the navigator."

I climbed into the white Taurus. Mmmm. It still had its new-car smell. I hadn't driven a car even once in the year I'd lived in the city, and it felt good to be behind the wheel again.

And I was very pleased when, ten minutes later, I was rolling the car through Main Street in Southampton, with its small shops and restaurants on both sides.

I'd been here two Sundays ago for my thrilling interview at Country Modes. But I hadn't had time to look around.

This must be a movie set for a chic little beach town, I thought. If I look behind the stores, I'll see that it's all fake fronts.

I passed a Saks Fifth Avenue, across the street from a

couple of antiques stores. The sidewalks were crowded
with shoppers and casual strollers. I passed a bookstore,
a fudge store, several jewelry stores. I wondered, do people really come out to the beach and go jewelry shopping?

I pulled into a parking spot in front of an old-fashioned-
looking hardware store. There were black Mercedes
parked on both sides of me. Glancing down the row of
cars, I saw Mercedes, Jaguars, a few Range Rovers, lots of
other expensive SUVs.

Hildreth's Department Store stood a few stores down
from the hardware store. Abby told me it was maybe
the oldest department store in the country, from like
the 1800s. English people started settling Southampton
in the 1690s. I guess they couldn't resist the beautiful
beaches, either.

The little department store looked friendly and invit-
ing, the way I'd pictured old-fashioned shops. I stopped
to look into the big display windows in front. Talk
about a time warp—canopy beds and bolts of cloth and
brightly patterned curtains.

People strolled by in shorts and T-shirts and sandals.
A young man walking a gray standard poodle stopped
to talk to two girls wearing Wesleyan sweatshirts. The
girls fawned over the dog and pretty much ignored the
guy.

It was a warm day for the beginning of June. But suddenly, I felt a chill. The back of my neck prickled.

I spun around. Why did I feel that someone was
watching me?

Shielding my eyes from the sun with one hand, I
glanced up and down the street. Such a strange feeling.
It came over me so quickly, like a warning.

But no one seemed to be paying any attention to me.

I climbed the wooden steps and pulled open the windowed front door. A bell rang above the door.

I pushed through the kitchen housewares department jammed with people outfitting their summer homes. I wandered toward the back of the store. Again, the hairs on the back of my neck tingled.

That feeling again.

I spun around, my eyes surveying the crowd of shoppers. No one watching me.

I took a deep breath to calm myself. Ellie, what is your problem?

I found the linens department near the back.

Abby had ordered some sheets and pillowcases over the phone and wanted me to pick them up. I went to the register at the back desk and looked around for someone to help me.

In the aisle across from me, a platinum blond woman in black tights and a silvery sweater-top—maybe the skinniest woman I'd ever seen!—held up an orange-and-yellow throw pillow. "Do you have one that isn't stained?" she was calling across the store. "Do you have two that aren't stained?"

I sighed and leaned against the counter. This could be a long morning. I saw dozens of shoppers and only two salesgirls.

"Oh!" I jumped as a hard, cold hand grabbed my wrist.

"Hello. I've been looking for you."

13

I turned quickly—and found myself staring at an elderly woman. Her round face was very pale, her white hair piled up in a tight bun. She wore square glasses with very thick lenses that caught the light from the ceiling and made her pale blue eyes look enormous.

"I've been looking for you," she repeated. Her voice was smooth and somehow younger than her appearance. She wore a navy blue jumper, a lacy white blouse with a red, jeweled flower pin on the collar, and a blue-and-yellow-striped scarf around her neck.

I squinted at her. Her face was powdery, etched with deep cracks and crevices. But her eyes were wide and alert, piercing. She didn't blink.

"Excuse me?" I said. She was standing too close, invading my space. I could smell onions on her breath. I took a step back.

She grabbed my arm again with those hard, bony fingers. "You're the Harpers' new nanny."

"Well . . . yes. Yes, I am." I took another step back. "Uh . . . why have you been looking for me?"

A dry-lipped smile stretched slowly over her craggy face. I thought of craters on the moon, so dry and pale and sandy.

"I'm the *old* nanny," she said, blue eyes flashing behind the thick glasses. "That's me. Mrs. Bricker. The old nanny."

"Really?"

She pulled my arm. Her grip was surprisingly strong. "Come, let's have a chat. What's your name? I've been watching for you. I want to tell you some things."

"Things?" I pulled free. "I'm really sorry. I—I can't. I have too many chores. I just arrived and—"

Her eyes narrowed. Her smile faded quickly. The powdery face seemed to grow hard, like cement drying fast. "Listen to me. I'm trying to help you, dear."

"Help me?"

"Yes. I'm Mrs. Bricker, the old baby-sitter. I came to help you. I know things."

I stared hard at her. Was she crazy? Totally whacked?

"Things? What kind of things?"

"Find another job."

"Huh?"

"It isn't safe there, dear. Listen to me. I know what I'm saying."

I took a deep breath. "I'm sorry, Mrs. Bricker. I really don't understand. You're telling me it isn't safe at the Harpers' house?"

She straightened the scarf with her bony fingers. Her chin quivered. The unblinking blue eyes locked on mine. "Listen to me. Get away from the boy. Stay away from him. I know. I know. It's in the guest house. The guest house. Get away now. *Now!*"

14

I didn't sleep well that night. The crisp, new bed-sheets were scratchy. The pillow was too hard. I kept kicking the quilt onto the floor.

But I knew the bed wasn't the problem. It was just being in a new place, in an unfamiliar room, with a family that wasn't mine.

A little after two in the morning, I climbed out of bed and walked to the window. I could hear the steady wash of the ocean waves beyond the dunes. A soft, cool wind fluttered the curtains beside me.

I leaned out and peered down to the backyard. A haze covered the pale half moon. The sky was an eerie yellow, and there were no stars. The tall grass on the dune rustled in the wind.

Yawning, I shut my eyes and let the cool, salty air caress my face. Relax, Ellie. Listen to the waves; feel that soft air. Let it relax you.

But when I opened my eyes, I gasped. I gazed down, openmouthed, as a figure floated into view from the pine trees at the top of the dune.

Who's out there?

I leaned farther out the bedroom window, squinting

into the darkness. Bathed in the hazy moonlight, the figure moved slowly closer.

A man.

Walking toward the house.

No. A boy.

As he floated closer, head down, I saw dark hair. A long coat, a raincoat, too long, trailing behind him on the ground.

He stopped suddenly, in the middle of the yard, the tall grass blowing around his ankles, and raised his face to the house.

Brandon?

Outside at two in the morning?

Has he totally lost it?

Shivering, I pulled my head in. I tugged down my long nightshirt with both hands, turned, and ran barefoot out of my room.

Down the hall, with my hands clenching and unclenching at my sides. I bumped hard into a little table against the balcony wall, invisible in the dark. "Ow!"

Pain shot up my side. Ignoring it, I crept silently down the stairs, holding on to the slender railing. A square of yellow moonlight spread over the living-room floor.

I turned and headed through the kitchen, alert now to every sound. The hum of the refrigerator. The clink of the ice maker beside it. The faint whistle of wind around the side of the house.

I turned the lock on the kitchen door, pulled the door open, and stepped onto the deck. Into the night air, cool and wet. A sudden explosion of noise—the chirp of a thousand crickets.

The deck felt cold under my bare feet. I hurried to the railing and peered through the milky light.

My voice came out in a choked whisper, "Brandon? Are you out here?"

Below the deck, a hedge of rhododendrons shivered and shook. The patches of tall grass in the yard shifted one way, then the other. The symphony of crickets grew louder.

The whole yard is *alive*, I thought.

But where's Brandon?

My eyes searched the darkness. No one there now.

"Brandon—are you hiding from me?"

I waited a few seconds. Watching. Listening. The only sound: the harsh grating of the crickets, all around me, warning me to keep away. Finally, I swung away from the deck railing and ran back into the kitchen. Still shivering, I carefully closed the door and turned the lock.

The wetness of the night air clung to my hair. I pushed damp strands of it back off my face with both hands.

And then I heard a sound. A soft breath. Somewhere in front of me in the dark kitchen.

"Brandon? Are you inside?"

No reply.

I held my breath and listened.

I could hear the steady breathing, slow, a whisper of air in and out. Closer now.

"Brandon? Are you trying to scare me?"

Silence.

And then the soft, steady breaths again. Close. So close.

"This isn't funny!"

I fumbled against the wall, searching for a light switch. None there. I didn't know this kitchen. It was all so unfamiliar, so strange.

I could feel him next to me. Feel someone there. Could hear the breaths, irregular now, growing harsh.

"Who's there?" My throat suddenly so dry. "Who's there? Who is it?"

And then the lights flashed on.

15

Abby?"

She stood in the kitchen doorway, in a satiny, pink robe, her hand still on the light switch beside the door. She squinted at me, her tanned face wrinkled with sleep.

"Ellie? You scared me to death. I heard someone in the kitchen. I thought—"

"I—I'm sorry," I stammered. "But Brandon . . ."

I turned, my eyes still adjusting to the bright ceiling lights.

No one there.

No one breathing beside me. No one in the kitchen.

"I thought I saw Brandon out in the yard. So I came down. But he wasn't outside. Then I thought I heard him in here. But I couldn't find the light switch, and . . ."

I stopped. I realized I sounded totally mental.

Abby pulled the front of her robe tighter. She tilted her head as she squinted at me. "Brandon? Outside in the middle of the night? Ellie, what are you talking about?"

"Really, I—"

"Let's go see." Shaking her head, Abby turned and trotted up the stairs. My legs trembling, I pulled myself up after her.

Abby pushed open Brandon's door. We both tiptoed in.

He lay sound asleep on one side, snoring softly, quilt pulled up to his chin, a small teddy bear clutched in one hand.

I gazed at him from the side of the bed. He wasn't faking. He was really asleep.

My mind spinning, I followed Abby out to the hall. "I'm so sorry," I whispered. "I don't really know how to explain it. I—"

"You're trembling, dear," she said softly. "Don't be upset."

"I didn't mean to wake you up," I muttered.

"Was it a dream, Ellie? That's very normal, being in a new house. You know. The stress of a new job. And . . . well . . . this is a difficult thing. With Brandon acting so strange and all."

"I . . . no . . . it wasn't a dream," I said. "I definitely saw something."

I thought of Mrs. Bricker, that crazy old lady in town. *Stay away from the boy. It's in the guest house. . . .*

That's what she had said.

The boy . . . the guest house . . .

I suddenly felt so weary. Weary and embarrassed.

"I'm really sorry I woke you up," I said, avoiding Abby's eyes. "I'm usually not crazy. I mean, I'm really very calm and responsible. You'll see. I promise."

"I'm sure of it," she replied. "Do you want some hot tea or some cocoa or something?"

"No. Thanks. You've been so nice."

"Let's forget this whole thing," she said, walking me down the hall to my room. "A fresh start tomorrow— okay?"

"Okay," I said. I thanked her again and returned to my room.

* * *

The next morning, sunlight poured through my open window. I glanced at the bed-table clock—nearly eight, and the room was hot already. My nightshirt was damp and twisted around me.

I could hear the crash of waves at the beach and, closer, Heather screaming for more juice downstairs.

I sat up in bed and stretched. I felt achy, still tired. I gazed around the unfamiliar room. Some of the shorts and tops that I'd bought in town were still tossed over the dresser.

My first words of the morning—"I'm not crazy."

I saw something last night.

I don't hallucinate. I've never hallucinated in my life.

Even during the long nightmare after Will died, even through all the guilt, all my crazy, irresponsible behavior, all the *bad* years, I always kept my hold on reality.

I never went crazy.

I never saw things that weren't there.

So what had I seen last night?

I shook my head hard, as if forcing the thoughts from my mind. I pulled on some of my new clothes—a pair of white shorts and a pink sleeveless top.

"I'm all new," I told myself. "A fresh start today." Isn't that what Abby said?

Okay. You got it, babe. A fresh start.

I brushed my hair, made my bed, gazed out the window at the sparkling sunlight, and started to the stairs. My mobilephone rang.

I felt a shiver of dread. Was it Clay?

I checked the caller ID. "Hi, Teresa," I said.

"Ellie, hi. You didn't change your number."

"No. Not yet."

"I'm standing outside my office. I don't want to go in yet. It's so hot here in the city. The sidewalk is melting. Really. My shoes are sticking. You're so lucky to be at the beach. Hey, I thought you were changing your number."

"I didn't get a chance. Everything took so long in town."

"Well, did Clay call again last night?"

"No. Actually, he didn't. Something else happened. I—"

"Yaaaay. Maybe he was hit by a bus and dragged for twenty blocks, then flattened under the tires."

I laughed. Teresa always made me laugh. "Always look on the bright side, right?"

"That's me. Miss Mary Sunshine. Listen, Ellie—"

My line beeped. Another call? I was popular this morning. "Teresa, catch you later. I've got another call."

"Later. Bye."

I clicked the FLASH button. "Hello?"

"Ellie, where are you?"

"Mom? Hi. I'm in my room. You know. My new bedroom. At the Harpers' house in Watermill."

"You mean . . . you really took that job? I didn't think you were serious. I mean, I hoped—"

"Mom, yes. I took the nanny job. And I'm really happy about it. I'm looking forward to a great summer."

"A great summer? How about looking forward to a great career?"

"Excuse me? Mom, the connection isn't very good."

"You're a baby-sitter? Isn't that a job for teenagers? Ellie, did you lie about your age?"

"Ha ha, Mom. We all know you're funny. How's Lucky? Did you send him to Marsha?"

"Yes, I sent him and his furballs to Marsha. Don't

change the subject. What's the family like? They're famous Hamptons people? Have I heard of them?"

"No, they're a young couple, Mom. He's some kind of financial guy. And she ... I'm not sure what she does. She has the summer off. She has two kids to take care of."

"I don't mean to pick on you, Ellie, but—"

The famous *but*.

"—but why take another dead-end job? I'm just asking. I can ask a question, right?"

"Mom—I just woke up. I don't need this now."

"Well, I'm calling with good news. You don't have to take an attitude."

"Good news?"

"Knock knock."

I groaned. "Mom, I don't have time for jokes."

"Knock knock, Ellie. It's not a joke. It's opportunity knocking."

"Groan. Groan. Do you hear me groaning? I've got to go, Mom."

"Listen to me. Your sister, Wendy, is expanding her real estate office. Madison is growing like wildfire. She's taking on two new people. There's a place for you, Ellie. A very good salary and a fifteen percent commission."

"Mom, you want me back in Madison? You practically tossed me out of the house, remember? You were so thrilled when I moved to New York."

"Thrilled? Don't say that, Ellie. That's not true. It was hard for me to send my daughter away. I went along with it. I wasn't thrilled. You needed a fresh start in new surroundings. But you made a flop of that, too. Pardon my French."

"Huh? Mom, that's really harsh."

"Harsh? Harsh is for laundry detergents."

"Listen to me, Mom. I'm keeping this job, and I'm going to make something of it. You may think it's beneath me or something, but I don't. I have some things to prove to myself before I can start thinking about a real career. And I'm starting right here. And I don't need any suggestions from you or Wendy."

"I was only trying to help," she replied in a mousy little voice, totally phony.

"Bye, Mom." I clicked off the phone and tossed it to my bed.

I turned. Brandon was standing in the doorway. He wore a sleeveless striped T-shirt over a baggy black swimsuit that came down over his knees. He had his skinny arms crossed in front of him. And he stared at me coldly.

How long had he been standing there?

"Brandon. Hi."

Why was he staring at me like that, his lips pressed together so tightly?

"Were you outside last night?" I asked. "Did I see you in the backyard late last night?"

He continued to stare. Then he slowly shook his head.

"Come on, Brandon," I insisted. "Wasn't that you?"

He shook his head again. He twirled his finger around his ear, signaling that I was crazy.

No point in continuing.

"Listen, I'm going to go exploring this morning," I said. "Would you like to come with me?"

He turned and darted away.

Abby took the kids into town to buy shoes. I had a nutritious bowl of Cocoa Puffs—the kids' favorite—and a cup of lukewarm coffee.

Then I pulled on my new flip-flops and stepped outside to do some exploring. I figured it was time to get familiar with the terrain.

Whoa. The morning sun was already high in the sky, and I could feel its heat on my bare shoulders. I hurried back inside to get my sunglasses.

Last night, I was so freaked out that I didn't see where I was. This morning, I had time to take it all in.

A beautiful, wide redwood deck stretched along the back of the house. A round umbrella table and white metal chairs stood at one end, and several chaises longues and matching chairs were arranged nearby. A large barbecue grill stood at the other end.

Steps led down to the small, sandy backyard, and a low, unpainted picket fence tilted this way and that on the left. A hedge of tall rhododendrons stretched along the bottom of the deck. The spring blossoms, all white, were starting to shrivel and turn brown.

I picked up a beach ball and tossed it back toward the house. An inflated inner tube and a silver-blue Frisbee lay near the rhododendrons.

I trudged up a steep dune, my flip-flops slipping, the sand already hot, burning my toes. At the top of the dune, a row of slanting pine trees. They stood in a perfect straight line, I noticed, as if deliberately placed to hide the guest house behind them.

I ducked into the shade of the trees and gazed at the little house. A dark cyclone of buzzing insects rose up at the side of the house. The tiny gnats—or whatever they were—spun furiously, millions of them, sending up a loud droning whine, such an unpleasant sound.

Though it was two stories tall, the house was nearly as small as a gardening shed. Its gray shingle siding was dark and weathered with age. The small windows at the back were frosted with dust. A thick carpet of dried pine needles stretched the length of the house, piling up like a snowdrift against the back wall.

As I drew nearer, a strong stench of mold and decay invaded my nostrils. I held my breath. Was it just normal house smell? Or was something rotting inside?

I let out my breath in a whoosh as Mrs. Bricker's warning flashed back into my mind. What had that crazy old woman said?

It's in the guest house. Stay away. It's in the guest house.

What could she have been babbling about?

And why the hell did I have such a talent for attracting crazy people?

I turned and made my way past the whirling insects and to the front of the house, which faced the ocean. The front door had been white at one time, but the paint had peeled and faded, revealing the dark wood beneath. The tiny octagonal window in the door had cracked in two.

A dark stain rose on the shingles beside the door like a shadowy ghost. A faded gray curtain covered the front window, which was also frosted with dust. Slates from the roof littered the ground.

This must have been a cute little house when it was built. Did someone live here once? Why was the place abandoned?

It's in the guest house. Stay away. It's in the guest house.

The old woman's velvety voice lingered in my mind.

What was in the guest house?

I had to check it out.

I held my breath again as I stepped up to the front door. To my surprise, the air suddenly grew chilly. As if the house gave off waves of cold.

"Huh?"

Through the broken window, I thought I saw something move inside.

I jumped back.

No. Wait. No.

It had to be my shadow on the glass—right? Or maybe my reflection.

Ellie, don't scare yourself. It's an abandoned old house. That's all. Are you really going to let that crazy old woman terrify you?

I stepped back up to the front door, and again I felt a wet chill seep from the house. I squinted through the tiny window in the door, but couldn't see anything.

I'm going in, I decided.

I grabbed the doorknob. The metal was cold. Cold despite the hot sunshine beaming down on it.

I squeezed the knob. Started to turn it.

And a voice shouted, *"Get away!"*

16

At first, I thought the cry had come from inside the house. But then I heard the crunch of footsteps behind me.

I spun around.

The glare of sunlight hid the person approaching, a figure in white, all white. And again, I thought of ghosts. I squinted hard, struggling to focus.

And then he stepped out of the glare, a grin on his tanned face. He wore a white polo shirt, damp from sweat, white tennis shorts, white sneakers, and he carried a tennis racquet in its case.

"Chip? Oh. Hi."

"Ellie, I didn't scare you—did I?"

"Uh . . . no," I said. Why did he shout like that? Did he deliberately try to make me jump?

"You should be careful. Stay away from here," he said.

He stepped closer, and I could see his broad forehead was beaded with sweat. "Dangerous," he said, a little out of breath. He grinned at me. "You're looking fresh and alive this morning."

"Well . . . thank you."

He pulled a handkerchief from the pocket of his

shorts and mopped his forehead. "You finding your way around?"

I nodded. "Yes, doing a little exploring. I saw the little guest house and—"

"Think I should rent it out? Ha ha. What a dump, huh? It looks like a bomb hit it. No kidding. It's kinda dangerous. You should stay away. And you should definitely keep the kids away. Don't let 'em play in here or anything."

"I won't," I said. I tried to act as if he wasn't staring at my top. But it was hard not to notice. The guy wasn't exactly subtle.

He put his hand on my bare shoulder. "I hope you like it here. Everything okay so far?"

"Yes, fine."

But I'd like it better, Chip, if you stopped staring at my tits.

"Shame about this little guest house," he said. He brushed a fly away from his face. "It was already a wreck when we moved in. Abby and I really should have it torn down, I guess." He scratched his crooked nose. "Probably cost as much to tear it down as rebuild it."

He grinned at me, his eyes lowering over my body. "You play tennis?"

"No. Not since high school," I said.

"Oh. You've got those strong, athletic legs. I thought maybe you played."

"I do the treadmill. You know. At the gym. When I can afford it."

He nodded. "Have you been to the beach yet?"

"No. I was just on my way to check it out."

I was tempted to tell him how uncomfortable his stare was making me, but I had the feeling he didn't care.

I turned and started up the dune that led to the beach. "I'll be back for lunch. Abby says I have the kids this afternoon."

And wouldn't you know it? He followed me. "Totally amazing day, isn't it? But, man, I sucked at my tennis match this morning. And I was playing a guy twice my age. Gotta get back in shape." He took my hand and pressed it against his stomach. "Still pretty tight, huh?"

"Uh . . . yeah."

I didn't like the way this was going. I pulled my hand free. "Chip, I ran into someone . . . in town yesterday. Mrs. Bricker? Actually, she came up to me. She said she used to be the nanny here."

"You're kidding." His face reddened. Rivers of sweat ran down his cheeks. "That crazy old bitch? What did she want with *you*?"

"She—she acted very strange. She—"

"She *is* very strange," he said. "She's totally nuts. I had to fire her. I caught her telling Brandon all kinds of frightening ghost stories. She was scaring the poor kid to death."

"Oh, wow. That's awful," I said.

"Can you imagine? Telling ghost stories to a four-year-old? Abby and I think maybe that's why he stopped talking."

I shook my head. "That's bad news." Then I added, "It's a good thing you hired me. I don't *know* any ghost stories."

I was just making a joke, but it didn't make him smile. "Enjoy the beach, Ellie. See you at lunch." He lowered his gaze. "Are you wearing a swimsuit under that?"

Yuck.

"No. I'm just exploring today," I said.

He saluted with his tennis racquet. Then he turned and started trotting toward the house.

"Weird," I muttered.

I heard a loud creak from inside the guest house. Did the curtain over the front window move?

No. Of course not.

I was imagining things.

Right?

17

I can't believe that I stood this close to her this morning, that she's in my house. That I see her every day.

She's so close.

Close enough to strangle.

Parading around in that tiny pink top, as if she had any tits. . . .

I really can't stand it. She's making me crazy.

Only two days, but she's making me crazy.

All the old feelings . . . They're all flooding back to me.

I'm only human. Every time I see her, every time I stand close to her, she brings it all back—all the bad feelings. All the anger.

How can she not remember me? How is that possible?

She looks at me and doesn't remember.

How insulting is that?

It proves that I was nothing . . . nothing at all to her.

I've controlled myself so well. I haven't let on a thing.

But I'm angry enough now. After two days of seeing her, I'm angry enough.

She's made me angry enough to kill her.

Sooner? Or later? That's the only question.

Sooner? Or later?

Or . . . perhaps I should torture her first. The way she tortured me.

18

After lunch, Abby and I rubbed the kids down with sunblock. Brandon stood still as a statue and let Abby goo him up. Heather made a giggling game of it and made me chase her around the house first. Then she kicked and screamed and pretended she didn't like it when I slathered her with the stuff.

"They make a spray sun lotion now," Abby said. "We'll have to get some. Then we can just line them up and spray them."

"In my eye," Heather complained, rubbing both eyes.

"Well, stop rubbing it, then." Abby took a tissue and wiped Heather's eye.

"Do you like the beach?" I asked Brandon.

He nodded, but his flat expression didn't change.

Abby pulled a blue-and-white Yankees cap over Brandon's curly black hair. He took it off. She put it on again.

She turned to me. "Since we're down at the end, our part of the beach is pretty deserted. No one for them to play with. So turn right when you get there and go where it's more crowded. The public beach is just a short walk."

"No problem," I said. I slung the bag of beach toys over my shoulder.

"Look for an au pair named Maggie. She has long red hair, and she's very tall, and has an Irish accent. You'll see her. She works for Hannah Lewis, a friend of ours. Maggie takes care of the two daughters. Sometimes Heather and Brandon like to play with them."

"Great. I'll find her," I said. "It'll be nice to have company."

"You can't miss her," Abby said, pulling a small tennis hat over Heather's blond hair. "She has the reddest hair you've ever seen and a face full of freckles. I think you'll like her." She patted Heather's head. "Are you going to keep your hat on today?"

"No way."

I couldn't stop myself. I laughed. Two-year-olds are so refreshingly honest.

Abby flashed me a scolding glance. "Don't let her get too much sun." She grabbed Heather playfully and started to tickle her ribs. "Heather's bones. I've got Heather's bones."

Heather giggled and squirmed. Then she thrust her little hands at Abby's ribs. "Mommy's bones! Mommy's bones!"

I turned to Brandon. He stood in the corner, tugging the waist of his swimsuit, watching the tickling match, his face as blank as ever.

Abby and Heather giggled together. "Mommy's bones! Mommy's bones!"

Then Abby said, "Enough." She pulled Heather to her and kissed her cheek. "You be good for Ellie, okay?"

Heather didn't answer.

Abby handed me a straw carrier full of beach towels and sun glop. "And here. Take some extra Pampers. You'll probably need them."

So now I had the pails and shovels slung over my back, the straw bag in one hand. Heather took the other hand. Brandon ran ahead, and we stepped out the back door, finally on our way to the beach.

As we passed the deck, I glimpsed Chip stretched out on a chaise longue, reading a Stephen King novel, a tall drink on the table beside him. He lowered the book and gave us a wave. "Have fun," he called.

"Daddy, come beach?" Heather called.

"Maybe later," Chip shouted.

We climbed the dune toward the guest house. The sun faded in and out. High clouds passed quickly overhead. The breeze off the ocean felt cool.

As soon as we reached the line of pine trees, Heather pulled off her tennis hat and handed it to me. I decided not to argue with her. I tucked it into the beach bag.

Brandon suddenly started to run toward the guest house, a determined expression on his face. He bent down and picked something up from the thick carpet of pine needles.

"Brandon? What have you got?"

"Bandon? What got?" Heather called, mimicking me. "Bad boy. What got?"

Stepping into the cold shadow of the guest house, I caught up to him and saw that he'd picked up a straight stick. He studied it for a moment, then began trotting toward the beach, waving the stick in front of him.

"Hey, you don't need that stick," I called. "What are you going to do with that?"

It was on the tip of my tongue to say, "Put it down. You'll poke your eye out."

But how many thousands of times had my mother said that to me?

I caught myself in time. *No way* was I becoming my mother!

"Brandon, wait for us. Don't run ahead." I practically dragged Heather up the dune to catch up to him. "Are you going to use that stick to help build a castle?"

He waved the stick at me.

"Shall we build with that?" I repeated.

He nodded. The steady ocean breeze fluttered his hair around his serious, pale face. He stared hard at me for a moment, lowering the stick to his side.

What are you thinking, Brandon? I wondered. What is going on in that troubled brain?

If only you would talk . . .

At the top of the dune, the ocean came into view.

"Wow."

I stopped and gaped at the wide band of golden sand, at the crashing waves. The beach stretched on forever!

Ellie, you're a long way from Madison.

The green-blue waves were high today, roaring to shore in twos and threes, exploding in burst after burst of white froth. Two terns picked at something in the sand. I watched them run when the surf rolled over their spot.

Chip and Abby's house stood alone down at this end of the beach. I could see the top of the guest house from here and, beyond it, the second story of the main house.

Brandon kicked off his flip-flops and left them in the sand. He went running down the beach, his bare feet splashing up sand and water.

"Pick me up! Pick me up!" Heather demanded.

What choice did I have? Somehow I managed to carry the beach toys, the straw bag, and the two-year-old.

"What's dat?" Heather pointed at a shiny black object half-buried at our feet.

"It's a crab shell," I said. "I think it's called a horse-shoe crab."

"Yucky!"

We passed several nice-looking older houses that faced the water, then came to the edge of a public beach. A few dozen people had spread out blankets and erected beach umbrellas. The tall, white lifeguard stand stood empty. Too early in the season for lifeguards, I guessed. Most of them probably weren't out of school yet.

Brandon had already found the au pair, Maggie. Abby was right. No way I could miss her. She was at least six feet tall and had flowing, carrot-colored hair that gleamed in the sunlight. She wore a long white cover-up over a green one-piece bathing suit. As I approached, she was handing juice boxes to two little blond-haired girls.

She smiled and greeted Brandon and then turned to me.

I groaned as I lowered Heather to the sand. "Are you Maggie?"

"Yes, hello. You must be the new nanny."

"Juice!" Heather demanded. "Juice!"

"Sure, I have one for you," Maggie said. She dipped into a red-and-white plastic cooler and handed Heather a juice box. "How about you there, Brandon, my lad?"

Brandon shook his head.

"I'm Ellie," I said. "I just started with the Harpers."

Maggie brushed her hair back. She had a warm smile. "At least they got rid of the old woman."

"Mrs. Bricker?"

"Imagine her coming here and telling me ghost stories. I'm from Limerick, you know. I could tell her a few ghost stories of my own."

I dropped the straw basket and the beach-toy bag to the sand. "She—she followed me in town," I said. "I think she wanted to tell me some kind of ghost story, too. She warned me to—"

"She's daft as they come," Maggie said. Then she lowered her voice. "She tried to tell me that Brandon there—that sweet, innocent boy—was haunted, possessed by something evil, and that's why he stopped talking."

The image of last night flashed into my mind. The sight of a boy shrouded in the eerie yellow haze. Then in the kitchen. The soft breathing, so close to me in the dark.

I shook away the thought. "Well, anyway, Mrs. Bricker is gone," I said to Maggie.

Heather and the two Lewis girls were handing their empty juice boxes back to Maggie. "That's Deirdre, and that little angel is Courtney." Maggie pointed. "Nice girls, so pretty with that fine, blond hair, but they're spoiled. Back home, we wouldn't wait on them hand and foot like royal princesses."

She shooed the four kids away. "Go play. Here. Take your shovels and things, and go busy yourselves. Go play with those other kids over there."

"You come, too!" Deirdre insisted. She tugged Maggie's hands. "You, too!"

"I'll be joining you in a moment. Shoo. Go." Maggie turned to me. She still had the crunched-up juice boxes in her hands. A stiff wind gust fluttered her white shirt. "Are you a local girl, Ellie?"

"No. Actually, I'm from Wisconsin."

Maggie chuckled. "I'd have to look that up on a map. I've been in your country only little more than a year."

"It's in the Midwest," I said. "It's a long way from here."

I turned and saw that the girls had joined up with some other kids a little ways down the beach. The kids had formed a circle. They were holding hands and moving together, circling something, moving slowly, clockwise.

"What on earth are they doing?" I asked.

Maggie tossed the juice boxes down, and we hurried over to them. "It's a gull," Maggie said. "A fat seagull. Oh, look. The poor thing has a broken wing. I guess it can't fly. It's just standing there while they dance around it."

We stood at a distance, watching the circle of kids. Step, step. Holding hands, they kept the circle tight as they moved.

The gull tipped its head, watching warily.

Some of the kids were laughing as the circle began to move faster. Some appeared to be singing.

And then I spotted Brandon, by himself, off to the side, far back from the circle.

Why hadn't he joined the other kids?

I cupped my hands over my mouth and started to call to him. But I stopped when I saw him raise the stick. He raised it chest-high in front of him, and then he went charging—

—Charging into the circle of kids.

I screamed, starting to run. "*Brandon! Stop! Brandon—no!*"

Kids cried out, startled, as Brandon broke through the

circle. Two girls stumbled into each other and fell to the sand.

Running hard, his head down, Brandon lowered the stick—aimed—and drove it deep into the gull's white belly.

The bird let out a hideous, shrill squeal. Its good wing shot straight up, fluttered frantically.

But it couldn't move, skewered on Brandon's stick. The bird cried out again, hoarser this time, like the caw of a crow.

Brandon jerked out the stick. With a loud grunt, he stabbed again, burying the stick deep in the gull's chest.

The bird's head fell back. The wings drooped to its sides. It groaned and toppled over.

Kids screamed and cried.

The Lewis girls, shrieking, tears running down their cheeks, ran to Maggie.

Grunting like an animal, Brandon poked the stick through the gull's belly again. Stabbed it.

Stabbed it again.

I hurried up behind him and grabbed his shoulder.

I pulled him back. Brandon toppled over, breathing hard. His face red, his dark eyes wide, blank, almost unseeing.

"Brandon—why?" I choked out. "Why? You killed it! Why?"

White gull feathers blew around my ankles, sticky with blood. Dark blood soaked into the sand, spreading into a puddle around the mutilated gull.

"Brandon, answer me! Answer me!" My throat stung from screaming. "Why, Brandon? Why?"

19

I sat across from Abby in the kitchen. I hadn't changed—I still wore my bikini with an oversize, white T-shirt on top.

Late afternoon sunlight slanted through the windows, making the room rosy and warm. We sat with our legs tucked under us at the small, square white table in the breakfast nook. The red straw place mats from breakfast were still on the table. A glass vase brimming with blue and white hydrangeas sat in the middle.

Abby leaned over the table to pour tea into my cup. She was wearing white sweats, which made her tan look even more sensational, and she had a white bandanna around her hair. She shook her head sadly as she slid into her chair.

"I don't know why Brandon has become so violent," she said. Chip was upstairs, watching a Disney cartoon video with the kids. So we didn't have to whisper.

She sprinkled a packet of Equal into her tea. "I just don't know what to think about that boy. I'm at a loss, Ellie. I really am." She sighed. "I feel so helpless. Why would he do a thing like that? What would make a four-year-old boy kill a bird . . . so brutally . . . in front of all those other kids? It's just sick."

I raised the cup to my lips and took a sip. "His doctor—?" I started.

"Yes, of course, I'm going to tell Dr. Kleiner about this," Abby interrupted. She was spinning her cup slowly in her hands, tapping her magenta-polished nails on the china, but she hadn't taken a sip. "I have to tell him about this right away."

She sighed again, tapping the cup some more. "But I don't know about these shrinks. I really don't. Is Dr. Kleiner getting anywhere with Brandon? Is he reaching him? I don't see any sign. The boy has killed two animals in the short time since you arrived."

Her shoulders shook. I thought she might cry. She stared into the steaming teacup.

Then, she reached across the table and took my hand. "He seems to like you, though, Ellie. You're the first one he's responded to."

I sure didn't see any signs of it. But if Abby said so . . .

"Well, thanks . . . ," I said.

She squeezed my hand, then let go. "I hope you'll stay, Ellie. I know it's kind of tough. Not your normal babysitting job. But I hope you'll stick it out. I think you can help Brandon. I really do." Her eyes watered over. She brushed the tears away with her paper napkin.

"I'll try," I said.

She took a sip of tea. The cup shook in her hand. Suddenly, her eyes went wide. She jumped up. "Oh, my goodness. I totally forgot."

She hurried out to the hall, her sandals clicking on the wood floor. A few seconds later, she returned carrying a long white box, tied with a satiny red ribbon. "These came for you, Ellie. Looks like roses." She handed the box across the table.

"Weird," I muttered. "Who would send me roses?"

I took the box from her. As I set it down, I saw a little white envelope tucked under the ribbon. I opened it and read the note, written in blue ink, very neatly, in a handwriting I didn't recognize:

Congratulations!
To the new nanny.
Love,
A FRIEND

Abby had walked to the kitchen counter and was sorting through some mail. "These must be from my friend Teresa," I said.

"Nice," she muttered.

I tugged off the ribbon, pulled open the lid—and let out a sickened groan.

20

I dropped the box to the table. The flowers weren't roses. They were carnations and lilies, I think. And they were spray-painted black.

The blossoms were withered ... shriveled ... and crawling with bugs.

"Ohhh—cockroaches!" I cried.

Abby hurried over. "What's wrong?"

Cockroaches—dozens of them—swarmed over the black flowers. Swarms of bugs began crawling over the sides of the box.

"Oh, my goodness!" Abby let out a cry. "Who—? Who—?"

"I don't know," I said. My stomach lurched. I felt sick. I slammed the lid back on the box. Too late. Cockroaches were scrambling over the kitchen table, darting over and under the straw place mats.

Abby ran to the sink, grabbed a roll of paper towels. She tore off some sheets and began slapping at the slithering cockroaches. "Sick," she muttered. "Sick ... sick ..."

I grabbed up the flower box. My arms prickled as roaches slid onto my skin. They poured out of the box. The back of my neck itched. My *hair* itched.

Were they crawling through my hair?

"Oh, help." I slapped the back of my neck and felt a warm, wet squish. "Abby, where's the trash?"

She swung a place mat off the table and slapped it at a fleeing roach. "In back. Under the deck. Hurry. Get it out of here!" Roaches scattered over the floor. Abby did a wild dance, stomping them under her sandals.

Clamping the box shut with both hands, I hurried out the kitchen door, down the deck stairs, and to the ground. I found three metal trash cans near the driveway and shoved the box into one of them.

"Oh, gross." Gritting my teeth, I frantically brushed cockroaches off my arms, off the front of my T-shirt, out of my hair. Did I get them all? I couldn't tell. My whole body tingled and itched. I could still feel their prickly legs all over my skin.

By the time I returned to the kitchen, Abby seemed to have everything under control. She stood behind the table, her arms crossed tightly in front of her.

I shuddered. I rubbed my arms, the back of my neck. I could still feel those fat bugs. "I'm so sorry," I muttered.

"What was *that* about?" Abby asked. "Was it a joke? Who would send such a horrible thing? Your friend Teresa?"

"No way." I let out a sigh and dropped back into my chair. A cockroach floated belly-up in my mint tea.

"Then who?" Abby asked.

"Probably my ex-boyfriend, Clay. I'm really sorry, Abby. He—he's been acting like a total jerk. I broke up with him in the city before I came out here, and he— well—he can't seem to take a hint."

"What kind of guy sends bug-infested black flowers? Is he crazy?"

I tugged at my hair with both hands. "Aggggh. I don't know. He's been acting crazy. I think he's very angry. He just won't take no."

She crossed the room and stepped up close beside me. "Is he dangerous? Can I help you call the police about him, Ellie? I'd be happy to help call. If you think it would do any good."

I hesitated. "I don't really—"

A cry from upstairs. Heather. I jumped up.

Abby pushed me back down. "No. I'll go. Chip is up there with them. He probably fell asleep. You sit for a while and get yourself together." She hurried down the hall.

I sat for a long moment, staring at the dancing dots of sunlight on the kitchen counter beneath the window. I shut my eyes, and I saw those disgusting shriveled flowers and the fat roaches scrambling, scrambling over the flowers, over the table, over me.

I pictured Clay's teddy bear face, the chubby, pink cheeks, the round, dark eyes under the furry eyebrows. Did he really think this was the way to win me back?

Or had he given up?

Was this his crude, angry way of saying good-bye? Did he hate me that much?

Well . . . maybe it means I'm rid of him, I thought.

Way to go, Ellie. Always look on the bright side.

And then, another scene with flowers flashed through my mind. Another time when flowers made me want to cry . . .

A dance recital at Miss Crumley's, the dance studio on Henry Street in Madison that my sister and I faithfully attended every Saturday morning. Wendy was eleven and I was eight. I was so excited about the recital because I knew I was a better dancer than Wendy. Our grandparents were going to come, and I'd have a rare chance to show off in front of them.

I was so nervous, I sweated right through my tutu. But I danced wonderfully. At least, I thought I had. I can still remember the applause, the feeling of exhilaration. And then there came my grandparents, leading my parents into the dressing room, everyone beaming, so many big smiles.

Arms outstretched, I ran to them—and then stopped. I saw that my grandmother held a bouquet of flowers—yellow roses—in her hands.

A bouquet she started to hand to Wendy.

"Oh, goodness, Ellie," Grandma Estelle said. "We completely forgot that you dance, too!" I saw her cheeks blush red. She lowered her eyes to the bouquet—my sister's bouquet—pulled out a single yellow rose, and handed it to me. Then she gave the bouquet to Wendy.

I held myself in. I didn't cry. I think I might've even thanked Grandma Estelle.

But later in my room, I ripped the petals off the rose one by one, and I said a dirty word for each petal.

Wendy kept her flowers in a vase in her room. She asked me several times if I wanted to come in and smell them.

Whoa. Amazing how memories jump back to you.

The card that came with the black flowers sat in a puddle of spilled tea. I grabbed it and ripped it in two. Then I jumped to my feet and carried my teacup to the sink.

I poured the cockroach down the drain and washed

the cup clean. Then I held my hands under the faucet and just let the hot water pour over them.

I was still standing there, leaning over the sink, when I heard someone come up quietly behind me. Then I felt a hand caress the shoulder of my T-shirt.

Thinking it was Abby comforting me again, I turned. And there stood Chip, with his crooked, sleazy grin.

"Oh. Sorry. Didn't mean to startle you," he said.

"I . . . didn't hear you. I didn't know you were home," I lied, taking a step to the side, drying my hands on a dish towel.

His eyes flashed. "I can be quiet as a mouse when I want to be," he whispered.

I let out an awkward laugh. "You missed all the excitement. I—"

"Check this out," he said, showing off the hip-length, brown leather jacket he was wearing. "I just bought it. In Easthampton. Like it?" He spun around, modeling it for me.

"Sure. Very cool," I said.

"It's Armani. The leather is not to be believed. Made from virgin calves or something. Here. Feel it."

I hesitated. Virgin calves? He was joking, yes?

"Go ahead, Ellie. Feel it. You'll fall in love, no kidding." He stuck out his arm.

I ran my fingers down the jacket sleeve. "Really soft leather," I said. That's what I was supposed to say, right?

"I put it on and I couldn't take it off. I just had to have it. A total impulse thing." He brought his face close to mine and whispered again: "You ever do anything just on an impulse?"

The question hung in the air between us for a moment. When he didn't get an answer, he changed the subject. "How about a drink, Ellie? It's almost late afternoon. And who's counting, right? I'm going to have a vodka tonic. Nice and summery, I think. What can I get you? We could go out on the deck and chat. You know. Get acquainted."

Down, boy! Down!

"Well—"

"Hey, I really like that swimsuit. I saw you down on the beach with the kids. You look great in it."

I straightened my long shirt. "Thanks, Chip . . . but . . ."

I heard Abby talking to Heather. Does Abby know what Chip is like? Would she be surprised to know that he's coming on to me while she's just down the hall?

"Uh . . . no drink for me right now. Thanks," I said stiffly.

His eyes went dull.

"I'd better change and help out with the kids," I said.

I brushed past him and started toward the stairs.

"Maybe later," he called. It sounded more like a threat than an invitation.

Late that night, I was in bed, thumbing through a stack of magazines I had dragged out from my apartment—mostly dance magazines and ballet journals. Fantasy time for me.

Even after the humiliating incident at Miss Crumley's recital when I was eight, I continued to dance. In fact, I took ballet lessons up till my senior year in high school—until the day the real world stopped the music for me.

It was hard work, and my leg muscles ached just about every day of my life. But I loved the feeling of floating in the air, turning and moving with such precision and beauty and grace.

Another reason I loved it: I was good at it, and Wendy was a klutz.

I wanted to be a ballet dancer in New York. I danced in my dreams and in my daydreams. I doodled dancing figures on all my notebooks instead of taking notes in class.

Then, after that night with Will, after I stopped dancing forever, the dreams ended. But I never gave up my subscriptions to all the dance magazines. I never stopped studying the wonderful photos of dancers frozen in beauty, defying gravity.

Yes, I guess that was my unconscious ambition—to defy gravity. To dance on air. To dance in the mirrors on the ceiling.

Ha.

A little after midnight, I shoved the magazines under my bed and called Teresa on my cell.

"I'm not calling too late, am I? I know you're a working girl."

Teresa sighed. "Don't remind me. The computers were down today, so they told us to write everything down on paper. I mean, what is *that* about? I can't wait to get to the beach this weekend. How's it going, Ellie?"

"Not great."

"Like, how not great?"

"Clay did the most disgusting thing yet," I said. "He sent me a box of wilted flowers painted black."

"No shit? What a creep."

"I haven't finished. They were crawling with cockroaches."

"Oh, gross. I don't believe it. The cockroaches were probably other members of his family."

"Easy for you to make jokes," I said. "The roaches got out of the box and were crawling all over me and all over Abby's spotless kitchen."

"Did she freak? Did she lose her tan when she saw them?"

"No. She was okay about it. She's been really nice to me."

"Well, that's a good thing."

It was my turn to sigh. "Teresa, I think I have the job from hell. I really do."

"Ellie, give me a break. You're living two steps from the ocean in a gorgeous summer house and—"

"The kid is a total psycho maniac," I interrupted. "I mean, he's like right out of *Bride of Chucky* or something. And his father keeps staring at my tits, telling me how great I look in a bathing suit, offering me drinks as soon as his wife is out of the room."

"Dad is a slut?"

"Dad is a slut."

"Jesus, Ellie. Is he hot? Are you going to sleep with him?"

"*Shut up,* Teresa. You are *so* not funny tonight!"

"Come on, El. Only trying to make you laugh. You just started this job, and you sound totally wrecked. Are you going to stay there?"

"I don't know. I guess. I mean, do I have a choice?"

"Well—"

"I *have* to stay here," I insisted. "Can you hear my mother if I tell her I've quit another job? Could I live through another lecture from her about what a quitter I am and how I'm aimless and juvenile, and it's time for me to start my life for real, and how I should use my sister, Wendy, the saint, the soon-to-be-millionaire, as an example? I don't think so."

"Okay. So you're definitely staying. Excellent. I'll be out Friday night. Saturday night, we'll hit some clubs."

"You mean, have actual fun?"

"Actual fun. I promise, El."

I said good night to Teresa and clicked off my phone. I placed it on the bed table and slid under the quilt. "Actual fun," I murmured, yawning. I suddenly felt so weary, that aching kind of sleepy where your eyelids feel heavy and even your hair hurts.

I yawned again. Pressed my head into the pillow.

And heard footsteps downstairs.

Rapid, heavy footsteps in the room below mine.

Was it Chip? Yes, the heavy thuds sounded like Chip. Pacing back and forth, back and forth, pacing furiously. I glanced at the clock. After twelve-thirty.

What was his problem?

21

Did you like the flowers, Ellie?

They didn't upset you, did they?

Once you got over the shock, did you think about what they mean? Or did you toss them in the trash—the way you trashed me?

Yes, they were funeral flowers. Black flowers to honor the dead.

They were for your *funeral*, Ellie dear. Did you figure that out?

Yes, I sent them early. But I wanted to be the first. I'll be there. I want you to know that. I'll be the first at your funeral—because I'm going to cause it.

But don't worry, you have a little time.

I want to torture you a bit more. Because the very thought of you tortured me for seven years. Because you were there torturing me. Even in my sleep. Even in my dreams.

Maybe tonight you'll dream about my present to you. Maybe you'll dream about cockroaches crawling up and down your body. Maybe in your sleep tonight you'll feel the prickle of their feet against your skin, their dry bodies as they move over you, swarm over you . . . cover that cute little string bikini of yours, cover your arms, *your legs, climb into your eyes, your mouth . . . choke you . . . smother you.*

Soon you'll be a playground for bugs and worms. Under the ground, in the dark, where the bugs and worms play.

Soon, Ellie. Soon.

22

A few mornings later—cloudy, gray, the ocean air heavy and wet—I dropped the kids with some friends on Noyac Road and then headed the Taurus toward town.

My tires splashed through deep puddles of rainwater. The trees on both sides of the road glistened and dripped. It must have rained hard during the night, but I hadn't heard the storm.

I'd slept a deep, dreamless sleep. And when my alarm went off, I'd blinked my eyes open, confused. I didn't know where I was.

Now I was on my way to Southampton to buy party supplies for Abby. She was having a small party—a barbecue if the weather cooperated—and she needed beer and wine, and paper plates, lemons and limes, and a long list of other items, which I had tucked safely in my bag.

Noyac Road bumped past woods and small frame and shingle houses set close to the road. I passed a homey-looking restaurant with a big sign that proclaimed AR-MAND'S, then a pretty marina with small boats bobbing in the choppy, gray bay water.

I searched the radio for some lively music, something to wake me up, and I settled on Party 105: dance, dance,

dance. I recognized Pink, singing a song from a couple of years ago— "Get the Party Started"—and I sang along with her at the top of my lungs.

The music cheered me up, and thinking about Teresa coming out made me eager for the weekend.

Oh, yeah. Get this party started, all right!

I was still in a good mood at the gourmet store on Main Street when I felt a tap on my shoulder.

I had a sudden heavy feeling in the pit of my stomach, a feeling of cold dread as I turned and stared at Mrs. Bricker.

So much for my good mood.

Her bony hand was still on my shoulder. She pulled it away slowly. She wore a blue-and-white flower-print dress, a little faded with age. She had the same scarf she'd been wearing last time tied loosely around her throat.

Her round face was heavily rouged, and as a smile formed on her scarlet lips, her cheeks appeared to crack and crumble.

"Ellie? I hoped I'd find you today." Her voice was soft and smooth, a young woman's voice.

Had she been coming to town every day hoping to run into me?

Leave me alone, you old freak!

No. Don't do it, Ellie. You're a polite, young woman. Especially to old people. Remember?

"Hi, Mrs. Bricker. Nice to see you," I said.

She licked her heavily lipsticked lips. Her teeth were smeared with red. "You're still working for the Harpers?"

I pulled two boxes of wheat crackers off the shelf and dropped them into my basket. "Yes, of course. It's been only a few days."

Her smile faded. Behind the thick-lensed glasses, her

blue eyes were sharp and cold. "Did you think about what I told you?"

"Well, actually—"

She grabbed my arm so hard I nearly dropped the shopping basket. "I need to talk to you, Ellie. I didn't get a chance the first time. You really need to hear—"

I raised my free hand, as if calling for a truce. "Please, Mrs. Bricker. I have so much shopping to do. I really can't today."

I tried to turn to the shelves, but her grip tightened. "You're in danger, Ellie. I must speak to you. Now. It really can't wait."

My heart started to pound. What did I do to deserve this? Didn't I have enough trouble back at the house?

"No, I'm sorry. Please," I said sharply. "I don't mean to be rude, but—"

She brought her face close to mine. The powder and rouge on her cheeks smelled like oranges. Her breath smelled like sour tea. "You have time to buy me a coffee," she whispered, giving me a tight smile. "When you're finished here, we'll sit down and have a coffee. It will take ten minutes, Ellie. And it may save your life."

She led me to a little bakery and coffee shop called The Golden Pear, at the end of the row of shops. A light rain had begun to fall, and she held my arm as we walked along the sidewalk to the restaurant.

She must have been in her seventies or eighties, but she didn't walk like an old woman. She wore black New Balance sneakers and had no trouble keeping pace with me.

"My family used to own most of that block," she said, pointing to a row of stores across the street. "But they sold it during the Depression for next to nothing. Can you imagine how rich I'd be today? I'd be taking *you* out for coffee."

"Your family has lived in Southampton a long time?"

She sniffed. "We're not summer people. I'll tell you that."

We found a cramped booth by the window in back and ordered coffee and croissants. The restaurant was noisy, the little square tables were jammed together, and a man on a cell phone at the table across from us was having a loud, embarrassing fight with someone. Probably his wife.

I shouldn't have been there with her. I had so much shopping to do, and I barely knew my way around town. But Mrs. Bricker promised she would never bother me again, if I would only let her tell her story.

"I wouldn't be nagging you like this if you weren't in danger," she said, those sharp blue eyes trained on mine.

"Well, why don't you start with that?" I said, leaning forward. "How am I in danger?"

She shook her head. "I'll have to start at the beginning," she replied.

23

Our coffees and croissants came. Mrs. Bricker pulled her croissant in two and carefully slathered both halves with butter and strawberry jam. Then she spooned two teaspoons of sugar into her coffee and stirred it slowly, staring into the cup as if thinking hard, trying to decide how to tell her story.

I wanted to scream. I glanced at my watch. How long was this going to take?

Luckily, the loud, angry man on the cell phone got up and left. He was replaced by two gangly teenage girls in midriff tops and short shorts. They both wore rhinestone beads in their navels.

I counted to ten as Mrs. Bricker took a small bite of her croissant. Jam clung to her upper lip. She raised her cup, took a long sip of coffee, and I noticed the ring on her ring finger. It was an oval ring, silver with a large, dark green stone—an emerald?—mounted in the center.

She saw me gazing at it and raised her hand to give me a better view. "Isn't that the most perfect emerald you've ever seen? See how it catches the light? My husband gave me that on our fortieth anniversary. He said it once belonged to Queen Victoria." She snickered. "He always was a fucking liar."

Whoa. Such language. I almost did a coffee spit.

"It's beautiful," I said. I glanced at my watch. "But please, Mrs. Bricker . . ."

Finally, she cleared her throat and started her story.

"I guess I'll start with the Harpers' house. You know, the little guest house was built first. You've seen the guest house by now, right?"

I nodded.

"Well, it was built sometime in the 1850s. Back then, Sag Harbor was a major whaling town. There's a museum there to this day with displays about the whales that were caught and the sailors who went after them. It's all gone today, of course. No more whaling boats. All gone. Like just about everything else that was real out here."

She sniffed again, frowning, and took another bite of the croissant.

"Well, the little house was built by a whaling captain, a man named Halley, who sailed off Montauk. The truth is, Halley was a dishonest old scoundrel. My great-grandfather had a whaling boat, and Halley robbed him of it. Promised to buy it on credit, then never paid. A typical Halley. My family never had any use for them from that day to this.

"Well, Halley wanted to build a house for his family. He had four children by this time. But he couldn't really afford a house. So he stole a lot of lumber. Would you believe he stole some of it from coffins? Don't look at me like that, Ellie. I'm only speaking the truth. The man stole wood from people's coffins."

I set down my coffee cup and stared at her across the table. "Mrs. Bricker, how do you know all this?"

She wiped jam off her chin with her napkin. "It's in

the family records, dear. Besides, it's all common knowledge around here."

Common knowledge. Yeah, right.

She really is crazy, I realized. Hel-lo, Ellie. Why are
you sitting here with her when you could be getting your
shopping done and picking up the kids?

Mrs. Bricker raised her coffee cup to her mouth and
slurped the last of it. She held the cup up to the waitress,
signaling for more.

"Halley's wife had left him," she finally continued.
"So when he went off whaling, he left the children in
the care of a nanny. Now, I really don't know if he was
humping the nanny . . ."

Humping? Gross! Please—spare me.

"The children loved the nanny. I think her name was
Ann-Marie, but I might be getting that mixed up."

You might be getting everything mixed up, you kook!

"One of the children in particular—Jeremiah, the
youngest boy—*really* loved the nanny. He was a frail,
sickly boy. Premature by two months, you know, and
never made up for it. He didn't speak much and was shy
around people outside his family.

"Anyway, the nanny took the place of the boy's
mother, and she was his best friend, too, I guess. I mean,
she meant a little too much to the child. He loved her
too much. It became obvious that he had crazy ideas
about her. Because one afternoon—and this is in all the
newspapers of the time, dear, so you can look it up—
Jeremiah Halley caught the nanny making love to her
boyfriend, a young Italian man from the village.

"Jeremiah was sickly and thin, remember, but he went
into some kind of ungodly rage. He picked up an old
whaling harpoon. It was much too heavy for him, much

heavier than he was. But in his rage, he lifted it off the wall. And he heaved it. Heaved it at her, hoping to kill her for betraying him.

"But Jeremiah's aim was bad. He was just a tiny thing, remember. He heaved the harpoon—shot it across the room—and plunged it through the *boyfriend's* heart. He killed the boyfriend instead of the nanny."

Yeah, sure, I thought. A sickly little boy picks up a huge harpoon twice his size and throws it across the room with such force that it goes right through someone.

Tell me another one, Mrs. B.

"That's a horrible story," I said, making like I believed it. "And you're sure it's true? It really happened in the Harpers' guest house?"

Mrs. Bricker nodded solemnly.

An image flashed into my mind: Brandon poking the seagull to death.

I forced it from my thoughts.

"The nanny ran for help," Mrs. Bricker continued. "She sent for the town constable. The boy admitted what he had done. He hadn't moved from the nanny's bedroom. He stood, staring at the boyfriend's corpse lying there in a pool of blood."

"And what happened to the boy?" I asked.

Mrs. Bricker cleared her throat. "They didn't know what to do with Jeremiah. The local police had never encountered a murderer that young. No one had. Four years old. And the boy was so frail, so sickly and silent. He almost never spoke."

She took a long sip of coffee.

I shifted in my seat impatiently. "And?"

"Wouldn't you know it," the old woman said. "Jeremiah died two days later. They found him lying dead in the nanny's bed. Some said he died from the strain of what he did. Others said the little boy died of a broken heart."

I spun my coffee cup on its saucer. Then I raised my eyes to the old woman. "It's a real interesting story. But I don't understand. Why did you follow me all over town to tell it to me?"

Behind the thick, square glasses, her blue eyes narrowed to slits. "Because it happened again," she whispered. "Listen to me closely, Ellie: *It happened again.* Jeremiah's ghost remained in the house. It never left. It—"

"Whoa. Wait." I touched Mrs. Bricker's bony hand with my own. I could feel the big, emerald ring on my palm. "Stop. I enjoy ghost stories. Really. But I have so much shopping to do."

I glanced out the window. Rain was still drizzling down. The sky had grown darker. I sat there for a moment before I realized that my eyes had slipped from the sky and settled on a man.

I was staring at Chip Harper. He wore a tan plastic rain poncho, raindrops rolling down the front, and a blue Yankees cap. He was staring hard at Mrs. Bricker and me.

He had an intense scowl on his face. But when he realized I was looking back at him, he nodded awkwardly, then hurried away.

"Please let me finish," Mrs. Bricker pleaded. "I'm not telling you this for my health, you know. It happened again. In the 1950s. You see, Jeremiah's ghost remained in the guest house. Because the boy wanted his revenge.

He had missed his target. He had missed the nanny and murdered the boyfriend instead. And his ghost couldn't rest until he finished what he intended—until he murdered the nanny. And so, Jeremiah struck again."

I squinted at her. "A hundred years later?"

I signaled to the waitress for the check. I'd heard enough.

"Listen to me, Ellie. A doctor owned the house. The guest house. The big house still hadn't been built. I don't remember the doctor's name, but it's in the newspapers. You can see for yourself. He had a couple of kids. A boy, four or five, a little boy. The doctor came out only on weekends. The kids were left with their nanny.

"Don't roll your eyes, Ellie. I'm not making this up. It happened again. Just like the first time. The little boy caught the nanny he adored with her fiancée. He picked up a harpoon mounted near the mantel. He had to be possessed. He had to be possessed by Jeremiah, seeking his revenge.

"He tossed the harpoon. He missed. He missed again. He murdered the young man. Jeremiah didn't get his revenge. Afterwards, the boy didn't remember a thing. Not a thing. And that's proof—"

"Proof that he was possessed by Jeremiah Halley," I said.

"Yes. And he's still there, Ellie. Jeremiah is still in the guest house, waiting. He can't rest until he murders his nanny. Don't roll your eyes. Believe me. Your life could depend on it."

She licked her lips. Her voice had become raspy and hoarse. "I started work at the Harpers' in March when they first started coming to Watermill. And a friend told me this story a few weeks later. You can imagine how I felt. I—"

"You started in March? Was Brandon talking then?" I interrupted.

"No. Not a word. Poor kid. He seemed frightened to me. Frightened and strange. Clung to his father. A real papa's boy. Seemed angry at his mother all the time. I don't know what she did to deserve it. She was the nice one, seemed to me."

The waitress brought the check. The restaurant had become crowded, louder than when we had entered. I leaned across the table to hear the old woman better.

"I started at the end of March. The boy wasn't talking. I remember my first day so well. Cold and gray, with the wind blowing something fierce off the ocean.

"The boy disappeared for a while. He did that sometimes. He liked to be by himself. Liked to collect things from the ocean, shells and stones, and things.

"Anyway, that day, my first day, I found him on his hands and knees behind the guest house. I asked him what he was doing back there. Of course, he didn't answer. He just stared at me, stared with cold, angry eyes."

"Weird," I muttered.

Mrs. Bricker grabbed my hand. "Don't you see? What brought Brandon Harper to the guest house? It's Jeremiah Halley at work again. I know it. I—"

"Is that why you left the Harpers?" I asked. "Because you thought Brandon was possessed?"

She snorted angrily. Her rouged cheeks turned even redder. "No. I was fired. Unjustly fired by Chip Harper."

"Why? If you don't mind my asking."

"I was telling the story about Jeremiah Halley and the guest house to a friend, and Brandon overheard me.

Chip Harper fired me on the spot. I was never treated so badly in my life. Luckily, I got another job down the beach. A better paying job, I might add, with normal kids."

I dropped a twenty-dollar bill on the check. "Well, thanks for telling me all this." What else could I say? That she's a crazy, superstitious old woman who probably shouldn't be allowed near kids?

I slid from the booth and stretched out a hand to help her up. Her powder and rouge had caked, and her skin showed a thousand tiny cracks. She looked a lot like one of those ancient mummies in a horror film.

"Keep an eye on the boy," she rasped, waving a bony finger at me. "He looks sweet, but he could be dangerous. And watch out for Chip Harper, too. He's a shifty one. There's something definitely wrong with him."

I laughed to myself and hurried back out into the cool, refreshing rain, eager to get away from the old woman and her ugly stories.

If only I had listened.

24

"Is that Christie Brinkley?"

Teresa spun around. "Where?"

"The one in the shimmery red thing. See? Way too tight for her?" I pointed to the other end of the long, curved bar.

"Yeah. She looks great, doesn't she? I mean, for her age."

Teresa tossed her hair off her bare shoulders. She wore a silvery low-cut top over straight-legged black slacks. She had a small, temporary, red-and-blue heart tattoo on each shoulder and large silver earrings that dangled down over her cheeks and kept getting tangled in her hair.

I was dressed for our big club night, too, in a new outfit Teresa had picked out for me in Southampton. I had on a tight, pink-and-blue tie-dyed midriff top over a short denim skirt, and clog-type shoes that made me walk about a foot off the floor.

I had even teased and tortured my hair, trying to make it look like a do Nicole Kidman wore in a photo in *People* magazine.

It had all been Teresa's idea, and I couldn't say that I was quite comfortable with the look yet.

"Is my hair okay?" I asked Teresa. "Do I look like Raggedy Ann or something?"

She tugged a tangled strand off my face. "The waif look," she said. "Guys love it, Ellie. Seriously. You're Winona Ryder without the criminal record."

"Ha ha."

We were at Pulsations, a new club on the beach in a little town past Easthampton called Amagansett. It didn't look like much from the outside—a high, boxlike structure, like an airplane hangar, painted gray, without any decoration, not even a name sign. We stood in line for about twenty minutes, which Teresa said wasn't bad, and watched limos and expensive new cars pull up, and all these tanned, well-dressed guys and girls climbing out.

Music throbbed out every time the door was opened. An unhappy-looking crowd of ten or twelve had gathered across from the line. They were pleading with the guy at the door, gesturing wildly.

"They've got New Jersey written all over them," Teresa said. "They'll never get in."

A hot, humid night, and I knew my eye makeup was starting to run and my hair was frizzing up like crazy. I motioned to the guy at the door. "Think he'll let *us* in?"

And before Teresa could answer, he was giving us the big wave, holding the rope aside, and we were hurrying into the club, my shoes clonking on the concrete walk.

We stepped into a narrow, mirrored entry hall where we paid our admission and a music cover charge— thirty-five dollars before we even entered the club—and then into a cavernous room. My eyes adjusted to the low lights, the blue spotlights sweeping pale light over a crowded dance floor, the blue walls, the endless blue bar curving along one wall.

"I'm beginning to get the color scheme," I said, keeping close to Teresa, who was surveying the room, her eyes moving from face to face at the bar.

"See, it's cool, not hot," she said.

"Don't we want to be hot?" But she didn't hear me.

The deejay was fading a Mary J. Blige song I recognized into some dance hall reggae. The dancers seemed hesitant, then found the beat.

I saw a girl dancing with a cigarette in one hand and a martini glass in the other. A lanky guy in a sweat-drenched T-shirt with ABERCROMBIE blazing across the front waved his arms wildly, singing loudly, seemingly dancing by himself. Despite the fast beat of the music, a couple danced slowly, faces pressed together, his hands gripping her ass as they swayed.

On the other side of the dance floor, at the far end of the club, I saw tables, tall blue booths—a restaurant. "Do we want to eat?" Teresa asked.

"I think we just want to drink," I replied.

We pushed up to the bar. Two guys holding bottles of Red Stripe beer were arguing about the Mets. A really tanned guy with black hair slicked straight back was trying to impress a girl: "No, for real. I know *two* Baldwin brothers."

I heard snatches of conversations.

"I traded in the Hummer. Too hard to park."

"My wife is at Jet East tonight. We don't always go out together."

"Steven was at the next table. He eats there all the time. He had the smoked salmon, but he sent it back."

"Sure, he's a cokehead, but at least he can afford it."

The bartender was tall and drop-dead gorgeous—and he knew it. Women practically crawled over the bar to get his attention. I was going to order my usual—a glass of chardonnay. But then I thought, Get out of the rut, Ellie. Try to be different tonight. So I ordered a Hennessy sidecar, same as Teresa.

She lit a cigarette and gazed around. I took a long sip of my drink. I felt a little overwhelmed—the pounding music, the voices, the energy, the tension.

All this talk, all this dancing and moving and all this frantic, noisy, sweaty activity—just to get drunk and go home with somebody.

"See those two young blond women?" Teresa poked my shoulder with her glass. "No. Not those. The ones over there, the trampy-looking ones."

"They're not trampy. They're kinda attractive," I said. "Who are they?"

"They're the famous Hilton sisters, Nicky and Paris."

"Huh?" I squint into the blue light at them.

"Don't you ever read the 'Styles' section in the *Times*? They're in every week."

"Yeah, I read it. Well, okay, sometimes. But why are the Hilton sisters in every week?"

"Because they're rich and beautiful, and they go everywhere. They're at every party. Every charity event. Every dance club, every restaurant. They're *everywhere*. They're even here tonight. You can't go anywhere without seeing them. And they get their pictures taken wherever they go."

"And what do they do?"

"Do? They don't do anything. How could they do anything? They have to *be* everywhere!" She stubbed out her cigarette. "Hey, okay! I see two guys from my house. Come on."

She pulled me over to the two guys at the edge of the dance floor. They looked like they could be brothers. They were both short but had pumped-up bodies—big shoulders and muscled arms, as if they worked out all the time. They both had wavy, light brown hair. One of them wore a green-and-yellow T-shirt with a martini glass on the front under the name DEWAR'S. The other had a silky, shiny red sport shirt, unbuttoned nearly to his waist, gold chains hanging to his chest.

Teresa introduced them. I think their names were Bob and Ronnie. I couldn't really hear. We were already practically on the dance floor, so it was pretty easy to start dancing. I danced with the one in the T-shirt, and then Teresa and I traded, and I danced with the open shirt, who turned out to have fabulous rhythm.

It felt good to dance again. It had been so long.

I danced with Bob or Ronnie or whatever his name was under the blue lights. And then Teresa found some other people from her share house, and I danced with some other guys, had another sidecar or maybe two, danced some more, feeling light again, moving to the steady, booming beat, feeling lighter than ever under the blue lights, so blue and cool.

Then I fell out of one of my shoes.

I knew I would. They were just too high and clunky for dancing. I started to fall—and someone caught me. A dark-haired guy in a collarless black shirt and black denim jeans.

I saw his brown eyes, his slender, smiling face, glistening with sweat, so close to mine. He steadied me and then dropped away. I stood on one shoed foot, my bare foot dangling in the air.

He bent, picked up the loose shoe, lifted it to his ear, and spoke into it. "Hello? Who's calling?" He handed me the shoe. "It's for you."

I took it from him, raised it to my ear, and listened. I said, "They hung up."

I leaned on him as I tugged the shoe back on my foot. He felt solid. He smelled nice, of cologne and sweat, something lemony.

It took me a while to realize I was still leaning on him. "Oh, sorry." I took an unsteady step back. How many sidecars had I had?

I glanced over his shoulder for Teresa. Was she still dancing? I stared into a haze of blue, the dancers suddenly shadows moving up and down in the haze.

I grabbed his arm again. "Is it hot in here? I thought it was supposed to be cool. Isn't this supposed to be a *cool* place?"

"I'm sweating, too." He had a tiny scar under his chin and tiny dimples, just specks, when he smiled. He had a nice face, I thought. His eyes were warm and seemed to be laughing. I've always liked laughing eyes, people who saw the joke in things. I haven't known too many guys like that.

"Follow me." He took my hand and started to lead me around the crowded blue dance floor to the back door. "Want to cool off on the beach?"

"No, wait." I pulled free. The floor tilted a bit around me. "My friend. I can't leave my friend."

And then I spotted Teresa at one end of the dance floor, dancing with Bob or Ronnie—or was it both of them? I saw a jumble of arms and bodies and legs, moving as if they were underwater.

Yes, I'd definitely had a few sidecars too many. The problem is, you just think you're drinking fruit juice. You don't realize . . .

Well, Teresa was having fun and wouldn't miss me if I ducked out for a short while to get some air. I took the tall guy's hand and let him lead me out the back door, past a girl who was dancing in what looked like a red bra and panties, a swooping bird tattooed across her back. Past a table where I jumped, startled, thinking I heard the explosion of gunfire, but then saw it was only a group of guys slamming empty shot glasses down.

He pushed open the back door, and we stepped outside. A restaurant terrace faced the beach, tables jammed with people drinking pitchers of beer, downing big plates of chicken wings. The ocean looked like a wide black stripe under the purple night sky.

I took a deep breath. The air was cool and fresh and salty. Wooden steps led to the beach. I felt dazed, as if I had stepped out of myself, into a different life, allowing this stranger to pull me down to the sand.

"Hey, stranger, what's your name?" I blurted out.

He turned. His eyes were as dark as the ocean. "Jackson. Jackson Milner."

"Hi, Jackson. I'm Ellie Saks."

He took my hand and shook it formally. "Nice to meet you, Ellie. Want to walk?"

As my eyes adjusted to the darkness, I could see other couples walking slowly along the shore. I kicked off my shoes and left them beside the steps. "Sure."

We made our way closer to the water. The wet sand

felt good under my bare feet. The cool air, sweeping off the ocean, helped clear my head.

Music floated faintly from the club far behind us. "Are you out here for the summer?" I asked. I slipped in the sand, and we bumped shoulders.

"Yeah, I'm staying with a guy from school. How about you?"

I nodded. "I have a nanny job. I'm living with a family in Watermill."

His eyes studied me. "You like kids?"

"Probably not after *this* job!"

I liked his laugh. I liked the solid way he felt when I bumped into him. "Are you working, too, or just hanging out?"

He kicked a stone into the water. "I'm mostly hanging out. But I'm working part-time at a bicycle store in Southampton. It's called Spokes. Have you seen it? On Jobs Lane? But I'm kinda taking the summer off. Fall is going to be tough."

"How come?"

"Law school. I'm starting end of August."

"Where?"

"Cardozo." He sighed. "I thought I was a lock for NYU, but I didn't get in. I think they get like sixty thousand applications for about six hundred places."

"Well, Cardozo is supposed to be good," I said. As if I knew anything about law schools.

We stepped into wide circles of light. I turned and saw that they were spotlights from another club above us on a high dune.

Jackson grabbed my hand suddenly and slid his arm around my waist. He started to dance, spinning me with him. "I can't resist being in the spotlight," he shouted.

I tossed my head back and laughed as we danced in the circle of light.

Danced. Yes, danced.

I was dancing again, feeling so light and giddy and . . . free. I hadn't felt so happy in a long time, and I knew it wasn't just the drinks.

We stepped out of the spotlight and walked, hand in hand now, along the shore. As we talked, I realized I felt really comfortable. Jackson had an easy sense of humor. He didn't seem to take himself so seriously. He didn't seem aimless. You know, not a beach bum type. But he wasn't crazy intense, either.

He was solid.

Did he like me? I couldn't tell for sure, but he seemed to.

I told him some stories about my first days in New York, how confusing and foreign it was after Madison. I mean, when I went into a coffee shop, I had no idea what a bagel with a *shmear* was! And was a *regular* coffee with milk or without milk?

Was I talking too much? He seemed interested in me, but was it for real? Did he just want to get laid tonight? Who knows?

I'm always amazed at how you can keep two conversations going at once: one with the other person, one with yourself.

Finally, he started doing the talking. He grew up on the East Side of Manhattan. He went to Riverdale High School in the Bronx, then graduated from Wesleyan two summers ago with a degree in Comp Lit. "A worthless degree," he joked. "You can't go out and get a job doing Comp Lit."

He spent most of last year with Habitat for Humanity,

helping to build houses for poor and homeless people. "And the next exciting chapter will be law school. Stop yawning, Ellie."

"I'm not yawning!" I protested. "I'm just a little out of breath."

"Want to turn back?"

Actually, I wanted to keep walking with him all night.

But we turned and slowly strolled back toward the club. After a while, the yellow circles of light on the sand came into view. I wondered if Jackson would want to dance again.

But to my surprise, he stopped while we were in darkness, the world so dark and still except for the steady low wash of the waves. He stopped and pulled me close and said, "I'm sorry. But I've wanted to do this since I first saw you."

He held my chin in his hand, so gently—no one had ever done that before—and brought my lips up to his.

And as we started to kiss, I saw the figure walking into the wide, yellow circle up ahead.

The boy. The blond boy. Stepping into the circle, bobbing slightly—the way Will had always walked.

Will.

No.

Of course it couldn't be. But it was Will. Poor, dead Will.

And I pulled away from Jackson, pulled out of his arms, and started to run. "Will? Will?"

I heard Jackson calling to me. I could still feel the taste of his lips on mine.

But I couldn't stop. My bare feet pounding the wet sand, I ran toward the spotlights, ran toward Will, gone for so long, dead for so long. But there he was. I saw him so clearly.

And now where was he?

I ran through a circle of light, my feet kicking up sand, my heart thudding against my chest. Into darkness now. And no sign of him.

"Will? Will?" I'm too breathless to shout.

And he is gone once again.

I lowered my hands to my knees, gasping for air, my eyes still gazing down the purple-black ribbon of beach.

Why did I suddenly see Will again?

It took so long to stop seeing him. All those years of seeing him everywhere I went.

Is it starting again?

25

Why did I sleep with Frankie Munroe?

I don't really know. Why do you do anything when you're seventeen years old?

I guess it had something to do with being in the popular group at school. Knowing I was in demand, at the top, so cool, just so damn cool. I guess it was a feeling of invulnerability.

What could happen to me, right?

Mandy Groves had been doing it with Colin Crowe since freshman year. And the Everson twins—they bragged about the guys they'd had as if it was some kind of competition between them. And, of course, I'd slept with Will a couple of times, including that feverish afternoon he got his notice from Princeton.

No big deal, right, when you're popular and on top and *immortal*?

And I guess all the while—all four years—I had the sneaking suspicion that I didn't really belong in the popular clique. I mean, I fit in okay and was friendly with just about everybody and all that. But I always had the feeling I was tagging along with my friends, who were prettier and hipper and smarter and richer. Like they were tolerating me for some reason—and I wasn't sure why.

Typical teenage self-doubts, I guess.

So, did I feel I had to prove myself? Is that why I slept with Frankie Munroe after the party at his house when his parents were in Puerto Rico?

It happened so fast. It didn't really feel as if we had done it. Frankie came so fast, while we were still messing around, rolling around on his parents' bedspread. He shot it all over my leg. I mean, that's not even really doing it.

And afterwards, I didn't feel anything.

Not even guilt.

And then a few days later, Will and I sat in his car after school, the windows frosting up from our breath, and Will steaming, too—steaming because some guys at school told him about Frankie and me.

Did I really think Frankie wouldn't brag?

And Will so angry, so red-faced angry, slamming the steering wheel with both hands and demanding to know why.

My voice was trembling: "You've been smoking, haven't you? You're high, Will, aren't you?"

"Don't change the subject," he screams. "Why did you do it? After what we promised each other."

I feel bad that I've disappointed him. But I don't feel much more.

He sweeps back his white-blond hair, the hair I love to run my hand through. His chin is quivering. He's so intense. He feels this so much, feels the hurt, my betrayal.

I wish I could feel it more.

I say I'm sorry again and again. All I want is for him to calm down and stop yelling at me. Should I climb out of the car? Should I just say sorry one more time and walk away?

No. I care about him. I really do. I just don't care as much as he does.

Who could care as much as he does? He's so intense. His eyes burn into mine, like glowing blue lasers. "How can I ever trust you again?" he asks.

I take a deep breath, and I say, "You're too serious, Will. You've got to lighten up. You've got to back off a little. You know. Cut me some slack."

Does that help calm him down?

No. He starts the car. He slams his foot on the gas pedal.

He's in a rage now. I know he's stoned. And now he's in a total rage.

I touch his shoulder. He brushes it away.

The car slides over an ice patch in the road. We're roaring away from the school, past snow-covered lawns, kids on sleds—

"Slow down! You're driving too fast! Will, I mean it. This is crazy!"

His eyes are narrowed on the frosty windshield now. The car goes into a slide at a stop sign. He furiously spins the wheel. We spin out into the intersection. Luckily, no other cars around.

"Will, please!" My heart is in my throat, every muscle tensed. I'm shaking, my whole body shuddering. "Will, stop—!"

He ignores me. Straightens out the car. Stomps on the gas again. We squeal away, tires spinning, bouncing onto the snowy curb, then back onto the street.

He's out of control. What does he think he's doing?

Now I'm frightened. Really frightened. I've never seen this kind of anger.

And now I'm screaming, "Let me out! Let me out, Will!" I'm pleading, begging him to stop the car.

The car bounces hard over a rut in the road. My head hits the roof. "Will, you're going to get us killed!"

"Why did you do it, Ellie?" he asks again, through clenched teeth, his voice strained, strange. "Just tell me why."

He starts to turn. The car goes into a slide. We're skidding so fast. I see the embankment, the snow-caked guardrail.

I grab the wheel. In panic. In horror. I grab the wheel.

"Will, stop the car! Stop it! Will—!"

We go crashing through the guardrail.

Flying. We're flying over the snowy ground. Everything white.

Then everything red as the pain jolts me, and I hear the clatter of glass and the hard crunch of bending metal.

Then black.

And when I slowly open my eyes in the hospital, two days later, my first thought is this: I grabbed the wheel. I did it.

And I see my mother's tearstained face, her cheeks so swollen and red, mascara running, teardrops on her glasses. That's the picture I'll never forget—those teardrops on her glasses. She's leaning over me, laughing and crying at the same time because I've finally awakened after two days.

I grabbed the wheel.

That's all I remember.

I blink hard, trying to focus. It takes so much effort to

open my mouth. And my first raspy words are, "Is . . . Will . . . okay?"

My mother shakes her head. The tears roll down her cheeks. She doesn't say a word.

She doesn't have to. I know the answer from the slow shake of her head, from the tears that drip onto my bed-sheet.

I know the answer.

Will is gone.

Because I grabbed the wheel.

26

Sunday morning was rainy, showers that started and stopped and forced us to stay inside. I read the kids some picture books, and we watched cartoon videos.

I turned on *Sesame Street*, and both kids laughed at Bert and Ernie and Elmo. They did a funny skit about *over* and *under*—teaching the kids the difference between the two words.

Wow. I saw this same skit when I was a kid, I remembered.

Heather started chanting, "Over, under, over, under," and then laughing, as if it were a great joke.

Brandon sat very close to me and held my hand with both of his. Maybe Abby was right. Maybe he *is* starting to like me. He stared intently at the *over-under* skit, and I felt a shiver run down his body.

Did I think about Jackson? Of course. I felt so embarrassed, so humiliated. He started to kiss me—and what did I do?

I ran off after a ghost.

When I couldn't find Will, when he had vanished once again—as all ghosts do—I started back to find Jackson. But I felt so embarrassed . . . so confused and . . . well, *crazy*. The drinks, the excitement of meeting someone new and fun and interesting, Jackson, like a light on a dark beach. That's what he was. A light on a dark beach.

And I turned and ran away from him.

I was too embarrassed to search for him. I ran to the club and found Teresa. I made her drive me home to the Harpers'. I told her I'd explain later. She didn't ask a single question.

Now I definitely wanted to apologize to Jackson. I definitely wanted to see him again, if he didn't think I was a total mental case. I decided I'd call him at the bike store.

Still thinking about him, I gave the kids lunch in the kitchen: reheated macaroni and cheese, applesauce, and a Fruit Roll-Up for dessert. My mother called on my cell while I was cleaning up the dishes.

"Ellie, happy birthday," she yelled.

"What? Oh, my goodness! I completely forgot."

"You forgot your own birthday? That's a new one. You're only twenty-five, dear. You don't have to start forgetting your birthday till you get to my age."

My head spun. How could I forget my birthday?

And was I really twenty-five today? It sounded so old.

My mother's voice droned on. I realized I hadn't heard a word she'd said. I pressed the phone to my ear, forcing myself to listen.

"Twenty-five. I already had two kids when I was your age."

Go ahead, Mom. Rub it in. You had a life, and mine hasn't started yet. Please don't cut me any slack—even on my birthday.

"So you're so busy with your baby-sitting, you don't have time to remember your birthday? It's a quarter of a century, El. I take it you're not doing anything to celebrate?"

"Well, I went to a club with my friend Teresa last night. That was a nice celebration."

"I'll bet it was."

"Excuse me? What does *that* mean, Mom?"

"Nothing. Why are you jumping down my throat? I didn't mean anything. I said I'll bet you had a nice time, that's all. Where was it? One of those trendy Hamptons dance clubs where people get high on lord-knows-what and back their cars over each other in the parking lot?"

"Yuk yuk. Right, Mom. That kind of club."

"Well, listen to me, El: Have a good time in that crazy place. You're still pretty young, so you *should* enjoy life. Go out. Meet guys. Go to clubs. But, please—don't do a lot of drugs and get yourself date-raped."

"You've been watching *Ricki Lake* again, huh?"

"No, *Jerry Springer.*"

"Well, thanks for the charming birthday wish. That's so sweet."

"Sarcasm. I always get the sarcasm. Ellie, if you could bottle sarcasm, you know how rich you'd be?"

"I'm sorry. Really. But—"

"Did you get my package? I sent you a present."

"Well, no. It hasn't come. I'll watch for it. Oh—hey, the baby's crying. I have to run."

"Well, happy birthday, darling. Kiss kiss kiss. Dad and I love you. You know he'd get on the phone, but he isn't here. He has his golf game."

"Love you, too, Mom. Bye."

I clicked off the phone, tucked it into my shorts pocket, and hurried to see why Heather was crying. I could smell the reason immediately. Her diaper was real full. I hurried to change her—not exactly my favorite part of the job.

"Hold still. Hold still, Heather. I can't get this side closed." I turned and saw that Brandon had entered the room. He was holding *Hop on Pop*, one of his favorite Dr. Seuss books. I had already read it to him about a hundred times that morning. Did he really want to hear it again?

"Brandon, hi. Did you know that today is my birthday?"

He stared at me blankly.

"Maybe you'll sing 'Happy Birthday' to me later. What do you say?"

His expression didn't change. His eyes were glassy and blank, a dead man's eyes.

I stared back at him. What could I do?

What could I do to get through to him?

"Ellie, two things came for you."

It was about four on Monday afternoon. The kids were napping. I was in my room, lying on my back in bed, legs up, bare feet on the sea blue wallpaper, reading about Keanu Reeves in *People* magazine. I was thinking about how Jackson looked a little bit like Keanu, when Chip's voice from downstairs interrupted my thoughts.

I hurried out of the room and peered down over the balcony. He was standing in the living room in baggy khaki shorts and a white sleeveless T-shirt, holding up a rectangular white box to me. "I think it's a cake."

"My mother sent it," I called down. "Yesterday was my birthday." I made my way down the stairs.

"Oh," he said. "Sorry. We didn't know. Happy birthday, kiddo." His lopsided smile was a clue that he'd had a few drinks. He sang out: "Happy birthday to yoooooo."

I made a clumsy curtsy. "Thank you very much."

I was wearing a scoop-necked, blue-and-white-striped tank top over white shorts. I could see his eyes lower to my tits as I took my bow.

"How about some champagne?" he said, still balancing the white box in one hand. "A little celebration?"

"Well . . . not right now," I said.

My rejection seemed to sting him. He suddenly looked so sad. His face just crumbled. "Hey, I'm not a bad guy," he said. "I'm just being friendly, that's all. Sometimes—well, it's a little lonely here."

I stared at him, struggling to think of a response. Why was he telling me this? What was I supposed to say?

He shook his head as if shaking away his sadness. Then he pulled an envelope from his back pocket and handed it to me. "This came, too. In the mail." He carried the white box to a narrow table behind the couch. "Look at the label. It's from the French bakery in Southampton."

He had a drink on the table. He picked it up and took a long sip, his eyes avoiding me. "How old are you, anyway? Twenty? Twenty-one? You're not still jailbait, are you? You're legal, right? Ha ha."

Yikes.

"Twenty-five. And would you believe I forgot my own birthday?" I said, pulling open the envelope. "My mother is the only one who remembered."

But I was wrong.

I tugged a birthday card from the envelope. The front showed hands clapping, dozens of hands clapping, and it read, CHEERS ON YOUR BIRTHDAY!

I didn't bother reading the rest of it. Because, when I opened it, I saw the signature on the bottom. *Love, Clay.*

And then, written under the signature, the words: *See you soon, babe.*

See you soon?

A chill tightened the back of my neck.

See you soon?

I tossed the card onto the table.

"That card from Mommy?" Chip asked. He tilted the glass to his mouth. He was standing really close to me. I could feel the heat off his body.

"From a guy I know," I said.

He squeezed my hand. "Your boyfriend?"

"No. I don't have a boyfriend."

He grinned. "A hottie like you? You're kidding, right?"

His hand lingered on mine. I carefully slid my hand free.

"Open the box," he said. "Let's see what Mommy sent."

His arm brushed mine. The way he kept saying *Mommy*, it was like he was coming on to me and making fun of me at the same time. What a jackass.

The bakery box had pink-and-white string around it, knotted at the top. I worked the string off one side and then pulled open the lid.

"It's not a birthday cake," I said.

The box was packed with shredded newspaper.

"Must be something fragile," Chip said, setting down his glass. He peered into the box, his face close to mine.

Carefully, I dug both hands in. At first, I didn't feel anything in there. I burrowed deeper—and felt something.

I squeezed it, and it was hard. Kinda warm.

"What is it?" Chip asked, leaning against me. His breath smelled of gin.

"I don't know."

I wrapped my fingers around the object and carefully lifted it out. The shredded newspaper fell away.

And a moan of horror escaped my throat.

I tried to scream, but no sound came out.

A hand! A human hand!

I was holding a human hand!

It's a fake, I thought. A mannequin hand.

But no. I could feel the soft skin, the hard bone underneath. I could see where the hand had been cut off at the wrist. Bone poking through, damp, red flesh, yellow tendons.

I finally found my voice. I let out a shrill scream.

The hand fell to the floor. It hit with a soft *plop*, bounced once, and landed on my bare foot. The limp fingers fell across my foot and wriggled—*as if still alive!*

And as I frantically started to kick it away, I saw the ring on the ring finger. The oval, silver ring with the big emerald in the center.

"Mrs. Bricker!" I shrieked. "Mrs. Bricker! Mrs. Bricker! Mrs. Bricker! Mrs. Bricker!"

27

Teresa, I'm so terrified."

I dropped breathlessly into my seat. I felt as if I were on the deck of a swaying ship, the floor tilting and shifting to a strange rhythm. The faces around the restaurant bobbed and swayed like stringed balloons. Why did I have the feeling they were all staring at me?

I blinked them away and, holding on to the edge of the table to steady myself, turned back to Teresa. "I'm just shaking. What a frightening week. A fucking nightmare. I really should get away from there. I should just pack up and—"

Teresa signaled to the waitress. "Let's order some drinks. Then we can talk about it. What do you want?"

"Oh, I don't know. Rum and Coke, I guess."

Teresa ordered two rum and Cokes. She turned back to me. "You look like total crap."

I groaned. "You're trying to make me feel better?"

"Ellie, you poor thing. I've never seen you so strung out. Those lines under your eyes—"

"I can't sleep. You'd have lines under your eyes, too, if someone sent you a human hand!"

I didn't mean to shout. People turned to stare. I

ducked lower in the booth and held the menu in front of my face.

Teresa and I were at Bobby Van's in Bridgehampton. It was Friday night, and the restaurant was jammed. We'd taken a booth at the back of the bar where we could hear each other.

I had spoken to Teresa for only a second on Monday. Now I knew she was eager for me to catch her up. But I wasn't sure I could talk about it.

The waitress brought the drinks. "You ready to order?"

Teresa ordered soft-shell crabs. I decided to have them, too. I took a long swallow of my drink. The rum felt warm on my throat. "I'll need a few more of these," I said.

Teresa tsk-tsked. "You poor thing."

"I can't sleep at all," I moaned, holding on to the glass with both hands. "When I close my eyes, I see that fucking hand. I see the fingers, crawling up my leg, crawling up my body. One night I—I—this is so awful—I dreamed the hand was around my neck, strangling me."

"Oh, my God." Teresa pulled nervously on her hair. "Oh, my God, Ellie."

I took another long swallow of my rum and Coke. "The police haven't left me alone for an hour. First it's the town police, then the village police. They can't decide which of them is in charge. So they ask the same questions over and over.

"And the TV reporters are even worse," I said. "They hound me. They follow me. They ask the most horrible questions. I—I just hope my mother hasn't seen any of this."

"You haven't told her?"

"Of course not. If my mother had any idea that some-one had cut off a woman's hand and sent it to me with a threatening note, she'd be here in two minutes, pulling me by the hair back to Wisconsin!"

Teresa nodded solemnly. "You're probably right." She pushed her hair off her face. "And the old woman? She's alive?"

I nodded. "They found Mrs. Bricker in her living room in a pool of blood. She nearly bled to death, but somehow she hung on. She called 911 with the hand that was left. Do you believe that?"

Teresa downed her drink. "Wow. She is a strong old bird. Where is she? Is she home?"

"No. She's still at the hospital in Southampton. She was in a coma for a couple of days. They didn't think she'd pull through. I went to visit her there, but she was still out. Hooked up to a million tubes and wires. No one had any hope for her. But she woke up on Wednes-day. She surprised everyone."

"Why'd you go visit her?"

I shrugged. "I don't know. It's weird, you know. I mean, I guess I feel kinda responsible."

"Huh? Responsible? Hel-lo. *You* didn't cut off her hand. Some crazy bastard did!"

"But if I wasn't here, she'd still have it. See what I mean? I mean, someone cut off her hand because they wanted to scare me."

"Well, did the old woman tell the police anything? Could she help them? Did she know who did it to her?"

The waitress brought our food. I waited for her to leave. I stared down at the soft-shell crabs. I hadn't eaten much all week. I just hadn't felt like it. My stom-ach growled.

"Mrs. Bricker couldn't remember much. She said she saw a flash of brown. Maybe the guy was wearing brown. But she couldn't be sure. She didn't remember seeing the knife or anything. I guess she went into some kind of shock."

Teresa leaned over the table. "And have the police arrested Clay? It *was* Clay, right? That sick idiot."

I shook my head. "It wasn't Clay." I put down my fork. I couldn't talk about this and eat at the same time.

"Of *course* it was Clay," Teresa insisted. "Who else could it be?"

The question sent a chill down my back. Yes. Who *else* could it be? Who else hated me so much? Who wanted to terrify me so badly?

What *insane* person had reason to threaten me like that?

"Clay was in Philadelphia the whole weekend. He went to a Sixers game with one of his brothers and visited his other brother there. Both brothers swore to it. They even had the ticket stubs."

Teresa swallowed a chunk of crab. "Bullshit. They're lying, right?"

"No. A bunch of neighbors were at the brother's barbecue Sunday afternoon, and they all said that Clay was there."

"Maybe they're all lying."

The waitress brought two more rum and Cokes. I took a long sip. "All the neighbors?"

"But, Ellie, you told me the hand—you said it came with a birthday card. From Clay. And the card had hands on it. And—"

I sighed again. "Looks like a coincidence. A stupid coincidence. Clay told the police he bought the card a long time ago and had it in a drawer. Besides, Clay hasn't been out to the Hamptons. And he's never heard of Mrs. Bricker."

I realized I was tapping my fork on the table. I let it drop. "The police questioned Clay for hours. They say he isn't a suspect. Besides, it doesn't make sense for it to be Clay. Clay is in love with me, right? He says he wants us to get back together. So why would he chop off that poor woman's hand? He wouldn't—"

"Because he's crazy. He's totally whacked, Ellie. He's been stalking you. He's been calling you day and night, hounding you, threatening you—"

"It isn't Clay. Let me finish. There was another card with the hand. In the box. We—we didn't see it till later."

Teresa gasped. "Another card? Oh, my God. What did it say? Was it signed or anything? Where is it? Do you have it?"

"No. The police took it. For evidence. It was hand-written. I—I remember every word. It's—so horrible, Teresa."

I felt my eyes brim with tears. I didn't want to cry in front of everyone in the restaurant. I'd cried enough all week.

I rubbed the tears away with my napkin. "It was a lit-tle card. You know. A white card. The handwriting was kinda scrawled, big letters, very sloppy. And—"

"And what did it say?"

"It said, 'Guess what? I'd give my *right arm* to see you dead. So, this is a start.' "

Teresa tugged her hair with both hands. Her mouth dropped open. "Oh, my God. Oh, my God."

*   *   *

After dinner, we drove around aimlessly. We ended up at a beach called Sag Main in Sagaponack. We walked barefoot in the sand along the dark, tossing ocean—high waves tonight, rising up like fingers over the beach, and no stars in the sky—and we tried to talk about other things.

But how could I think about anything else? I was so frightened, I kept turning back to make sure no one was following us.

"Ellie, are you going to stay?" Teresa asked.

I shrugged. "I don't know what to do. Abby and Chip are begging me not to leave. They say the kids are upset. They know something weird is going on. Abby says they need me now. Chip offered me a raise to stay, a really good raise. They both promised to watch out for me, to protect me."

"So you're staying here?"

"I guess. It's so hard to think straight. I really don't want to go back to Wisconsin. And . . . if someone wants to kill me—" I swallowed. My throat suddenly felt so dry. "—if someone wants to kill me, they'll follow me to Madison, right?"

"Who would want to kill you, Ellie? Who?"

I tossed a stone into the dark water. "That's what the police asked me over and over. Do I have a clue? No."

Teresa invited me to her share house the next Saturday for a barbecue party. I started to say no, but then changed my mind. I needed something to take my mind off what had happened, something to help erase that pale, bony hand from my thoughts.

"Maybe I'll invite this guy I met," I told her.

"Guy?" Her eyes flashed. She tossed her cigarette onto the sand.

I told her about Jackson, how nice he seemed, so solid, so laid back, not like the other guys I'd been with. I didn't tell her I ran away from him, chasing after a ghost.

"Yes, tell him to come by," Teresa said. She laughed her throaty laugh. "Tell him to bring a friend for me."

She dropped me back at the Harpers' a little after one. The house was silent and dark and smelled of popcorn. I stepped into the kitchen to see if any of it was left. But the bowl on the counter was empty except for a few unpopped kernels.

Yawning, I made my way upstairs. I started to get undressed, then heard a sound outside my bedroom window. A voice. A man's voice.

Who was out there at this time of night? I hurried to the window.

The backyard was dark. A thick haze curtained the sky. No moon or stars. I heard the crash of the tall ocean waves beyond the dunes. And over that sound, a man's voice. Coming from where? From the guest house?

I poked my head farther out the window. I gazed over the backyard. Shadowy black shapes against black. Nothing moving. No one there.

Had I imagined the voice?

No. I heard it again. A murmur of words. I couldn't make them out. And then a woman's voice. I didn't recognize either of them.

The ghosts of the guest house? I thought of Mrs. Bricker, of the crazy story she was so desperate to tell me.

Sorry, no way. I don't believe in ghosts, Mrs. B. It wasn't a ghost who cut off your hand and wrapped it so nicely in a box for me.

The voices again, both speaking at once. Voices from an empty, abandoned house?

I pulled my jeans back on and crept down the stairs. Out the kitchen door, onto the deck.

I waited for my eyes to adjust to the darkness. The backyard lay perfectly still.

But wait.

A dark form, moving fast, slithering across the sandy ground. A chipmunk. I watched it dive into a hole.

A loud crash of an ocean wave, loud as thunder. And then, in the stillness that followed, I heard the man's voice, low and gentle, clearer now, although I still couldn't make out the words.

Not Chip. I could hear that it wasn't Chip.

Besides, Chip was in the city. He had driven off in the Porsche right before Teresa picked me up tonight.

Squinting into the darkness, I stepped off the deck, into the yard. The sandy ground felt cold under my bare feet. Patches of long grass tickled me as I crossed the yard, climbing the dune.

I stopped halfway to the line of pine trees. I could see the dark outline of the guest house behind them. The voices had vanished.

Ellie, why are you out here?

Curiosity?

Some kind of force, pulling me here? An invisible force pulling me against my will to the guest house?

Oh, Christ, Ellie. That's such bullshit.

And then a chilling thought: Is it the killer?

Is it the man who wants to kill me?

Is he waiting for me up there? Luring me to the guest house, luring me, pulling me . . .

Why am I out here?

I hugged myself to stop my shivers. My teeth chattered. The ocean wind suddenly felt damp and chilling.

So silent. No voices now. Everything still, as if the earth had frozen.

I started to turn back to the house.

"Oh—" I gasped as I saw something move behind the trees at the top of the hill.

A flash of color.

Someone stepped out, walking fast down the dune.

I saw dark hair, a slender body. A woman in white shorts and a white midriff top, swinging her arms as she walked.

Abby!

"Ellie?" she shouted. Seeing me, she started to run. "Ellie? Did you hear it, too?"

I still had my arms wrapped around my chest. My teeth wouldn't stop chattering.

Abby ran up to me, her sandals kicking up sand behind her. "Did you hear the voices, too?" she asked breathlessly.

I nodded. "Y-yes."

Abby put her arm around my shoulder. "You're shivering. Are you okay? It isn't that cold out. Let's get you inside."

"I—I'm totally freaked," I confessed.

We started back to the house. "I was sound asleep," Abby said, still breathing hard. "I heard voices. A man and a woman, coming from the guest house."

"Yeah, so did I," I said.

"I pulled on my clothes and went running up there," she said. "I could hear the voices so clearly."

I stopped and turned to her. "And? Did you see anyone in there? Did you see who it was?"

"Ellie, it was empty. No one there. No one."

I stared hard at her, my mind whirring. Finally, I whispered, "Abby—do you believe in ghosts?"

She didn't answer. I saw her chin tremble. Then she turned and strode quickly into the house.

28

The next Friday morning, I met Maggie at the Lewises' house. We packed her two girls and my two kids into her Suburban, along with the usual gear—blankets, coolers, sand toys, and so forth. Then she drove us to a freshwater lake—about a ten-minute ride—for a picnic and a swim.

The Lewis girls sat with Heather in the middle seat. The three of them had fun tickling each other, throwing each other's hats on the floor, singing songs at the top of their lungs. Brandon sat in the back by himself, gazing blankly out the window.

It was still morning, but the parking lot was already crowded. I could see kids playing and running in the gentle blue-green water.

"It's very shallow for a good bit," Maggie said. "So it's safe for the kids to swim. But then it drops off suddenly, to about twenty feet deep."

The sun burned the back of my neck as we unpacked the kids and all the equipment. It was a humid day, hot for June, a taste of the summer days to come.

"You look tired, girl," Maggie said as we lugged everything across the asphalt parking lot to the narrow beach. "You've been partying too much?"

I laughed. "Partying? I wish."

I guessed she hadn't seen the TV or newspapers. Well, good. I wasn't going to bring it up. Why spoil her day, too?

The beach was rocky, covered with large, round pebbles and washed-up shells. Heather complained it hurt her feet, so I picked her up and carried her along with all the other stuff.

"Do you have lakes where you come from?" Maggie asked.

I nodded. "Dozens of them. This looks just like a Wisconsin lake. Especially with all the tall trees around it. The Hamptons are amazing, aren't they? The ocean, the bay, and even a lake."

"Swim! Swim! I want swim!" Heather began the chant, and the Lewis girls picked it up. Brandon tagged along behind us, picking up stones and tossing them into the water.

"You can't swim until I get your floaties on," I told Heather. I turned. "Brandon, are you going to swim today?"

He nodded.

"Well, I need you to take good care of your sister. Will you help me watch Heather?"

He stared at me blankly.

Yes, I confess. Sometimes I just wanted to pick Brandon up and shake him and shout, "Talk, damn it! Just *talk*!" It was so frustrating. If only there were some way I could reach him.

And then, as if reading my mind, he came up and took my hand, and I instantly felt sorry for thinking my violent thoughts. The poor guy. What could be troubling him so badly?

We found a spot and set down our stuff and spread some blankets and put up a beach umbrella. I slid the plastic floaties onto the kids' arms and inflated them, not easy with Brandon and Heather squirming and pulling away, eager to get to the water.

I was eager to get in the water, too. The sun beat down. I was dripping with sweat. Maggie and I led the kids to the edge of the shore. We passed a little red-haired boy dragging a big, black inner tube across the pebbles to the water. Ahead of us, two kids were fighting over a red Styrofoam pool noodle. Their tug-of-war ended in tears when they snapped the pool noodle in half.

I saw Brandon snicker as we passed the crying kids. Why did he enjoy seeing them cry?

The four kids had fun splashing and jumping about in the flat, warm water. Even Brandon joined in.

But, of course he had to frighten me. He kept floating facedown, doing the dead man's float, holding his breath until my heart started to pound. Then he'd raise his head and stare at me, a strange grin on his face, as if he knew he had scared me and was pleased about it.

Maggie and I took turns watching them. First, she did lifeguard duty so I could go out to the deep water and have a good swim. Then I relieved her.

"I like your swimsuit," Maggie said, as we were toweling off later. "Very bold."

I laughed. "Bold? Do you think so?"

I was wearing a bright red bikini. Of course, Chip had complimented me on it as I was leaving the house.

Okay. He had backed off a bit since the severed hand incident. And he kept telling me he would do everything he could to protect me from whoever was threatening me. But I could still feel his eyes on me all the time, see him watching me while pretending to read the newspaper or a magazine.

I wondered if he would make a real move. Would he corner me sometime when Abby was away and tell me again how lonely he is? Tell me how his marriage is falling apart, how he desperately wants me, how he has to have me? . . .

And then what would I do?

I'd have to quit.

I'd have to push him away and tell him I'm outta there and let *him* explain to Abby.

And then what?

I go back to New York with a few hundred dollars to my name and try to find an apartment and a job.

Or . . . back to good old Madison with Mom and Dad.

Uh—no.

Maybe Chip will lay off. Maybe he feels sorry for me, knowing that someone out there hates me—hates me enough to cut off an old woman's hand and send it to me—hates me enough to want me dead.

Maybe Chip won't make a move. He says he wants to protect me, after all. Wow, he's such a loser. He's probably just a watcher, a daydreamer.

And why isn't Abby enough for him? They're both so young. They couldn't have been married very long. How can he be so horny? Is he just a total slut?

A ringing sound interrupted my thoughts. My phone. I rummaged through the beach bag searching for it. Finally, I found it. I checked the caller ID, then raised it to my ear.

"Hi, Teresa."

"What's up, Ellie? Everything okay?"

"Yeah. Not bad. I'm at a lake with the kids, so I can't really talk."

"We still on for Saturday afternoon? Party at my house?"

"Yeah. I called Jackson. He said he'd stop by."

"Cool. Wait till you see the house, Ellie. Thirty people jammed into five bedrooms. It's insane!"

"I'd better go, Teresa. Can I call you later?"

"Yeah. No problem. Everything okay? Nothing weird going on?"

"Okay so far," I said. "The police were back yesterday. They asked a bunch of questions, but they don't have a clue. And Clay has called me every day. But I see his number on my caller ID, so I don't pick up."

"Good. Maybe he'll get the message in a year or two."

"Let's hope. Later," I said. I clicked off the phone and tossed it back into the beach bag. Then I turned toward the water.

Deirdre and Courtney were piling up stones a few yards in front of the blanket, building some kind of stone house. And Heather and Brandon—

Heather and Brandon?

Oh, no. I turned to Maggie. She was bent over the cooler, pulling out wrapped sandwiches for our picnic. "Maggie? Do you see Brandon and Heather?"

She jumped to her feet and, sheltering her eyes with her hand, squinted down the beach. "They were just here, building rocks with the girls. They couldn't have gone far."

I stepped over the beach blanket and hurried up to the girls. "Have you two seen Heather and Brandon?"

They looked up from their rock pile, blond hair gleaming in the sunlight, blue eyes looking up at me so blankly, as if they'd never heard of Heather and Brandon.

"They went away," Deirdre said finally, in her tiny voice.

The words sent a chill down my back. *Went away?*

"Where? Went away *where*?"

They both shrugged their little shoulders.

I stepped away from them, slipping on some rocks. Squinting hard behind my sunglasses, I searched up and down the beach. I saw dozens of children that could have been them—but weren't.

My heart racing now, my throat achingly dry, I cupped my hands around my mouth and shouted. "Brandon? Heather? Where are you? Brandon? Heather?"

I turned to the water. No sign of them. I spun around slowly, surveying the whole beach.

Finally, trembling, my stomach knotted in fear, I turned to Maggie. "Maggie," I choked out. "They're gone."

29

"Are the little devils hiding from us?" Maggie asked. "Playing a game, I'll bet." Her voice was light, but her face revealed her concern.

She said something else, but I didn't hear it. I started to run. On trembling legs, I trotted along the crowded beach, slipping on the wet rocks, searching each face, fighting the sunlight, the bright white light that faded every face, that made every face so vague and hard to identify. Fighting the white light radiating off the sand and stones, such a strong light that seemed to want to surround me, to hold me, keep me from finding the right faces.

Fighting the sunlight—or my overwhelming dread?

I cupped my hands around my mouth and shouted. "Heather? Brandon?"

This isn't happening.

This is *not* happening.

And then I saw a shadow in the water, far out in the water, where the shallow bottom dropped off. The shadow became a figure. I recognized the baggy, black swimsuit, the T-shirt Abby insists he wears when he swims.

A boy with a big, black inner tube.

Yes. It's Brandon. Squinting through my sunglasses, I could see him perfectly now. Where did he get the inner tube? And why is he pushing it to the deep water?

"Brandon? Come back here! Brandon? It's dangerous out there! *Come back!*"

I leap into the water and run over the wet rocks, waving my arms frantically. And then I stop, water only up to my shins. I stop because I see what Brandon is doing.

I mean, I see his passenger clinging to the big tube. I see Heather's back. And I see her tiny hands gripping the side of the tube. She's on her stomach, clinging to the wet rubber, kicking her feet furiously, holding on for dear life.

And Brandon is pushing her, pushing her out to the deep waters.

"Brandon! No!"

Brandon, why are you doing this?

I gasp as he gives the black tube a hard push. It bobs out into deep water, tossing on the low waves.

"No—please! No!"

As I start to run, I see Heather slide off the side of the tube. Her little body sinks quickly—so quickly and smoothly—into the blue-green water. I see her legs disappear, then her waist, her head. Her tiny arms are the last to go under. I see her hands on the surface, like tiny white flowers. Then they disappear, too.

The tube bobs in place, and Heather is gone.

Brandon stands in the shallow water, watching intently, not moving.

The inner tube bobs, and there's no sign of his sister.

I run to the end of the shallow water. I kick off, using the bottom to propel me. Swimming hard, I pull myself along the surface and search for her.

Heather, come up!

Behind me, I glimpse Brandon just standing there, watching. I take a deep breath and dive down. Where is she? The water is thick with weeds. The tendrils wave and wriggle and reach out like dark snakes.

Where *is* she?

And then I see a foot—a pale, white, tiny foot, tangled in long black weeds. I need to breathe. How long have I been underwater? My chest feels ready to explode. I picture an inflated paper bag being popped.

I grab for the foot. I see Heather's body now, her pink swimsuit. I see her wide eyes, her startled face—not frightened, but startled and confused, as if wondering how this happened.

I tug once, twice, and wrench her leg free of the tangle of weeds. And then I am pulling her up, pulling her with strength I don't have, my chest exploding, the whole world red now, bright red.

We burst over the surface. I hold her up above my head. I gulp in breath after breath, choking, sputtering, spitting out water, my whole body heaving with each breath. The red fades. All color fades in the white sunlight, the pure, white sunlight that I am so happy to see again.

I hold Heather high. Without even realizing it, I am holding her up to the sun, warming her, returning her to the light.

Is she breathing?

Is she alive?

Yes. She thrashes her arms, kicks her legs, chokes, and spits out grimy green water. Water runs off her body, onto my shoulders. Her blond hair is matted to her head. A tuft of thick grass clings to her swimsuit.

I feel her shake as she starts to cry. She opens her mouth in a long, high wail, and then shudders with sob after sob.

"It's okay," I tell her. "Heather, it's okay now."

My muscles aching, I stumble to the shallow water. She's crying uncontrollably now. I pull her close to me.

"Where are your floaties?" I cry. "Who took off your floaties?"

She's crying too hard to answer. Brandon hasn't moved. He stands nearby, skinny arms crossed over his chest, staring at us with no expression at all.

I cradle Heather under one arm. I grab Brandon with my other hand and tug him sharply toward shore.

"Why did you do it?" I shout, squeezing his arm, wanting to hurt him, wanting to pay him back for trying to kill his sister.

I have to get through to him!

"How could you do such a horrible thing?"

A smile spreads over his face.

Furious, I jerk his arm and drag him to shore. Heather is still wailing, thrashing her arms and legs again.

"Heather, you're okay. You're perfectly fine." I set her down on the pebbly shore.

I turn to scold Brandon, but something catches my eye. A long white skirt. I look up and realize someone is standing beside us. At first her face is hidden behind a white wide-brimmed hat.

She is dressed entirely in white, a ghostly figure.

And then she turns, and I recognize the wrinkled, rouged face in the shade of the hat.

My breath catches in my throat. "Oh. Hi, Mrs. Bricker," I finally manage. "I heard you were out of the hospital. I—"

Her eyes are on Brandon. She stares at him for the longest time.

Then she slowly turns to me and raises her arm. I see the tight, white bandages. I see her bandaged stump.

Her eyes narrow to slits. She waves the stump at me and rasps, "It's started, hasn't it. It's started."

PART THREE

30

Teresa's share house was a tall, white stucco building on Noyac Road. The house was completely hidden from the street by a tall, perfectly manicured hedge.

The Harpers dropped me off a little after five. I thanked them for the ride and walked up the curving gravel driveway jammed with cars and SUVs. I could see the sparkling water of Peconic Bay behind the house.

Music blared from the back. I heard shouts and laughter. A red Frisbee came flying past my head. Two guys in swimsuits grabbed for it, bumping each other out of the way.

Teresa greeted me at the front door. "I hope you came to party," she said, pulling me inside. "This place is out of control!"

She pulled me into the living room crowded with guys and girls in shorts and bathing suits, talking, holding drinks, lots of laughter. Two guys were carrying a beer keg toward the back. Two couples were all tangled up, totally lip-locked on a low, tan couch that stretched the length of the back wall.

"Wow. My first party in a glamorous share-house in the Hamptons!" I said. I sounded as if I were being sarcastic (when don't I?), but I really was excited.

"Well, let me give you the glamorous tour," Teresa said, taking my arm. She led me past five bedrooms jammed with cots toe to toe, sleeping bags cluttering the floor. On the other side of the living room stood a large den where a group of guys was playing PlayStation 2, which they had hooked up to a big-screen TV. They were shouting and cheering as if they were at a stadium.

There were sleeping bags and cots in every room in the house. Thirty people had shares here, Teresa explained, and they were allowed to bring two or three guests a season.

"Not a whole lot of privacy," I said as Teresa led me out to the terrace in back.

"You got that right!" she replied. "But you're never lonely. And you do get to meet some okay people." She pointed to the glass doors at the back. "Come check out the pool."

I glanced around. "Where can I change?" I had a T-shirt and shorts over my swimsuit.

"Just drop your stuff in any corner," Teresa said.

We stepped through the glass doors. Pounding dance music greeted us. A beautiful swimming pool came into view. "Ta *da*! Not too shabby, huh?" Teresa said.

The pool was dark green and enormous, filled with people. I saw round hot tubs at both ends. And beyond the pool, I could see the beach and the bay, golden and green in the fading sun.

"Wow."

Teresa grinned and pushed back her hair. "I spend most of my time back here working on my tan."

I heard a squeal as a man tossed a woman into the pool. The tidal wave of a splash made several people sitting at poolside scream. And though the pool was really crowded, no one was swimming. Everyone was standing in the shallow end, drinking and talking.

Nine or ten people jammed the first hot tub. They had all taken off their swimsuits and tossed them onto the terrace. I saw a group of people leaning over a dark-wood picnic table, having a serious shot-drinking contest.

Three guys struggled to get the beer keg going. On the deck on the other side of the house, a guy and a girl in white aprons manned two barbecue grills. I watched them turning enormous racks of ribs. Smoke floated up from the grills. The wonderful, tangy aroma reminded me of the annual Brat Festival back in Madison, the streets filled with the aroma of barbecued brats and ribs.

Teresa and I poured ourselves glasses of white wine. Then we found a free space by the edge of the pool and dropped down with our feet in the water.

"I entered you in the wet T-shirt contest," Teresa said.

I sputtered wine down my chin. "You *what*?"

She laughed. "Kidding. Would I do that to you?"

I gave her a soft shove. "You are *so* not funny."

I glanced toward the house and saw someone I knew walk out through the glass doors. It took me a few seconds to realize it was Jackson. "Hey, he's here!" I exclaimed.

"Is that what's-his-name?" Teresa lifted her sunglasses to see him clearly. "Hey, Ellie, he's a total babe!"

I waved to Jackson, but he didn't see me. I leaned on Teresa's shoulder to help pull myself to my feet and went running over to greet him.

We shook hands awkwardly. "Hey, glad you came."

His eyes flashed. "I wanted to see how long it would take you to run away this time."

"Cut me some slack. I already apologized five times. Do you really think I'm crazy or something?"

He nodded. "Yes." If he hadn't chuckled, I would have believed him.

He wore faded denim shorts and a navy sleeveless T-shirt. When he shook my hand, I saw a tattoo near his right shoulder. Chinese letters.

"What's that tattoo?" I asked. "Something deep and mysterious?"

"It's my name in Chinese."

I ran my finger over it. "Why'd you get it?"

He shrugged. "I couldn't think of what else to get."

Teresa walked over, straightening the top of her bikini. I introduced them, and we chatted for a while. Jackson said he had three roommates in his apartment in college, but couldn't imagine having twenty-nine.

"We have better parties this way," Teresa told him.

Jackson glanced around. "When does the orgy start? Ellie promised me an orgy."

I gave him a shove. "Did not."

Teresa motioned to a couple at the far end of the pool. They were both dripping wet from the pool. He was on his back on the concrete, and she was on top, straddling him, locking him in a long kiss.

"Jeez," she said. "I think it's already started."

I narrowed my eyes at Jackson. "Don't get any ideas."

He grinned. "I have *plenty* of ideas!"

The keg was finally tapped, so we went over to get beers. Then we talked and hung out by the pool, met some guys who recognized Jackson from the bike shop. We swam and had platefuls of smoky ribs and potato salad, danced a bit and had a few more beers.

I realized later on that I never stopped to wonder if I

was having a good time or not. My mom is always telling me I think too much, that I overanalyze everything. And I know she's right. But tonight, I was as laid back as Jackson and didn't ruin my good time by wondering if I was really enjoying myself or not.

The party was still going strong at 1 A.M. Some couples from another house were just arriving. But I'd had a full day of the kids and the beach, and I was starting to yawn.

"Did you drive?" Jackson asked. He had his arms around my waist, and we were slow-dancing at the side of the pool.

"No. I thought I'd call a taxi."

He pressed his warm cheek against mine. "Let me take you home?"

I snickered. "On the back of your bike?"

He pulled his head back and frowned at me. "Just because I work in a bike store doesn't mean—"

"Okay. Thanks. I have to say good night to Teresa." I pulled away from him and started to search for her. But he pulled me close again.

"Listen, Ellie, I—uh—know what's been going on with you. I mean, I saw it on TV. When I saw you with the police, I—I couldn't believe it. Really. I felt so bad for you."

"Jackson, I—"

"No. Let me finish. I guess you don't want to talk about it. I mean, you haven't all night, and I don't blame you. But, I just wanted to say—well, if you ever *do* need someone to talk to. Or if you ever do need help of any kind, I—"

I didn't let him finish. I threw my arms around him and pressed my cheek against his neck. "Thank you!

Oh, you're so sweet. Thank you!" Then I pressed my lips against his and held his face while we kissed.

Maybe things were going too fast. Maybe I was jumping to conclusions—trusting him too soon. I mean, I'd just met him. But he seemed so much calmer than any guy I'd ever been with. Like a real grown-up. Hell, I'd ditched him on the beach in the middle of the night, and he understood and didn't think it was the end of the world.

We said good night to Teresa. She was sitting on some guy's lap, a drink in one hand, her other arm draped casually around the guy's neck. Her hair had fallen over her face, and her eyes were heavy-lidded and spacey. I don't know if she heard me or not.

Jackson and I made our way through the jumble of people in the house, carefully stepping around couples on the floor. In front, cars had filled the driveway and spilled onto the lawn.

We walked arm in arm, leaning against each other. "I'm parked on the street," he said. "By the time I got here, there had to be twenty cars lined up!"

Parked cars lined both sides of the narrow street. The windows of one car we passed were totally steamed up, and we could see the heads of a couple in the backseat bobbing up and down.

"That's my car down there," Jackson said, pointing to a new white Thunderbird convertible across the road.

"That's yours? You're kidding!" I cried.

He nodded. "Yes, I'm kidding. I'm driving a bright red Passat I borrowed from my brother."

We walked past a curve in the road. "Stop," I whispered. I held him back and pointed. "Look."

A large deer stood in the woods, still as a statue, staring at us through the cars. Its dark eyes sparkled. It lowered its head slowly, watching us warily.

"Oh—!" I cried out as a bright light swept over us.

I clamped my eyes shut, blinded by the white light. I heard the squeal of brakes.

I forced my eyes open. The deer was gone. Vanished into the safety of the woods.

Jackson pulled me hard, and we stumbled against a black Mercedes. The car behind the headlights slowly came into view—a black SUV.

Before the car had even stopped, the driver was climbing out. He left the car door open. He came at us, stepping through the twin headlights, a rapidly moving shadow who quickly became real. Too real.

Clay.

I stepped away from the Mercedes. My throat tightened with anger. "Clay—what are you doing here?"

He ignored me. He kept his eyes on Jackson. "Keeping my girl warm for me?"

He was dressed in city clothes—a long-sleeved white shirt that had come untucked on one side, necktie loosened, pleated khakis. He strode up to Jackson, as if I weren't there. "That what you're doing? Getting my girl warmed up for me? Are you the warm-up act for tonight?"

Jackson turned to me, confused. "Who *is* this guy?"

"Clay—get *out* of here!" I shouted.

Again, he ignored me. He was breathing hard, short, wheezing breaths. "Why'd you do it, Ellie?"

"Clay, just leave."

Jackson took a step forward. "You heard her."

Clay didn't back off. "Why'd you do it, babe?" Sweat poured down his forehead. His eyes were wild. His eyebrows kept flying up and down. "Why, babe? Why the fuck did you do it?"

"Clay, please—"

"Why, Ellie? I'm asking you a simple question. Just tell me why. Did you really think I'd chop up an old lady? Is that why you sicced the fucking cops on me? Why did you tell them it was me?"

"I didn't. I—"

"Oh, wait. I get it. I *get* it. You were protecting this guy. Is that what it was about?"

I felt Jackson tense at my side. "I'm warning you," he said softly.

"How could you do that to me, babe? I've got a job, you know. I've got a life. Do you think I'm crazy? Do you think I'm a fucking murderer?"

"You—you've been stalking me," I said, grabbing on to Jackson's arm. "What else could I think? First you sent me those disgusting black flowers and—"

"Huh? Flowers?" Clay wiped sweat off his face with his shirtsleeve. "I never sent you any fucking flowers. I sent you a birthday card. That's it."

"You're lying," I said. "You sent those black flowers. I had no choice. When the hand came, I—I had to tell the police about you."

"I don't know shit about any hand or any flowers, Ellie. I sent you a card, that's all. How come you didn't answer my phone calls? I called you every day. How come you didn't answer? Because you were fucking *this* guy?"

Jackson lurched forward angrily. I tugged him back. "No, please," I whispered. "He's high. He's totally trashed. He doesn't know what he's—"

"Yeah. I'm high," Clay broke in. "So what? So fucking what about it?" He strode up to Jackson. "And what are *you* high on, pretty boy? You high on her ass?"

Clay bumped Jackson hard with his chest.

He's out of his head, I realized. He's dangerous. I was wrong. He's much crazier than I thought. He really could be the one. Sure, he had an alibi set up. But he's crazy enough to attack Mrs. Bricker.

"You want to do something about it?" he challenged Jackson. "You want to fucking do something?" He bumped Jackson again.

I still had hold of Jackson's arm, but he pulled away from me. His face was tight with anger. He let out a low growl and grabbed Clay by the front of his shirt.

Clay threw a wild punch that sailed over Jackson's head.

Jackson pulled Clay up by the shirt, dragged him across the street. Clay thrashed and flailed, trying to land a punch.

"No, please!" I screamed, my heart pounding, hands pressed against my face. "Please, Jackson—don't!"

31

Clay is stocky, built like a bear. But Jackson pulled him easily, jerked him roughly across the street, then shoved him onto his back on the hood of his SUV.

"This is between me and her!" Clay shouted. "Hey, punk—this is between me and her."

I could hear laughter up at the house. Music floated through the trees. It seemed a long way away.

"Let's just end this!" I called. "Please—"

Jackson grabbed Clay roughly, stood him up, then shoved him to his car door. "Drive away, man. Get in there and drive away. I don't want to hurt you. Just drive and don't come back, hear?"

"This is between me and her," Clay insisted.

But when Jackson let go of him, Clay stumbled into the SUV and climbed behind the wheel. Jackson stood beside the car, hands at his waist, breathing hard, until Clay started the engine.

Then Clay roared past him, nearly knocking Jackson over. Clay's hand thrust out the window, flipping us the bird as he sped away. The car zigzagged wildly down the narrow street, nearly smashing parked cars on both sides.

I watched it until it disappeared around a curve. Then

I ran to Jackson. "Are you okay? God, he's such an obnoxious shit."

Jackson wiped sweat off his face with his hand. He let out a long whoosh of air.

I kissed his cheek. "Have you been in a lot of fights or something?"

He snickered. "Sure I have. I'm a Comp Lit major, remember? We duked it out all the time over who's tougher—Beowulf or the Golem of Prague."

"No, but—"

"Yeah, sure. Walk across the Wesleyan campus. You wouldn't *believe* the fistfights! Major brawls. Blood on the grass. It's like a war zone. Take no prisoners. Really."

He had me laughing. I could see he was upset. I held his arm, and it was trembling—but he was trying hard to make a joke of it.

We stopped in front of his Passat. "Who *is* that maniac, anyway?" he asked, his dark eyes probing mine. "You go with him?"

I sighed. I turned away from his stare. "I used to. I broke up with him over a month ago. But he doesn't seem to get it."

"Maybe he'll get it now," Jackson said.

"He—he used to be nice," I said. Somehow I felt I had to explain. "I met him when I was temping at his office. He was okay for a while. But then he got into coke . . . and other stuff. I think it was pressure from his job. I don't know. He changed. He's not so nice anymore."

Jackson opened the car door, and I slid inside. I hugged myself to stop shaking. It felt good to sit down.

Clay did it. The words forced their way into my mind: Clay did it. He cut off that poor woman's hand.

He's crazy.

What is he going to do next?

But if it was Clay, did the note in the gift box make sense?

"I'd give my right arm to see you dead. . . ."

Did Clay really want to see me dead because I had rejected him? Was he *that* crazy and strung out?

I slid down in the car seat, feeling more confused than ever. Jackson lowered himself behind the wheel. He squeezed my hand. "Good party, huh?"

I laughed. "You are Mr. Sunshine, aren't you? Always look on the bright side."

He started the car. "The bright side is that your friend Clay didn't *waste* me. I was lucky he was so fucked up. I'm a bleeder, you know."

We drove in silence for a few moments. I stared out at the passing trees, waiting for my breathing to return to normal, trying to stop the whirl of ugly thoughts.

Noyac Road curved and dipped. It was rutted and potholed, and so dark, Jackson clicked on the brights.

The houses were all dark, and we passed through thick woods, trees overhanging the road, blocking the faint light from the late-night sky so that I felt as if I being pulled through a deep, winding tunnel.

"Man, it's dark," Jackson said, leaning over the wheel. "At least it isn't foggy. One night a few weeks ago—" He stopped as bright, yellow light invaded the car. It spread over the windshield, light from behind us, the glass glowing, bright as sunlight.

Jackson squinted into the mirror. "Whoa. Some dude is on our tail with his brights on."

I turned and saw the twin headlights approaching like two fireballs shooting toward us. "He's going too fast!" I cried.

"Hey, what's his problem?" Jackson grabbed the wheel with both hands as we felt a hard bump from behind. "The crazy bastard!"

Our car jolted off the road. Jackson struggled to hold on to the wheel. Before he could regain control, the car bumped us again—a hard crash of metal against metal that jolted us, tossed me forward and then back, sent us skidding, tires squealing.

"Whoa! Jesus! What the hell!" Jackson cried.

I turned and stared out the back. The driver was hidden behind the blazing light. But I could see that the car was tall, high off the road. An SUV.

The road curved. I bounced hard, my head hitting the low ceiling of the Passat. I turned again and squinted through the back window. I could see our pursuer's car clearly as it came around the curve. Yes, an SUV. A black SUV.

"It's Clay!" I gasped.

I heard the roar of his engine behind us. The yellow lights swept through our car again. Again, the clash of metal against metal, a hard, jarring thud as he bumped us hard.

Our car jumped, flew forward.

I braced myself, slamming both hands over the dashboard, as Jackson's car skidded again.

"The bastard! The fucking bastard!" Jackson screamed. "He's trying to kill us!"

Yes, he is. He's a killer.

At that moment, I knew that Clay was a killer. And the accident flew back into my mind. . . .

Seven years ago . . .

I grabbed the wheel, and Will's car went flying out of control.

Over the embankment, floating for a few fleeting seconds, floating in midair as if about to take off. And then sending Will and me plunging down . . . down . . . down into a darkness so deep . . .

For Will, the deepest darkness there is. For Will, darkness forever.

I started to scream.

My hands spread over the dashboard, my eyes gazing into the lights that swept over our windshield, my head tossed back, as if pulled by my ugly memories.

I screamed and screamed.

And the SUV slammed hard into us, a hard *crunch* of bumpers.

Our car leaped and spun off the road, and we went hurtling into the woods, hurtling into the deep, deep darkness, my screams echoing off the trees.

32

He—followed us. He tried to kill us!"

Abby turned in her chair and glanced up in shock as I burst into the living room. She dropped the book she'd been reading and jumped to her feet. "Oh, my God. What's wrong?"

I was so frightened, my senses were on super alert. An adrenaline rush, I guess. I could see every detail with such clarity.

Abby was wearing a pale blue tank top over faded jeans. A necklace of coral beads lay on the low table next to the couch, crumpled beside a glass of red wine. Blinking hard, shaking her head, she hurried over to me. "Ellie, are you okay? Tell me—what happened?"

I sighed and dropped my bag to the floor. "Jackson and I—we were almost killed. Our car skidded—into the woods. We could have hit a tree. We could have—"

"Oh, my God. Ellie, you're trembling." She put an arm around my shoulder and led me to the couch. "Are you all right? Are you hurt? Sit down. Here. Have some of this." She handed the glass of red wine to me. "Go ahead. Oh, my God. You're white as a sheet."

I took a long drink.

Abby sat down beside me. "What happened? You were in an accident?"

"No. It was Clay. My crazy ex-boyfriend. He—he bumped us off the road. He was trying to kill us! Luckily, our car came to a stop against some soft pine shrubs. Jackson drove me home and—"

"Jackson? Is that a guy you know?"

"I met him the other night. At a club. He was driving me home from the party. But then Clay came up behind us. He started bumping us, slamming into us—"

Abby grabbed the cordless phone off the coffee table. "We should call the police. Right away."

"No. I—" I hesitated, my mind spinning. I didn't know what to do. I didn't want to make Clay even angrier, even more dangerous. "I don't really know if it was Clay," I said.

Pretty lame, El.

I wasn't sure what to do. I'd spent too much time talking to endless police officers. I just wanted Clay and the police—I wanted them all to go away, to disappear.

I emptied the wineglass. The red wine felt so soothing going down my throat. I felt my heartbeat slow to normal.

Abby filled my glass and poured another one for herself. "Well, I'm glad you're okay, Ellie. It's been one thing after another since you arrived, hasn't it?" Her eyes were studying me intently.

I glanced down at my wineglass. "I'm sorry. I'm so sorry I've been such a problem. Maybe I should go."

"No. Please." She squeezed my hand. "We'll get through all of this. Chip and I don't want you to leave. It's nearly July. It would be so hard to find a replacement now. Besides, the kids would be very upset if you left. Brandon, especially."

I took a long sip of wine. I pictured the black SUV roaring behind us, slamming us, the clang of bumpers, and I heard my screams, my high, shrill screams as we slid out of control, into the woods, into darkness.

History repeating itself.

Again, I pictured Will—fair, blond Will. I'm sorry, Will. I grabbed the wheel, and we went flying.

Would I always picture Will?

Abby's voice broke into my thoughts. "Well, I do have some good news for you, Ellie."

Good news? I shook my head, brushing Will away.

"Your cousin called tonight. She found someone to drop off your cat. He's going to bring it here tomorrow."

"Oh, that's great," I said. "I haven't seen Lucky for so long. I've missed him *so* much."

Maybe Lucky will live up to his name.

I took a final sip of wine. Then I set the glass down and said good night to Abby. I thanked her for being so kind and so understanding.

"Get some sleep," she said. "You'll feel better in the morning."

The wine had calmed me, but I felt a little dizzy. I held on to the railing as I climbed the stairs to my room. Would I be able to sleep?

I tossed my clothes on the closet floor and pulled on a long cotton nightshirt. The bedroom window was open, and outside, the crickets were making a racket.

I crossed the room to the window, peered out into the backyard—and gasped.

At the top of the dune, a light flickered in the guest-house window. I blinked. Squinted hard through the line of pine trees.

Yes. I saw it again. A tiny red dot of light, like the tip of a cigarette, moving slowly.

"I don't believe in ghosts," I murmured, holding on to the curtains, gripping them tightly, holding on to something real—flimsy but real. A chill slid down my back.

"I don't believe in ghosts. I'm not going out there again."

I pulled the curtains over the window and climbed into bed.

I awoke to a dark and rainy morning. The curtains flew violently at the window. Rain had puddled on the windowsill and the floor in front of it.

At breakfast, Abby said, "I'll take Heather this morning. Why don't you drive Brandon to the Whaling Museum in Sag Harbor? I think he might like that. I don't want him sitting home watching TV all day."

So Brandon and I drove to the museum, the car splashing through deep puddles of rainwater, the sky dark as night. "The museum is very interesting," I said, trying to sound enthusiastic. "It's all about the old whaling ships and sailors who used to hunt whales in the ocean here."

Brandon's expression didn't change. He clicked on the radio and turned the volume up all the way.

The noise startled me, and I nearly swerved off the road. Music blasted through the car like an explosion. My hand fumbled for the knob. Finally, I clicked the radio off.

"Stop it, Brandon." I tried to keep my voice low and

calm, but I couldn't hide my anger. "That wasn't funny. You scared me."

He tilted his head back and laughed.

To my thinking, he had become more hostile and angry since I had arrived. And I still hadn't forgiven him for trying to drown his sister. For standing there so calmly and watching Heather sink below the waves.

Abby said Brandon's shrink was dealing with it all, but I didn't see any signs of progress. And I certainly didn't see any signs that Brandon liked me or was the least bit attached to me, as Abby claimed.

I admit it. He was only four years old, and I was growing to hate him.

I parked the car at the curb in front of the Whaling Museum. It was a white, Colonial-style building behind a closely trimmed lawn and a white picket fence. I glanced around. We were on a residential block of sprawling old houses, well-maintained treasures that people probably kept in their family for generations.

I grabbed Brandon's hand. Ducking our heads, we ran through the rain. I pulled open the door to the museum, and we darted inside.

I expected something out of the 1850s, dark and mildewy, with fishermens' nets strung along the walls or over the ceiling. But the museum was bright and dry. We checked our rain ponchos. I paid the admission, and we began to wander around.

The building clearly had once been someone's house. I tried to imagine what it would be like to live in such big rooms with the grand, high ceilings, the majestic staircase winding up to even more wonderful space.

To my surprise, Brandon seemed interested in the displays. He tugged me into the first room. Large black-

and-white drawings of whaling ships on the walls. An enormous blowup of an old engraving of a whaler leaning over the side of his boat to heave a harpoon at a fleeing, monstrous whale.

And in the center of the room, a small wooden boat that appeared hand-carved. A sign explained that once the whale was spotted, whalers used this small, sleek boat for fast pursuit.

Brandon slid his hand along the side of the boat. Then he turned and ran into the next display room without waiting for me. I found him admiring a long harpoon mounted on the wall. He studied the sharp metal point. Then he reached up to grab the handle.

"Don't even think about it," I said. "Do you know how much that harpoon must weigh? A lot more than you do!"

He gazed at it for another long moment. Again, he tried to reach it, this time on tiptoe.

"No way, Brandon. What is your *problem*?" I pulled him away from the harpoon.

We discovered a movie about whales running in the next room, a dark room with rows of benches for viewing. Two little boys sat in the back watching intently as a whale lifted itself over the ocean surface. Brandon immediately took a seat at the front.

I had a sudden inspiration. "Do you want to stay and watch?" I asked from the doorway.

He nodded.

"Then I'll be back in ten minutes," I said. "Don't go anywhere. Just watch."

He nodded again, eyes on the leaping whale.

I walked back to the front desk and asked if the museum had a reference room. The woman pointed to the stairs. "Room 203. I think Gladys is up there, if she isn't on her break. She'll help you find things."

Gladys turned out to be a trim, smartly dressed older woman with bobbed white hair and tight, smooth cheeks that suggested more than one face-lift. I told her I wanted to find information about a house built in the 1850s.

She tried to frown, but her face was too tight. "That would be hard," she said. "We've just started to computerize. Everything's just in card files and old scrapbooks. Maybe if you had a name? The owner of the house? I might be able to look up a name."

I shut my eyes, trying to remember the name of the captain in Mrs. Bricker's story. Halsey? No. Halley? "The name was Halley," I said. "A whaling captain." I spelled it for her.

"Are those Guess jeans?" she asked, staring at my legs. "Do Guess jeans fit that well?"

"Uh, actually, these are Old Navy," I said.

She sniffed, no longer interested. "Halley," she muttered. "Let me see."

A few minutes later, she pulled some frayed, yellowed cards from a cabinet. She waved them triumphantly. "Thomas Halley?"

"Maybe. I—I don't really know his first name."

Gladys walked to a shelf at the back of the room, bent, and pulled out two bulging scrapbooks. "I think there might be some old clippings. Let's check in these, dear."

She spread the scrapbooks out on a long library table and, checking back at the little cards, sifted quickly through the pages. "Hmmm . . . Halley. That's close to Halsey, isn't it. Halsey is a big family name out here.

Half the roads in the Hamptons are named Halsey this and Halsey that."

I wondered how Brandon was doing downstairs. Was I leaving him alone for too long?

"Oh, my goodness!" Gladys declared. "There appears to be a scandal, dear." She spun the old book around so I could see it.

The newspaper clippings were torn and brown with age. But the headline—YOUNG VILLAGE MAN MURDERED IN WATERMILL COTTAGE—was easy to read.

My heart started to pound. I suddenly felt light-headed. I pulled a metal chair out from the table and slumped into it. Then I let my eyes scan the old story.

Yes. Yes. It was all true.

Capt. Thomas Halley . . . His son Jeremiah . . . Jeremiah murdered the young man. . . . Heaved a whaling harpoon through his heart . . . Police find it mysterious. . . . How did the little boy lift such a heavy object? The father is a more likely suspect—but he wasn't home at the time of the murder. . . . The nanny ran to the police constables. . . . The nanny and the deceased were rumored to be courting. . . .

My eyes stopped at the bottom of the clipping. My eyes scanned the words, and my mouth opened in a startled gasp:

The boy, Jeremiah Halley, has gone silent and will not answer questions.

Mrs. Bricker, your story was true.

"Is something wrong, dear?" Gladys stared at me from the other side of the table. "You've suddenly gone so pale."

"No. I'm okay," I said, shoving the book away. "Thank you so much. Thank you for your help. I—have a little boy downstairs. I'd better get back."

I have a little, SILENT boy downstairs.

A boy who was fascinated by the big harpoon on the wall.

The museum was hot, but I suddenly felt so cold. A frightening cold, a chill from the distant past . . .

No!

I still don't believe in ghosts, Mrs. Bricker.

Well . . .

. . . maybe just a little.

I found Brandon sitting like an angel, hands clasped in his lap, watching whales spout and leap on the little movie screen. He was scrunched down on the seat and had the sweetest smile on his face. He seemed so tiny and frail and harmless.

I wanted to run my hand through that curly black hair and tell him I was sorry about all the angry thoughts I'd had about him.

What's troubling you, Brandon? What *is* it? Why don't you tell me?

I'm sure it has nothing to do with Jeremiah Halley. It can't have anything to do with Jeremiah Halley because he died over a hundred years ago. *And we don't believe in ghosts, right?*

The Whaling Museum is about two blocks from the town of Sag Harbor. We drove into town. The sky was starting to brighten, the rain having stopped, leaving the trees and houses glittery and dripping and shiny as new.

Abby asked me to pick up some things at the little IGA in town. Sag Harbor was crowded for a weekday, but I found a parking space in front of the old-fashioned looking five-and-dime, and pulled in.

I turned to Brandon. "Would you like to explore this old store before we pick up the groceries? It looks kinda cool."

He thought about it for a long while, then nodded.

I turned off the ignition, tucked the car key into my bag, raised my eyes to the windshield—and saw Will walk out of the dime store.

33

The first time I made love to Will was after the fall Homecoming dance. We did it in the backseat of his car, and it lasted only a minute or two, and I wondered what all the fuss was about. I think I would have enjoyed it more if I hadn't been so worried about staining my dress.

Will and I had been going together for such a short time. I guess I made love to him that night because Dawn Fregosi and Amy Kruschek—my two best pals and confidantes—said they planned to get laid after the Homecoming. In fact, they were double-dating, and the plan was for the four of them to do it at Dawn's house because her parents were in Florida—in the same bed side by side.

I was surprised about Amy because she said she'd never really done it, not even with Johnny Harmon, whom she was crazy about. She said she only gave blow jobs because that wasn't really sex.

So I don't know if it ever happened. I had a feeling maybe Amy had wimped out. But I didn't get the whole story because Dawn and Amy never talked about it, and I felt kinda weird bringing it up, even though I thought about it a lot.

I wasn't competitive with Amy and Dawn. I liked them and even trusted them, which is a hard thing in high school. But I always wondered why they wanted to be *my* friend. I never really accepted the fact that I was part of their crowd. I always felt as if I were some kind of an impostor, that I was just passing for cool, and someday they would find me out and expose me, humiliate me in some way, and then never talk to me again.

Typical high school bullshit, right?

Of course, we went to the Homecoming dance as a goof. Everyone I knew did. We were way cool and above such things as school dances, above *everything*. There was nothing we couldn't sneer at.

Except boys. We took them seriously, God knows.

Before the prom, Amy, Dawn, and I met at Dawn's house, and we put on our makeup in the dark. That's right. In the dark. Because, you see, we knew it would be dark at the dance. So we put on our makeup with the lights off to make sure we looked good in the dark.

We didn't think it was crazy. We thought it was totally necessary.

Will was a fabulous dancer. He had a natural grace. He moved so well, and it looked so easy for him. The same kind of grace he had on the basketball court when he'd stop and seem to fly back through the air as he sent up his jump shots.

He was very funny all night, dancing crazy, being silly, being a parody of a Homecoming dance date. But during the one slow dance, where we held each other and danced so close, I could feel him pressing against me, pressing against me. And I knew how the night would end.

Yes, I was excited. Because it was Will. Blond, graceful Will, who was so funny, who had picked me.

If only we'd had a place to go. If only it had lasted longer.

After that night, Will acted as if he owned me. And that's when it started—and when my feelings started to change. I didn't know it then. I didn't figure it out till much later.

But those two uncomfortable, sloppy minutes in the car changed everything.

Of course I still cared about Will. Of course I was still so thrilled and amazed that he had picked me. But did I really want to be owned? No. Did I want to be a possession, like one of those silly chrome basketball trophies he kept on his dresser?

Not really.

I didn't like the way he slid his arm around me when he came up to me in school. I'd be talking to someone, and there would be Will, grabbing me, wrapping his arm around my neck, roping me in like a runaway calf.

Yes, suddenly there were things I didn't like. Even while he was kissing me, his hands under my sweater so gentle but needy, even with the excitement of being so special to someone, there were things I didn't like.

Why were his lips so mushy and wet? Did he really think it was sexy to slobber all over me?

Later, I felt guilty about every complaint.

Our whole time together was so short, so damned short, like the two minutes in the backseat of his car. I should have had more. More of Will. More time.

And now, there he was in front of my car in Sag Harbor, stepping out of the dime store.

I shoved the car door open—slamming the car parked next to me. "Will—! Hey!"

He turned. Did he see me?

He had a white plastic bag in his hand. He tucked it under his arm and started to jog down the sidewalk.

"Will—wait!"

I lurched out the door. Forgot about the seat belt. It jerked me back. I fumbled to unfasten myself.

"Will? Hey—Will?"

I saw his blond hair. Saw him dodge two bent old men with canes. The sidewalk was crowded. People moved slowly, window-shopping, chatting casually.

I saw the blond hair, saw the white bag in his arms.

Was he running from me? Why was he running away?

I leaped from the car and took off, my sneakers thudding the pavement. Forgetting about Brandon. Leaving the car door open.

"Will—?"

"Look out!" a voice shouted, and a lanky teenager in an open Hawaiian shirt roared past my feet on a skateboard.

I stumbled back, into a display sign in front of a clothing store.

"Will, please!"

People were staring now.

I stopped. He had vanished again.

I grabbed the back of a bench. Gripped it with both hands, leaning all my weight on it, and waited for my heart to stop pounding against my chest, waited for the sidewalk to stop tilting and swaying.

Will vanished again.

But it couldn't be Will, I told myself, still sucking in air, still searching the crowded sidewalk.

Will vanished seven years ago.

Will died, Ellie. He's dead. So you've got to stop seeing him.

You. Have. To. Stop.

My shrink back in Madison told me I'd stop thinking about Will someday. He said one day I'd stop seeing him. One day I'd put my ghosts to rest.

I believed him then. I really did. But I didn't believe him anymore.

My ghost was back.

I stood up. Pushed back the hair that had fallen over my face. Took a deep breath and started back to the car.

I saw Brandon still sitting in the passenger seat. He was fooling with the dials on the dashboard. The driver's door still hung open. I shut the door and made my way over to Brandon's side to let him out.

A horn honked. Someone shouted my name.

I turned and saw Clay, his head sticking out of his black SUV, waving to me. "Hey, Ellie. Hi!"

I wanted to scream, but I held it back. I balled my hands into tight fists and stormed up to Clay.

"You—you shit!" I shrieked. "How could you call to me? How could you *face* me?"

He froze for a second. Then his face reddened as his smile faded. He blinked at me, acting confused, acting as if he didn't understand. "Whoa, Ellie. Please—"

"You tried to *kill* me!" I cried. I slammed my fist on his car door.

Bad idea. Pain shot up my arm.

"Kill you?" He kept the confused look on his face. "Hey, I'm sorry. I came on a little strong last night. I was a little ripped, I guess. I didn't mean to give that guy a hard time."

"Clay, you shit! You liar!" I banged my fists against his car again.

People were staring. I didn't care.

"You crazy shit! You bumped us off the road. You could have killed us."

I glimpsed Brandon in the car. He had his hands pressed over his ears.

"I *what*?" Clay gave me the innocent, wide-eyed, baby boy look. "I bumped you? Have you fucking lost it, Ellie?"

"I'm calling the police. I'm going to file a complaint, Clay. You used your car as a weapon. You followed us. You crashed into us again and again. You tried to kill us."

"You're fucking crazy. I mean it. I didn't follow you. Why would I follow you? I drove back to the house I'm staying at. I never followed you."

"You liar!" I screamed. "Of course you deny it now. You tried to kill me. Of course you deny it."

I jumped back as he shoved open the door and slid out of the car. "You think I would dent up my new SUV? Huh? You think you're so hot, I'd dent up my new car for you? Is that what you think? Here. Take a look."

He grabbed my arm roughly and pulled me to the front of the car.

"Take a look. Check it out. You see any dents any-where? Go ahead. Look. You say I bumped you again and again? You want to accuse me? Take a good look, Ellie. You see any scratches? You see any marks on the car?"

I leaned down and examined the front of the car.

No.

No marks on the bumper. No scratches or dents on

the fenders. The headlights okay, not cracked. No marks anywhere. The chrome shiny and new. The bumper spotless.

"You want to call the police on me again? You really think I'm a fucking murderer? You gonna call the police again? Look at the car, Ellie. Look at the fucking car. I didn't follow you. You're crazy."

He bumped me out of the way and climbed back behind the wheel.

And then it hit me: I'm crazy.

He's right. I'm crazy.

The car was spotless. Not the tiniest speck on it.

I stood up straight and took a deep breath. "You could have gotten it fixed," I muttered.

"When? At two on a Saturday night? Yeah. Lots of garages are open then."

"Just stay away from me, Clay." My voice broke. "Just stay away from me, get it?"

"No problem," he said. He didn't say it angrily. He said it wearily, defeated. "No problem, El. I'm real sorry. I was crazy about you, you know. You want to turn me in to the police for that? Go ahead."

He rolled up his window. Then he squealed away. I saw the policewoman at the crosswalk turn angrily and watch the SUV roar down Main Street.

I stood there at the curb, feeling dazed.

It *had* to be Clay in the black SUV last night. It *had* to be Clay crashing into us, hitting us, bumping us until we slid into the woods.

But the car would have scratches. Even a tall SUV would have marks on the bumpers, some sign of the impacts.

And if it wasn't Clay . . .

If it wasn't Clay . . .

Who?

I climbed back into the car. I started the engine. I was halfway out of the parking space when I realized I'd forgotten to pick up the groceries for Abby.

I pulled back into the space. I turned and saw Brandon staring at me.

"I'm sorry I was screaming back there," I said. "I—had a misunderstanding with someone I know. You know. An argument? It was no big deal."

His dark eyes were so wide. His slender face was so pale.

"Brandon, are you okay?" I asked.

To my shock, he unbuckled himself, scrambled onto my lap, and wrapped me in a tight hug.

I had to park on the street at the Harpers' house. The gardeners' truck stood halfway up the drive behind Chip's SUV. Five or six men in sweat-drenched T-shirts were working over the front yard, weeding, trimming plants, cutting the patches of tall grass.

Brandon helped me carry the grocery bags inside. Chip met us in the front hall. "Oh, good. Here you are," he said. "Put it in the kitchen. Abby will be home soon."

We set the bags down on the kitchen counter. Chip slapped Brandon a high-five. "How's it going, bud? How was the whaling museum?"

For a moment, I thought Brandon might speak. But no. He flashed his dad a thumbs-up. Then he grabbed an Oreo off a plate on the counter and hurried from the room.

Chip flashed *me* a thumbs-up. "I think Brandon liked it. That's great. I haven't seen him so enthusiastic in weeks." He started pawing through one of the grocery bags; then he stopped. "Oh. I almost forgot, Ellie. They dropped off your cat."

"Lucky's here?"

Chip pointed to the kitchen door. "Yes. He came about an hour ago. He's in his carrier. On the deck."

Lucky! Yes!

I dashed out to the deck, letting the screen door slam behind me. I was so happy. I'd missed my old cat so much.

"Lucky! It's me!" I called, running across the deck.

His travel carrier was near the steps.

"Lucky! Hey, Lucky! Remember me?"

I dropped down beside the carrier. I unlatched the door in the side.

"Lucky?"

I lowered my head to the door and peered inside.

Whoa. No cat? I saw a fuzzy, black ball.

No. Wait. Oh, wait.

The eyes. Two glassy eyes stared back at me.

Lucky's eyes.

The mouth open, purple tongue drooping out.

Oh, Lucky.

My poor cat, my poor old cat.

I couldn't move. I couldn't stop staring.

Staring at Lucky's head on the floor of the carrier.

Just his head.

34

Sobs shook my body. I let the tears roll down my cheeks. I sat on the top step of the deck, holding myself tightly, swaying from side to side.

I shut my eyes and tried to picture Lucky alive. Tried to see him playing with his favorite toy, a little, pink-and-yellow rubber mouse. Tried to see him creeping into my lap and forcing me to put down the book I was reading and give all my attention to him. Tried to picture the delicate way he ate, his tongue carefully cleaning his mouth afterwards.

But I couldn't picture any of that. I could see only the round, furry head, the empty eyes, the tongue hanging limp and shriveled like a dead worm.

"Who did this?" I screamed at the top of my lungs. *"Who did this?"*

And then, without even realizing it, I was on my feet and back in the kitchen, confronting a startled Chip, who was leaning into the refrigerator, rearranging things on the shelves.

"Who did this? Tell me! Who brought the cat? Who was here?" I grabbed him with both hands and spun him around.

A plastic container of fruit salad fell from his hands and splattered on the floor.

Chip stumbled back, holding on to the refrigerator door. "Ellie? What the hell?"

"My cat!" I wailed, and more sobs took my breath away. "Who brought it? Who was it?"

His eyes narrowed in confusion. "Some guy. In a Volvo station wagon. A young guy. Tall, with his head shaved and a little beard. He said he was a friend of your cousin's."

"But the cat is dead! Don't you understand! My cat is dead!"

Stepping around the puddle of fruit salad, Chip crossed the room. "Ellie, calm down. Ellie, let's deal with this." He raised his arms to wrap me in a hug—uh, no way—I backed against the counter.

"Lucky—he—he was murdered! Someone cut off his head!"

Chip gasped. The color drained from his face. "No. That's impossible." He grabbed the back of a kitchen stool. "I heard the cat scratching against the case. Really. And I heard it meowing."

"It *can't* meow!" I screamed. "Its *head* was cut off!"

"No. That's crazy. That's impossible. I heard it," he insisted. "You poor thing. You're shaking." He came at me again. I was trapped against the counter. He wrapped his arms around me. He smelled of coconut suntan lotion.

I let him hug me, and I cried, sobbed onto the sleeve of his polo shirt. It felt good to be held. I think he was genuinely trying to comfort me. Okay, maybe not. But I didn't care.

I couldn't think. I didn't know what to do.

What do I do next?

Choking on my sobs, I pushed him back. I ripped some paper towels from the dispenser next to the sink and wiped my face.

He stood with his hands at his sides, watching me, biting his lips. "We have to call the police," he said. "We have to let them know that someone . . . has struck again."

The police haven't been helpful at all, I thought. They ask a lot of questions and then fill out reports.

"Who was home?" I asked. "The cat was okay when it arrived? Then, who was here, Chip? Just you?"

He nodded. "Yeah. Just me. I took the carrier to the deck. I thought the cat would like fresh air until you came home. I—"

"And no one else was home?"

"No. No one. I think Abby was in Bridgehampton with Heather, and—oh, yeah. Maggie stopped by. With those two little girls. She was looking for you."

"Maggie—?"

"She stayed only a second. She left when I told her where you were."

"Maggie?"

My brain felt all cottony. I kept blinking, trying to clear the fog. Sunlight washed through the kitchen windows, but I felt wrapped in darkness, drowning inside a dark, swirling cloud.

Maggie wouldn't murder my cat.

Chip was the only one home.

He says the cat was alive. *And he was the only one home.*

It was too much. Too much to bear.

A scream burst from my throat. I heaved myself away

from the counter, pushed past Chip, his mouth open with shock, and ran screaming to the front of the house.

"I can't stay here! I can't stay here!"

I heard Brandon laughing upstairs. Was he laughing at a cartoon video? He wasn't laughing at me—*was* he?

"I can't stay here!"

I heard Brandon's laughter, and then I was out the front door, leaping down the stairs, and nearly knocked over one of the gardeners pruning the hedge. He cried out in surprise and dropped his hedge-cutters.

"Sorry!"

The other workers raised their heads to watch me. I ran over the flagstone walk, my chest heaving, tears burning my cheeks.

To the driveway.

Where was I going?

What was I doing?

I didn't know. I couldn't think. I only knew I had to run.

Run and keep running.

Someone was ruining my life. Someone hated me—hated me enough to kill me.

I had no choice. I had to run.

I reached the driveway. Behind the house, I could see two blue-and-red kites dipping and rising in the sky. Someone at the beach was having fun, flying kites in the strong ocean wind.

I want to be one of those kites, I thought. I want to fly high and free. I want to cut the string . . . sail away . . . float away from this heavy, dark fog . . . fly to sunlight.

I have to run.

But I stopped just past the SUV. Stopped and stared at the front bumper.

Chip's SUV. A black TrailBlazer.

The bumper was scratched in several places and dented on the left side.

The glass on the left headlight was cracked.

I stopped and ran my fingers over the dent on the bumper. Flakes of red paint came off in my hand.

Red paint?

Jackson's Passat.

Chip's SUV was black.

Chip was the only one home today . . . and his SUV was black and dented.

I raised my eyes to the house in time to see Chip stride out the front door.

He stopped at the bottom step and called to me.

"Ellie? Can we talk?"

35

I'm getting so handy with the knife.

I never knew it was so easy. I guess pure hatred makes a lot of things easy.

Poor kitty cat. Poor Ellie.

Such a lovely old cat. He hardly put up a fuss. Sure, he kicked and hissed a bit when I grabbed his throat. He was used to being treated well. He trusted people.

Foolish creature. Trusting people? Never a good idea.

I trusted people once, a long time ago. I trusted people—and then Ellie came along. And destroyed my trust forever.

But today, I feel so bad for Ellie. To see a loved one murdered in such a cruel, callous way. A beloved old family member. Part of her childhood. Part of her youth, sliced away forever.

Where's my youth, Ellie?

Where?

I guess the years on the farm toughened me, gave me a more realistic view of animals.

Animals are just animals; that's what you learn on a farm. Dad killed every pet I ever had. Even Billy, my little goat, my favorite pal.

Well, kitty cat is dead. His head would make a lovely

table ornament. If only those eyes weren't staring so accusingly.

I once read a story in which the murderer's face was trapped forever in his victim's eyes. The police gazed into the victim's eyes and saw the murderer, captured as if on film.

Well, I checked the cat's eyes. Believe me. I'm not superstitious, but I check everything. Those eyes were as dead as the rest of the carcass, which I carefully buried beneath the rhododendrons.

Is Ellie superstitious? I don't know.

Is she finally beginning to catch on? Does she realize that she's next?

I think she does.

Watching her run out of the house, screaming her lungs out, tears running down her little lemon face, made me think that maybe she's finally catching on.

She'll want to leave now. She won't want to stay.

But—no way, Ellie.

I've waited so long for this.

Have you heard the phrase, "No more Mr. Nice Guy"?

Well, you'd better believe it.

No more Mr. Nice Guy.

No more fun and games, sweetheart.

Now it gets real.

36

I still had my bag over my shoulder. Ignoring Chip's cries, I fumbled for the car keys as I ran down the front yard to the Taurus.

Was he coming after me?

I reached the curb, pulled open the driver's door. I turned to the house and saw Chip, still at the front door, motioning wildly, shouting for me to come back. The gardeners had all stopped working. They were standing up now, tools at their sides, silently watching the drama.

Chip screamed at me, "Where are you going? Ellie, we have to call the police."

Those were the last words I heard before I slammed the car door, turned the ignition, and roared off.

Where *was* I going?

Away. That's all I knew.

Well, I knew a few other things. I knew that Chip had a black SUV, and the front was dented, and the paint in the dents was red.

And he was the only one home when Lucky was murdered.

Chip.

But why?

I struggled to think of a reason why Chip would hate

me. Was he just crazy? Did Abby know about him? Would Abby live with someone so crazy?

I was sobbing again, my foot pressed hard on the gas, roaring down Flying Point Road, past a blur of tall hedges and green trees and sprawling brick and stone houses.

I saw the green van coming toward me. I swerved at the last minute. I didn't realize I was driving in the middle of the street.

The van honked a long warning as it sped past. I pulled to the side of the street. Jammed the gearshift into PARK. Sat stunned for a moment or two.

And stopped sobbing.

I just stopped.

Maybe it was the shock of almost being hit.

Or maybe there's just a time when sadness turns to anger.

That's what happened to me. I knew I was all cried out. Someone wanted me to cry. Someone wanted to terrify me.

But suddenly, I felt only anger. Anger that someone thought he had the right to ruin my life.

My jaw ached. I realized I was gritting my teeth. My hands throbbed from gripping the wheel so tightly.

I forced myself to relax, forced my muscles to ease up, let go. And I tried to think clearly.

The police had been no help. Poor Mrs. Bricker lost a hand, and the police still didn't have a clue.

Not a clue.

I suddenly had some ideas. Totally Nancy Drew ideas. But Nancy always got her man, didn't she? Nancy always solved the crime.

Now that my crying was over, I knew it was time to get to the truth, to find out what this was all about.

I circled around Southampton for a while and found only one flower store, a small shop on Hampton Road between a travel agency and a clothing boutique. Hand-printed signs covered the front window, advertising specials on long-stemmed roses and orchids in pots.

The store was crowded, and an elderly, white-haired woman with bright blue eyes and a harried expression seemed to be the only one minding the store. She tried to take customers' orders and answer the phone at the same time, and it was obvious from the disgruntled, impatient expressions on everyone's faces that she wasn't keeping up too well.

The shop was deep, bigger than it appeared from the street, with long refrigerated cases of flowers and a glassed-in greenhouse at the back. I took a deep breath and inhaled that sweet smell you find only in flower stores.

I had a lot of time to study the flower cases and inhale the sweet aroma before she finally got around to me.

"Can I help you, dear? I'm so sorry you had to wait. What a day. Both Arthur and Jimmy came down sick this morning. I don't even have a delivery boy, and how am I supposed to make the arrangements and wait on people at the same time?"

"I promise I won't keep you long," I said. "Do you sell flowers painted black here? You know. For funerals."

Her face changed, suddenly full of pity.

"Well, yes, of course. Arthur makes some lovely wreaths or arrangements. We've had a fresh shipment of lilies—did you see them in the back case? Of course, lilies are always appropriate and—"

"Actually, I don't want to order flowers. I need to know about an order from about three weeks ago."

She scratched her white hair. Then she pulled a white Life Saver from a pack on the counter and popped it into her mouth. "An order for funeral flowers?"

I nodded. "Black flowers, actually. You know. Sprayed black. The flowers were shipped to our house without a card. And I'd really like to know who was kind enough to send them."

She sucked on the Life Saver. "Without a card? We don't usually slip up like that. Especially with funeral flowers."

"Do you have any kind of record? Do you keep the sales slips or anything?" I asked.

"Well, yes. We don't have them in the computer or anything. We just have names and addresses on the computer. You know. Regular accounts. It's quite handy, you know."

"But you do keep sales slips?"

She bit down on the Life Saver. I could hear it crunch. She chewed it as she disappeared into the tiny office behind one of the displays. A few seconds later, she returned carrying a long wicker basket.

"I keep all the slips in here for about a month. Let's take a look. What did you say the name was?"

Before I could answer, the bell over the door rang, and a middle-aged man and woman, in designer jeans and matching red-and-yellow floral shirts, walked in. "Hi, Alma. How's it going?" the man asked.

Alma sighed. "You wouldn't believe it." She handed me the basket. "Look through it, dear. Let me talk to my good friends here. Did you two hear about Arthur and Jimmy?"

I took the basket to the end of the counter and began to paw through it. My hands were trembling. Was I about to learn who had sent the bug-ridden flowers and that disgusting note?

The sales slips and credit card receipts had been tossed in carelessly. But the dates were easy to see, the most recent sales at the top.

It didn't take me long to find the order for the black flowers about halfway down the pile. The credit card receipt was stapled to the yellow sales slip. I lifted it from the box, brought it up close to my face, tried to steady my shaking hand.

And let out a silent gasp as I read the name on the receipt.

37

Chip Harper.

Yes, the credit card receipt was in the name of Chip Harper. I squinted at it, reading it again and again.

Hadn't the police been here? Hadn't they tried to track down the sender of those disgusting flowers?

I wanted to ask Alma, but the phone had rung and she was writing an order, and her two friends were waiting to finish their conversation. So I tucked the receipt into my bag, slid the basket across the counter, and headed out of the shop.

"Did you find what you wanted, dear?" Alma called after me.

I hesitated. "Well, not exactly." I closed the door gently behind me and stepped out into the hazy afternoon sunlight.

Had I found what I wanted?

Not really. Did I want it to be Chip who sent those awful flowers and that frightening note?

Of course not.

Why did he hate me? Why was he doing this to me?

He'd been coming on to me almost since the day I arrived. Coming on to me—and then trying to terrify me?

It made no sense at all.

Is he totally psycho?

Oh, wait. I forgot one thing. I dipped my head back into the flower shop. "I'm sorry to bother you again," I said. "Is there a bakery nearby?"

Alma turned away from her friends. She pointed. "Yes. A very good French bakery. Right across the street. You'll see it, dear. It's right next to La Parmigiana restaurant. Try the raisin scones. The scones are out of this world."

I thanked her and started across the street. Some people had stopped to admire an old Cadillac convertible. It was bright yellow and enormous, more like a boat than a car, with swooping tail fins.

A lot of people collected vintage cars here in the Hamptons. I'd even seen an entire car lot where they sold only vintage cars.

Why didn't Chip have a normal hobby like that? Why didn't he collect old cars instead of torturing me?

The bakery smelled of butter and cinnamon. A young woman wearing a white apron over her T-shirt and tights looked up from her *Hamptons* magazine as I entered.

My eyes stopped on the tray of scones on the counter. But I had no appetite. I didn't really know what to ask. The young woman didn't get up from her canvas chair. She waited patiently for me to speak.

"I want to ask you about an order from about two weeks ago," I started.

She brushed back her short, streaky blond hair, but her expression didn't change.

"Do you remember—? Did anyone come in here and ask for an empty cake box?"

She tilted her head, as if thinking hard. "An empty

box? *Mais non.* No one orders an empty box." She had a heavy French accent and spoke with a slight lisp.

Okay, so maybe there was a cake in the box originally.

"Do you keep a record of orders?" I asked. "You know. A record of your deliveries."

"*Oui.*" She stood up, closed the magazine, and stepped up to the register. "What kind of a cake was it?"

"I—I don't know. I only know where it was delivered."

She frowned at me. "You did not like the cake?"

"Oh, no. No. That's not the problem."

This was harder than I thought.

"I just want to find out who sent it," I said. "It was a delicious cake. Really."

She continued to stare at me. "It was a delicious cake, but you do not remember what kind it was?"

Oh, boy. I knew I sounded like a total asshole.

I sighed. "Could you please just tell me who sent the cake?" I gave her the address on Flying Point Road.

She stepped over to the computer on a little table against the wall. She sat down and typed for a long while. Finally, she found it.

"The cake was sent to the Harper residence? On Flying Point Road?"

"Yes. Yes, that's it." My heart started to pound.

"And let me see . . ." She leaned closer to the monitor and peered closely at the blue screen. "It was purchased by Mr. Chip Harper."

38

"Mom, I'm coming home."

My bedroom door was shut tight, but I whispered into the cell phone anyway. I'd crept into the house and made sure that Chip wasn't home. I saw Abby on the deck with the kids, but her husband was nowhere in sight. I grabbed a bottle of water from the fridge and hurried to my room to call home and plan my escape.

"You're *what*?" My mother reacted with her usual cool. "Oh, my God. Oh, my God. What are you telling me?"

"I want to come home. I don't really have anywhere else to go."

I'd called Teresa first, my only friend in New York. When I tried her phone, I just got her voice mail. So I called her apartment, and May Lin, one of her roommates, told me that Teresa was in South Orange, helping her cousin move. May Lin didn't know if Teresa was coming out to the Hamptons this weekend or not.

I didn't want to go back to the Harpers' house. I didn't want to see Chip again. But all my stuff was here. I couldn't just run away.

Now I knew I really wasn't safe here. I was living with a maniac. I decided I would be safe in Madison, as far away from Chip as I could get.

"Mom, I have to come home right away. I'm packing my stuff and—"

"Ellie, slow down. What's this about? Why are you whispering? Take a breath, okay, honey? And tell me what's happening."

"I can't really explain, Mom. It's just . . . Well . . . the job hasn't worked out, and—"

"Oh, my God, Ellie, did something terrible happen? Are the children okay?"

"Yes. They're fine, Mom. It's not about the children."

Jesus. Leave it to my mother to imagine the worst kind of tragedy—caused by *me*.

"I'm quitting the job," I continued, my voice trembling. A noise outside my door made me jump.

Chip?

"I'm quitting, and I don't have anywhere to live. I gave up the apartment in the city, and—well—I want to come home for a while. You know. Try to regroup."

Silence on the other end.

Finally, "We don't really have much room for you, Ellie. Your father is using your room as a study. We didn't think you'd be coming back so soon."

"I'll sleep on the couch in the den, Mom. Really. It's just for a little while so—"

"It's not that we don't want you. Of course we do. It's just that . . . Don't you think just for once you should stick with something? You quit every job. Even your temp jobs."

I started to lose it. "A few days ago, you told me to quit and come home. Now you tell me to stay?" I was shouting into the tiny phone.

Of course, darling, come home at once and we'll take care of you. Isn't that what a mother should say instead of arguing? Did she really think she was arguing with me for my own good?

"Ellie, don't lose your temper. I know how much moving to New York meant to you. And now—"

"I can't stay here," I said, lowering my voice again to a whisper. "I just can't, Mom. It—it's not good here. I'll explain when I see you. Bye."

I clicked off before she could reply. I sat on the edge of the bed, trembling, my mind spinning.

I was living in a house with a murderer. A crazed, psycho murderer. Chip had sliced off Mrs. Bricker's hand, murdered my cat, and tried to kill Jackson and me by battering us off the road.

I knew I should call the police. But I was so frightened, so totally panicked. I just wanted to escape from this nightmare.

But what about Abby?

I have to tell her about Chip, I decided.

She has to know what she is living with. She and the kids might be in danger, too. I can't just run away without saying a word. I have to warn her.

How will she react? Will she believe me? I folded the flower shop receipt in my hand to offer as proof.

Then I took a deep breath and made my way downstairs. I found Abby on a chaise longue on the deck. She had Heather on her lap and was reading a Dr. Seuss book to her. Brandon crouched on his knees at the other end of the deck, playing with a bunch of action figures.

She glanced up and read my face instantly. "Ellie? What's wrong?"

"Read. Read," Heather insisted, slapping the book.

"I have to talk to you," I said, my heart suddenly pounding. "Right away."

Abby closed the picture book. Heather let out an unhappy cry. Brandon didn't look up from his action figures. "Is everything okay?" Abby asked.

"No," I said.

Her eyes locked on mine.

My chin trembled. My legs suddenly felt rubbery.

Keep it together, Ellie. You have no choice. You have to tell her.

Holding Heather, Abby climbed to her feet. "Wait here," she told me. "Come with me, kids."

Both kids started to whine. They didn't want to move.

"I'm sorry," I whispered.

She pulled Brandon to his feet, then took them both upstairs. A few minutes later, she returned, carrying a bottle of water. Regaining her place on the chaise longue, she tilted the bottle to her mouth, her eyes on me the whole while. "What's up, Ellie?"

I cleared my throat. I had my hands jammed in the pockets of my shorts. "This isn't easy to say."

She motioned for me to pull up a chair. "Are you leaving? Is that what you want to tell me? I don't blame you. It's been so horrible for you here."

"Yes, I have to leave," I said, sliding a deck chair up close to hers. I dropped onto it and gripped the wooden arms, my hands cold and wet. "But there's more, Abby."

She pulled herself up. "More?"

"It's about Chip," I said, my voice breaking. "He's the one—the one who's been torturing me."

I expected her to scream or protest or get angry or call me crazy. But she stared back at me, suddenly very still. A fly landed on her forehead. She made no attempt to brush it away.

"I can prove it," I said. I shoved the receipt at her.

"Those black flowers crawling with cockroaches—he sent them. And Mrs. Bricker's hand . . . I went to the bakery. It was Chip's name on the receipt for the cake box. He—"

Abby let out a long breath.

Was she going to defend him? Was she going to argue?

When she didn't speak, I forced myself to continue. "The black SUV is dented. And I found flakes of red paint on the bumper. It was him. . . . It was Chip who tried to kill Jackson and me. And my cat—"

She clamped her eyes shut. The water bottle fell to the deck and rolled away. "Not again," she whispered. "Oh, no. Not again."

I swallowed hard. My throat felt dry as sand. What was she saying? *Again?*

She leaned forward and grabbed my hand. "He's doing it again," she whispered. "He promised me. He promised me he was taking his medication."

"What do you mean?" I asked. "You mean he's done this before?"

Tears welled in her eyes. "I stuck it out with him last time. He begged me to stay with him. He swore it would never happen again. Of course, he never went this far before. Never like this."

For a long, horrible moment, we just stared at each other. When she wiped away the tears, I could see the fear in her eyes. She jumped to her feet and turned to the house. "The kids," she whispered.

She grabbed my arm again. "Ellie, I know you want to get away from here as fast as you can. But, please. I've got to think of the kids. I've got to make some arrangements, find some place for us to go. Some place where he won't find us."

Did she realize how tightly she was gripping my arm? "I really can't stay," I said. "I don't feel safe. He—he—"

"Just two more days," she pleaded. "Just till I can make a plan, make sure we will be safe from him." A sob escaped her throat. "Please, Ellie. Two days, that's all. I'll protect you from him. I can. I know how to work him. I know how to keep him down. I've—done it before."

"Well . . ." I hesitated. This poor woman. I could see she was totally panicked.

"Just two days," she said. "I'll make some phone calls right away. I'll get the kids away from here. Then I'll call the hospital from the last time this happened and find some help for Chip. Two days. I'll keep him away from you, Ellie. You'll be safe. I promise."

"Okay," I whispered. "Okay. Two days."

"Oh, thank you. Thank you. You're wonderful." She leaned forward and hugged me. Her hot tears rubbed off on my cheek. "You'll be safe. Don't worry. Just act normal, okay? That's the main thing. Just act normal."

A killer in the house.

Just act normal?

39

Saturday night, about nine o'clock, thunder roared over the house; I stood for a while at the kitchen window, watching lightning crackle over the dune. Sheets of rain poured down, battering the windows, driven by a strong, gusting wind off the ocean.

Heather and Brandon were in bed, but I wondered for how long. I sat in the living room, watching a DVD of *Sleepless in Seattle*, waiting for the storm to wake up the kids and start them calling for me.

I turned and saw Abby and Chip in the front entryway. He pulled an umbrella from the front closet, waited for her to arrange her rain poncho over her dress, and then handed it to her.

Abby had kept her word. I'd had no contact with Chip all day. He had spent the afternoon at his tennis club. When he returned home for dinner, I went upstairs with the kids.

Abby made a lot of phone calls during the day. When Chip was away, she didn't hide how tense she was. But as soon as he walked into the house, I saw her force a big smile onto her face and act happy to see him.

Now, I couldn't wait for them to leave for their party.

"Great night for a party on Dune Road," Abby grumbled. "We'll probably all float away."

"After a few drinks, I'll be floating anyway. I won't care about a little rain," Chip said. He'd already had a few drinks. A pregame warm-up, he said. I saw Abby take the car keys.

Chip opened the front door in time to let in a deafening burst of thunder. Abby poked her head into the living room. "We'll be late, Ellie. Hope the storm doesn't keep the kids up all night."

She followed Chip out the door, raising her umbrella. A gust of wind sent the door slamming against the wall. Chip reached in and pulled it shut.

Lightning crackled overhead. The lights dimmed, then flashed back on.

Oh, great, I thought. Just what I need tonight—a power failure.

What I do need is some popcorn, I decided. Or maybe some potato chips.

Thunder roared. I listened for the kids' cries. No. So far, they were okay.

I made myself some microwave popcorn in the kitchen and poured it into a big bowl. Then I settled down in front of the TV to watch my movie.

"Oh." I jumped, startled by a tap on the living-room window.

Just the rain?

No. Another tap—hard and loud. I jumped to my feet. What *is* that?

Another tap. Not the rain.

Tap tap. Like a fist rapping the glass.

I crossed to the window and tried to peer out, but rainwater had smeared the glass. Nothing but darkness out there—until lightning flashed high in the sky, making the ground bright as day for an instant.

In the flash of white light, I saw . . . no one.

No one there.

A knock on the front door made me jump. A single knock, hard. Then two knocks.

Not the rain. Definitely not the rain.

I stepped to the door and called out in a high, shrill voice, "Who's there?"

Silence now, except for the steady drumming of rain.

"Is anyone there?"

I pulled open the door. A wave of cold water greeted me. My sweatshirt and jeans were drenched. The porch light was on. It sent a dim triangle of light over the front stoop.

No one there.

I shut the door and locked it, shivering from the cold rainwater.

I glanced up the stairs, expecting to see Brandon staring down at me. But no. Somehow both kids were managing to sleep through this.

Another tap at the window. The side window this time.

Tap tap. Tap tap tap. A rapid rhythm.

A boom of thunder shook the house.

Then two hard taps on the front window. This time a slapping sound, as if someone was pounding on the window with an open hand.

My heart began to race. My throat felt tight and dry. Someone was out there, running back and forth from the windows to the door. Trying to terrify me? Trying to break in?

A wave of panic washed over my body. I stood frozen

in the middle of the living room, waiting, waiting for the next sound, waiting to see what happened next.

I stared hard at two blue candlesticks on the coffee table, stared at them until they became a blue blur.

If I stare hard enough, I can make everything else go away.

No. Another series of taps on the window. Then a few seconds later, someone pounding on the door.

Breathing hard, I ran from the door to the window, following the frightening sounds.

No one. I couldn't see anyone.

A hard knock on the door. Then three taps on the window by the dining room.

I ran to the window and pulled it open. "Who's there?" I shouted into the roar of the rain. "Is somebody out there? Please answer me! Who—?" My breath caught in my throat. My whole body tingled with fear.

Another hard boom of thunder—and the lights flickered and went out.

"Oh, no." I stood frozen in darkness. I slammed the dining room window shut.

I pressed my back against the wall.

Ellie, don't panic. Stay calm. It's just a storm. You're frightening yourself.

No. Someone was out there. Someone was frantically trying to break in.

And now I stood in total darkness.

Where are the flashlights? I wondered, waiting for my eyes to adjust to the dark. Where do they keep them? Where is the phone? Who can I call for help?

Lightning flickered across the sky. Was that a face outside the window?

Yes. It was. I saw a face out there, pressed against the glass.

Oh, no. A hard pounding on the front door.

The lights flickered back on, orange at first, then back to normal. I stumbled to the front door and pressed my ear against the wood. "Is anyone there? Who's out there?"

The wind howled in reply.

I was shivering so hard, my knees started to fold. I gripped the door. And heard a voice, a soft voice, carried on the wind, *"Elllllie . . . Elllllie . . ."*

I let out a cry. And jumped back from the door. My name? Someone calling my name?

A crackle of lightning, so close, as if right in the living room. And then another long howl of wind, like a cry, like an angry cry.

And again, my name, carried in the wind like an angry, bitter threat. *"Elllllie . . . Elllllie . . ."*

Panting hard, my dinner rising to my chest, I stumbled to the window and squinted out.

No one.

"Elllllllie . . . Elllllllie."

A ghostly cry.

Someone is out there. Someone is torturing me. Someone is breaking in.

I'm calling 911.

Will they get here in time? Will they?

I stumbled into the kitchen, grabbed the phone off the wall.

And let out a scream of horror as the back door crashed open.

A man stepped into the kitchen. A black umbrella hid his face.

Rain ran off the umbrella, splashing at his feet. I could see a dark raincoat over dark slacks. I took a step back, my fist pressed to my mouth, holding back another scream.

He lowered the umbrella slowly, shook it, sending a spray of water over the kitchen floor. Then he raised his face to me.

"Chip!" I gasped. "What are you doing here? Why did you come back?"

40

He stood the umbrella next to the door. He wiped his shoes on the floor mat. He grinned at me, closing the door behind him.

A sick grin. An evil grin.

I stepped back, my body tingling with fear.

Alone in the house with a maniac. All alone.

Abby's frightened words from yesterday rushed back to me: *Not again. He's doing it again!*

I gazed around the kitchen, searching for a weapon—*anything* I could use to protect myself. The knife holder was on the counter next to the sink. Behind him. I'd never get there.

What could I use? What should I do?

Should I run out the front? He would catch me before I got very far.

He shook his head. "Wouldn't you know it? I forgot the wine." He moved toward me, toward a small, white shopping bag on the table beside me containing two bottles of white wine.

"We were already at the party. Abby made me drive all the way back."

"Abby's at the party?" I asked. I pictured her lying

dead on the side of the road. He murdered her so he could come back and murder me.

"Of course," he replied.

I didn't like the way he was moving toward me. I didn't like the grin on his face.

I slid around him, edging to the sink. If I could grab a large knife from the holder, maybe . . .

Chip grabbed up the shopping bag. The shoulders of his raincoat were soaked. He turned back to me, and his grin faded. "Ellie, you look so pale. I'm sorry. I didn't scare you, did I?"

Of course you scared me, you creep.

You *wanted* to scare me.

And now what's on your disgusting, psycho mind?

"I heard noises—" I blurted out. "Someone tapping on the windows and—"

He set down the wine. "Are you okay? You look so frightened."

Oh, no. Please, no.

He walked over to me slowly. His wet shoes squeaked on the floor. He placed his hand on my shoulder. "You sure you're okay?"

His touch made me shudder. He was pretending to be concerned. But his eyes were laughing at me, and his sick grin had returned.

"You heard noises, Ellie? Was it the kids? Did the storm wake them up?"

"No . . . I don't think so."

I could smell the gin on his breath. He squeezed my shoulder. He had me trapped against the counter. The knives . . .

Too far to reach.

"You're shaking," he said softly. "Are you always afraid of thunderstorms?"

"No. I'll be okay. Really."

"Maybe you need a drink."

"You startled me—that's all. I'm all right." I edged closer to the knife holder.

Please take your hand off me.

I glanced at the wood block holder, just a few feet out of my reach at the sink.

When I turned back, I saw that Chip had followed my glance. He was staring over my shoulder, staring at the knife holder.

A chill tightened the back of my neck.

Did he plan to grab the carving knife now? Is that what he had planned for me? To slice off my head the way he sliced poor Lucky?

You twisted bastard.

What if I get to the knives *first*? Are you thinking about that now? Is that what's spinning through your sick mind?

He let go of my arm.

"Uh, Abby must wonder where I am. I don't hear any strange noises now. Do you?"

"No."

The tapping and knocking stopped when you came in the house. Three guesses what that means.

"At least the kids are sleeping through the storm," he said, his eyes still on the knives. He picked up the wine bag. "Go back to your movie, Ellie. Sorry I startled you."

I didn't move. I stood rigid, pressed against the counter as he picked up the umbrella. He gave me a nod and opened the kitchen door. Then he disappeared back into the rain.

My whole body shuddered. I realized I had been holding my breath. Now I sucked in air, letting it out slowly, trying to calm my racing heart.

Out the window, I saw headlights sweep across the backyard as the car rolled away. Was he really gone?

Did he come back here to kill me?

Did my glance at the knife holder push him back?

I took another deep breath. Then I opened the fridge and pulled out a beer. I popped the top, tilted the can to my mouth, and took a long drink.

I could use a few of these.

I carried the beer into the living room and, still shaky, dropped into the armchair.

And heard a loud knock at the front door.

41

I set the beer down on the table. I didn't move from the chair. I sat still, my body tensed, listening.

I heard the patter of rain. The clink of the ice maker in the kitchen fridge.

And then another knock on the front door. Harder, more insistent.

I forced myself out of the chair. Moved on tiptoe to the living-room window, and peered out. I couldn't see the front stoop. But I saw a dark station wagon parked in the drive.

Someone pounded hard on the door. The doorbell rang.

I stepped up to the door. "Who's there?" I had to shout over the steady rush of the rain.

"Ellie, it's me! Open up!"

I pulled open the door. "Teresa! Hi!"

She probably wondered why I threw my arms around her wet rain poncho and hugged her. But, hey—I'd had a long night.

I pulled her into the house. She had three friends with her from her house, two girls and one of the guys I'd met at the club, either Bob or Ronnie, I couldn't remember which.

"We thought maybe you'd come out with us," Teresa said. "We're going to this bar in Hampton Bays. The Drift Inn. It's supposed to be a wild scene."

"I can't," I said. I motioned upstairs. "The kids."

"Hey, I love this movie," one of Teresa's friends said. She dropped down on the couch. "Check it out. It's the best scene. They're at the Empire State Building."

Bob-or-Ronnie and the other woman moved to the TV. Teresa took a sip of my beer, then pulled me aside. "Are you okay? You look kinda weird."

"No, I'm not okay," I whispered. "I tried to call you. I—I have to go. I mean leave. Right away. I already told Abby."

Teresa's eyes widened in surprise. She brushed wet tangles of hair off her face. "Omigod. What happened?"

"It's too long to tell. I—I'm not safe here, Teresa. I'm very frightened. It was Chip. The whole time. I told Abby, and she said, 'Oh, no—not again.' He's a psycho. She admitted it."

"Oh, wow. Oh, Ellie. I'm so sorry. You've got to get the hell out of here. Why are you still here?"

"Abby promised to protect me. She needs time to make arrangements for the kids. I'm going to leave Monday probably."

"But where are you going to stay?" Teresa didn't give me time to answer. "You'll stay at my apartment. May Lin is moving out in September. She's going to live with her boyfriend. So there'll be a room for you."

"But . . . how will I pay the rent?"

"You'll find a job. No problem."

I hugged Teresa again. "You're the best!" I told her. "You're saving my life. Really."

I begged them all to stay for a while. I really needed

company tonight. But they were meeting some guys at the bar in Hampton Bays, so they had to go.

"Listen, Ellie, call me on my cell," Teresa said, lingering at the front door. "And get that look off your face. Everything will work out. You'll be outta here in two days."

Yes, in two days, I thought.

I can keep it together for two days, can't I?

42

Sunday morning, the storm had passed and the sky was sunny and blue, marred only by a few puffy clouds. Gazing out my bedroom window, the whole world appeared glittery and green and fresh, the tree leaves, the shrubs and grass, even the sandy ground sparkling from the rain.

Abby and Chip were having their breakfast on the deck. I grabbed a plain bagel and gulped down a cup of coffee in the kitchen. Then I herded the kids to the beach as early as I could.

No way I wanted to hang around the house and run into Chip.

As I led the kids down the stairs, Abby and Chip were reading the Sunday *Times*, laughing together about something they'd read.

Abby's doing a good job of acting normal, I thought. Better than I could ever do. No way Chip could guess that she's on to him.

From my first day in their house, I thought they had an odd relationship. She treated him like a naughty kid. She was always scolding him about his drinking and his general laziness, lounging around on the deck, never doing anything.

He'd just grin and act as if it were all a joke.

Sometimes it seemed to me that she didn't care enough about Chip to take him seriously. She wasn't very affectionate—at least, not that I could see. He was in the city most of the time, and she never commented that she missed him.

It was like when he was away, she only had *two* kids to deal with, not three. Whenever he left, she went off to the spas and had her massages, and her manicures, and her facials—sort of like a celebration. She was definitely happier.

Of course, I had no way of knowing all that she had gone through with Chip earlier. How she had stuck with him when he had gone psycho before. How she had somehow managed to live a normal life, knowing he could explode again at any time.

Of course, everything I'm saying is probably total bullshit. How can you ever really know anything about a couple? There are always so many secrets between them.

The ocean waves were high and frothy, still wild from the storm last night. They crashed like thunder against the beach. Heather grabbed my hand. "Don't be scared," I said. "We'll find a nice place high up on the beach."

Brandon lingered behind as usual, dragging a slender tree branch, making a long line behind him in the wet sand like a snail's trail. He seemed even more glum than usual. When I asked him a question, he refused to raise his head.

We were approaching the public beach when my cell phone rang. I pulled it from the beach bag and read the caller ID.

Clay?

I clicked it on. "Listen, Clay," I snapped. "We said good-bye, remember? I want you to delete this number from your phone. Do you—?"

"Ellie, I just called to apologize," he said softly. "Give me two seconds. I want to apologize. Then I'll never bother you again. Promise."

"Clay, I'm on the beach with the kids. I can't talk."

"But, Ellie—"

"I can barely hear you. The ocean—"

"I'll make it quick, Ellie. I'm so sorry. That's all I want to say. I've been a total asshole—I admit it. I don't know what happened. I just snapped or something. It's not like me. Really. So before I go back to the city, I just wanted to say I'm sorry. I'd like to come over and we could say good-bye in person. You know. As friends."

"I don't think so, Clay. But thanks for the apology. And have a nice life, okay? I—"

"What did you say? It cut off. Ellie? I can't hear you. Should I come see you? I can't hear."

"Clay? Can you hear me?"

Now it cut the connection completely. I clicked the phone off with a sigh and dropped it back in the bag.

Clay had sounded sincere, and I guess it was decent of him to call. I felt a little guilty for accusing him now that I knew the truth. But why couldn't he just go away and disappear? How many times did we have to say good-bye?

"Courtney! Dee Dee!" Heather saw her friends, the Lewis girls down the beach, walking with pails, collecting shells that had washed up in the storm. She let go of my hand and took off, waving to them, her bare feet kicking up clods of wet sand.

Maggie was struggling with a beach umbrella. I hurried to help her. The powerful waves crashing onto shore sent up a fine spray of cold mist over the beach. The sun felt strong, but the wet air off the ocean carried a chill.

"That was a whale of a storm last night," Maggie greeted me. "I had both girls in my lap, don't you know."

"My two slept right through it," I said. We forced the umbrella into the hard sand and managed to push it open. "Did your power go out?"

Maggie nodded. Her red hair blew behind her like a pennant in the wind. "For nearly an hour. The girls liked walking around with candles. Now they want to do it every night."

I watched Heather walking with the two little girls, bending to find shells for them. And Brandon? Where was Brandon? Sitting by himself high on the beach, in the shade of a low dune, poking his stick into the sand and pulling it out, again and again.

How much fun can that be? I asked myself. Poor guy. What is his problem? If only he would speak to me.

And then I reminded myself that I was leaving tomorrow. I would never find out what troubled Brandon Harper. I would never hear him speak.

I watched him for a moment, shielding my eyes from sand blown up by the wind. And then I saw a young guy jog past Brandon. I saw legs at first, then black bike shorts, a white, sleeveless T-shirt, and then blond hair over pale skin.

I watched the slender young man as he passed behind Brandon, jogging slowly, hands swinging at his sides. And when he turned, and I glimpsed his face through the mistlike sand, it took me a few seconds to recognize him.

Will.

I heard Maggie gasp as I took off running. I think I kicked sand on her. But I didn't turn back to see.

I had my eyes on Will, who jogged past the volleyball net, tilted from the storm, and kept trotting past the parking lot. And I knew this time I would catch him.

This time I would stop him. Turn him around. Make him look at me.

After seven years, make him look at me. And say, "You're alive! Oh, Will, how are you alive and jogging on this beach when I killed you seven years ago?"

I grabbed the wheel, and I killed you. And you have lived only in my mind for seven long years.

But now here you are.

How did you come back? And why are you always running from me? Don't you see me? Don't you remember me?

Here you are, Will.

And I'm catching up to you. This time, you won't outrun me. You won't vanish into thin air.

This time, I'm going to catch you and make you look at me and talk to me. And tell me how you came back.

"Hey!" I came up behind him, running hard, and grabbed his shoulder.

He let out a startled cry. His shoulders flinched. He stumbled to a stop. Then, breathing hard, sweat rolling down his face and hair, he turned to me.

"Hi, it's me," I said in a breathless whisper.

43

He squinted at me, his mouth open, still breathing hard. He wiped a thick strand of blond hair off his forehead.

"Omigod."

My mouth dropped open. I wanted to scream, but I felt too weak.

Too stupid and fucked up.

Too crazy.

It wasn't Will.

He looked a lot like Will. He *could* have been Will.

But he wasn't Will.

"Do I know you?" His eyes—not Will's eyes at all—studied me. I could see him struggle to remember me.

"No, I'm sorry," I choked out. I took a step back, retreating, retreating from my stupid dream. "I saw you jogging. I . . . thought you were someone else."

He shook his head. "You nearly tackled me. I thought maybe you were in trouble or something."

I *am* in trouble, I thought. After seven years, I'm still chasing after someone who is dead.

Dead. Will is dead, Ellie.

You didn't see him after Teresa's party on the beach

with Jackson that night. And you didn't see him walk out of the hardware store in Sag Harbor.

You saw *other* blond-haired boys. Because Will is dead.

Maybe this will convince you once and for all.

"I'm really sorry," I said. "You're not hurt or anything, are you? I shouldn't have grabbed you. I just thought—I thought you were this other guy."

"No problem," he said. But he didn't smile or anything. He still stared at me as if I were crazy.

"Well—have a nice day," I said. So fucking lame.

"Yeah. Have a nice day." He turned and trotted away.

"You're not eating," Jackson said, gazing down at my plate. "Your omelet is getting cold."

"I'm not hungry," I said, pushing the plate away. "My stomach is all knotted up. I feel like a big rubber band—all twisted and ready to snap."

He raised his fork and began eating the home fries off my plate. "Well, I'm pretty hungry," he said. "You know. Tough day at the bike store."

He grinned at me. He was trying to make me laugh, trying to cheer me up. Not an easy job.

We were in a small booth at the Driver's Seat, a popular restaurant-bar in Southampton. It was a warm, clear evening and most people were eating out back on the patio. But I had pulled Jackson into the darkness of the tall wooden booths inside, where we could talk more privately.

I'd called him at the bike store that afternoon and practically begged him to meet me for dinner. I wanted to spend as little time at the Harpers' house as I could.

When he picked me up in the red Passat, I was so glad

to see him, I kissed him and thanked him a dozen times. He got a wry, lopsided grin on his face and said, "Hey, seeing you isn't exactly a hardship, you know."

But his grin faded as I began to tell him why I was leaving the Hamptons, what had been happening to me since I arrived. He kept shaking his head, his eyes on the road, muttering, "I don't believe it," under his breath.

"I don't believe it, either," I said, my voice breaking. "But it's all true. And I can't wait to get away from here. Tomorrow is my last day."

We drove in silence for a few minutes. I could see he was thinking hard. "How are you getting back to the city?" he asked. "Can I give you a lift?"

"Huh? You want to drive me to the city? No, I couldn't—"

"There are some friends there I've been meaning to visit," he said, turning into the parking lot behind the restaurant. "This would be a good excuse."

I'd stared at him. "Do you mean it? That would be great!"

Now, he hungrily finished my home fries and half my omelet. He reached across the table and held my hand. "Sorry you've been living through such a nightmare, Ellie. I wish there was something I could do."

"You already are," I told him. "You're taking me away from here."

The waitress brought our coffee, and she set down a slice of cheesecake for Jackson. "We can still see each other in the city, right?" he asked. "I mean, I got my orientation materials in the mail from Cardozo today. You know. It's in the Village. I'll be in the city full-time, so—"

I squeezed his hand. "I'm really happy about that," I whispered.

He drove me back to the Harpers'. It was only ten o'clock when we pulled up the driveway. Through the front window, I could see Chip pacing back and forth, alone in the living room.

"I—I don't want to go in yet," I said.

We climbed out of the car. I pulled Jackson up the driveway and around the side of the house. Did Chip see us? I glanced into the window as we passed. He was still pacing, a drink in one hand.

I tugged Jackson into the deep shadow of the house, and we made our way across the backyard, up the dune that led to the guest house, hidden in a pool of darkness behind the line of pine trees, and to the ocean.

Clouds covered the moon. No stars in the sky. The air felt heavy and wet. We pulled off our sneakers and walked barefoot along the shore, hand in hand, leaning against one another as frothy, cold water washed over our feet.

I stopped and leaned against Jackson to pull away a clump of seaweed that had tangled around my ankle. And as I stood up, he pulled me close and kissed me. I didn't pull away. He tightened his arms around me. The kiss didn't end—I wouldn't let it end. I opened my mouth to him, and we pressed against each other and kissed and kissed.

And I found myself thinking, This is so romantic.

And that's all it was. It wasn't about anything else. It wasn't about him trying to prove something to me or me trying to find something in him.

It was just romantic.

And when I finally ended the kiss, so breathless, so wonderfully fluttery and breathless, and I whispered in his ear, "Let's make love—right here on the beach," it was just romantic, not anything else.

"Yes," he whispered, and kissed me again. And, still kissing, we were on our knees on the cool, damp sand. He pulled me tight and pressed me against him. I could barely breathe.

I wanted him. I wanted him so badly. I lowered my hands to his waist.

And felt a tap on my shoulder.

And then another. And then a cold, wet tap on my forehead.

"Rain," I whispered, gazing up.

Without warning, it started to pour. Large raindrops pattered the sand.

Jackson laughed. "Talk about poor timing." He pulled me up, and holding hands, we started to run.

Gusts of wind slapped the rain at our backs as we hurried up the dune. We were both drenched by the time we reached the top.

I pulled Jackson to the guest house door. "It's dry in there," I shouted over the roar of rain.

He squinted at me. "You sure you want to go in there?"

I didn't even think about it. I wanted to make love to him so badly. I grabbed the knob, twisted it, and pulled open the door. I put aside the curse and Mrs. Bricker's ghosts and her stupid warnings, and I pulled Jackson into the guest house.

Holding on to him, I glanced around, startled, disoriented because I had never been inside. And now here I was, clinging to Jackson, kissing his cheek, kissing his neck, his skin so salty from the ocean winds, gazing over his shoulder around the front room in the ghostly gray light, everything black and gray as if we'd stepped into an old movie.

I glimpsed a deer's head mounted on the wall. A low stack of firewood in front of the narrow fireplace. And yes, a long harpoon—*the* harpoon?—leaning against the mantel.

I didn't care about that now. I cared only that I had hold of Jackson, and we were so close, so close, our bodies pressed together, and we were kissing . . . kissing . . . Staggering over the floor together, bumping an armchair, then a couch.

And in the back room, a bed. An old quilt tossed over it, and even two or three pillows against the headboard. And I pulled Jackson's T-shirt over his head, still kissing him, kissing his chest now, wanting him so badly.

My skirt dropped to the floor, and he was tugging off my T-shirt. Kissing my shoulder, my breasts, and I felt I couldn't breathe. And then, still holding each other, we were on the bed, and I lowered my lips down his body and took him into my mouth, and he let out a soft cry of surprise, and a few moments later, we were making love, rocking up and down so gently on the old, abandoned bed, so gently, but the ancient springs creaked anyway, creaked with each loving move.

This is the first time *I* wanted it, I thought.

The first time it wasn't because the guy wanted it, the guy needed it.

The first time . . . the first time . . .

I pressed my mouth against his neck as he moved above me. He tasted so salty and sweet.

"Yes . . . oh, please . . ." The first time . . .

I raised myself to him, raised myself.

I froze when I heard the cough. Muffled. Across the room.

"Oh, my god! Jackson—someone's in here!"

44

Jackson slid off me. Our bodies were hot and bathed with sweat, stuck to each other.

I turned and squinted through the hazy light. "Who's there?"

Footsteps. I heard running footsteps. Heard the front door slam.

"Hey—!"

Jackson leaped to his feet and ran naked to the front. I saw him push the front door open. I sat up, pulling the quilt around me.

"Who is it? Can you see?"

Jackson returned to the room, shaking his head. "I didn't see anyone. I heard someone running. But I couldn't see him."

He dropped beside me on the bed and slid his arm around me. He pressed his forehead against mine. "Are you okay?"

I kissed him. Then I whispered, "Let's get out of here. This place gives me the creeps."

I lingered with Jackson behind the house until I saw all the lights go off. Then I guessed Chip had gone to bed, and it was safe to go inside.

"See you tomorrow night," I whispered, and then he was gone. And without him, I suddenly felt chilled. As if all the warmth had been taken and I had been dropped back into this cold, frightening place. I hurried inside through the kitchen door and then tiptoed up to my room.

My last night in this room, I thought. My last day in this house.

I could still feel Jackson's salty, warm skin against mine. I could still taste him on my lips.

I clicked on the light.

And saw Brandon sitting on my bed.

I let out a startled cry. "Brandon? It's so late," I said, louder than I'd intended.

He raised his dark eyes to me slowly. Like two black holes, I thought, leading where? To the mysteries of the universe? What did he see with those vacant eyes? What had those eyes seen that made him suddenly stop speaking?

He wasn't dressed for bed. He wore a yellow Poké-mon T-shirt over baggy gray shorts.

"Brandon? What are you doing in here? Why aren't you in your pajamas?"

Hunched on the edge of the bed, he continued to stare at me. The dark eyes glowed. He didn't blink.

I started across the room, but stopped halfway to the bed. "Let's get you tucked in, okay? It's very late."

"I saw you," he said.

Yes, he spoke. Brandon spoke, for the first time since I'd arrived.

The words were accusing, his voice raw and raspy, not a little boy's tiny, high voice, but an angry, throaty voice, coming from deep inside his chest.

"*I saw you.*"

"Brandon! You—you're talking!" I cried. "Oh, Jesus. Brandon, I don't believe it!"

His expression didn't change as he climbed to his feet, stood so erect, his eyes still accusing and cold.

"*Don't call me Brandon,*" he rasped. "*My name is Jeremiah.*"

45

Jeremiah?

Jeremiah Halley?

How could Brandon know that name?

Did he hear it from Mrs. Bricker? Is that how he knew it? And was he using it now to frighten me?

I dropped down beside him on my bed. I started to put a hand on his shoulder. But his eyes were so cold, his stare so ugly, so *inhuman*, that I drew back.

"Brandon, talk to me," I said, keeping my voice low and firm. "Who is Jeremiah? Where did you hear that name?"

He didn't answer. He shut his eyes, and I felt as if a chill had been removed from the room. When he opened them, his gaze was softer. The color slowly returned to his cheeks.

"Brandon? Why did you say you were Jeremiah?" I demanded, leaning over him. "Please, keep talking, honey. Don't stop. Come on. Please explain. Where did you see me? In the guest house? Were you in the guest house just now? Brandon, please talk!"

But he had sunk back into silence. I could see from his blank expression that he wouldn't speak again.

He yawned. He looked around the room as if surprised to be here.

"Brandon—?" I tried one more time. "Honey, can you speak again? Do you want to tell me something?"

He shook his head. His whole body slumped. He suddenly looked like a tired little boy, helpless, confused.

I picked him up in my arms and carried him to bed.

I hurried downstairs the next morning to tell Abby that Brandon had spoken. I ran through the kitchen to the deck. No one around.

Back in the kitchen, I found a handwritten note from Abby on the breakfast table:

E—Be back soon. Drove Chip to the Jitney. He'll be in the city all day. Please take kids to beach. —A

Wow, a break for me, I thought. No Chip today.

I threw the note in the trash. Then I rounded up the kids for breakfast.

I stared across the table at Brandon. Did he remember that he spoke the night before? Would he speak again?

He spooned his Cheerios with his head down and acted as if I wasn't sitting there.

Heather, meanwhile, was in a playful mood. She kept sneaking up behind me, tickling my sides really hard, and crying, "Mommy's bones! Mommy's bones!"

"Heather, sweetheart—please—give me a break," I groaned. She was only playing her silly game, but I wasn't in the mood. I'd been awake most of the night, thinking about Jackson, thinking about Brandon— unable to turn my mind off. I was exhausted, not at all ready to start the day.

My last day.

After breakfast, I dressed the kids for the beach, packed up all the equipment, and we started our trek to the beach. Heather was still in a good mood, having a great old time riding my shoulders, pulling my ponytail, kicking me with her sandals as we walked, and giggling her head off.

Brandon appeared as glum as ever. He held my hand and kept his eyes straight ahead. But as we started past the guest house, he grabbed the bag of beach toys I had slung over my back and began to tug it ferociously.

"Brandon—stop! It's wrapped around my neck! You're going to pull me over!" I cried.

I lowered Heather to the ground. I turned to deal with Brandon. But he managed to pull the bag open. He grabbed a plastic shovel and took off, running to a sandy spot behind the guest house.

He dropped to his knees beside a clump of weeds and began digging. The sand flew. He didn't raise his eyes. He dug rapidly, intently, pushing the shovel into the sandy ground with all his strength, then heaving the sand to the side.

"Unh . . . unh . . . unh . . ." He grunted with each hard plunge of the shovel.

At first, I tried to stop him. What on earth did he think he was doing? But when I saw how intent he was, how driven, I backed off and watched, hands pressed against my face.

Brandon jumped when he hit something hard.

And then he furiously began to scrape the sand away, groaning, grunting as he worked. And in a short time, something surfaced. Bones! Bones buried in such a shallow grave—a rib cage, gray-yellow bones poked up from the sand, glowing in the bright sunlight like something unreal, like something in a bad dream.

"Mommy's bones! Mommy's bones!" Heather chanted behind me.

Did she see them? Or was she just playing her game?

I didn't want her to see them. I grabbed Brandon's hand and pulled him up, pulled him away from the gruesome sight. And I swept Heather up in my arms and began to run.

Down the beach, I found Maggie with her two little girls. I breathlessly begged her to watch Brandon and Heather for me for just a while.

"No problem, dear," Maggie replied. "I brought extra sandwiches just in case you came."

I ran to the house, avoiding the back of the guest house, turning my eyes away from the yellow bones curling up from the sand.

How did Brandon know they were there?

Why did he suddenly need to dig them up?

"Abby? Abby?" I burst into the kitchen and raced to the front of the house, shouting her name.

She wasn't home. She was still out making arrangements for her escape.

Now what? Now what? My mind spun.

I picked up a phone. I called the town police. "I—I found a body. You'd better come quick."

Less than ten minutes later, two squad cars and an EMS ambulance pulled up the driveway.

Too late for the ambulance, I thought. Way too late.

How long had the body been buried there? Did it have something to do with Mrs. Bricker's ghost story?

How did Brandon know?

Three dark-uniformed officers and two EMS workers

in green scrubs hurried up the front stoop. I led them around the house to the back, then showed them the spot behind the guest house.

"The little boy I take care of—he dug them up," I said. "I don't know how he knew." My words caught in my throat.

I knew this had to be the scene of a horrible murder. Maybe Brandon had witnessed it. Maybe that's why he's been silent. Maybe I would soon learn Brandon's secret.

The officers squatted down around the yellowed rib cage. Sweat stained the back of their dark uniform shirts. They muttered to each other. I couldn't hear what they were saying.

One of them picked up Brandon's plastic shovel. He began to dig deeper, scraping sand away from the skeleton as he dug.

I suddenly felt sick. I turned away, pressing my hand to my mouth. I held my breath, trying to force down my nausea.

After a few minutes, I felt a hand on my shoulder. "Miss?"

I turned to the grim-faced officer. A curl of reddish brown hair was matted to his sweat-soaked forehead. His eyes were red-rimmed, bloodshot.

"Miss, the skeleton you found," he said softly. "I have a surprise for you."

46

A surprise?" I blinked at him, the sun suddenly so bright and blinding.

The other men had climbed to their feet. They formed a casual line behind the officer.

He nodded. "Those bones? They're not human. They're dog bones."

I swallowed. "Excuse me?"

"It's a dog skeleton, miss. Someone buried a dog back here. Pretty big one. A Lab or a shepherd, something like that."

"But—" I squinted at him. The sun burned my eyes.

"You might want to cover it up. Don't want to disturb the kids," he said. He motioned with his hand, and the others began to follow him to the house.

"Sorry you were upset," one of the EMS guys said. "Finding a skeleton must have been kinda scary."

"Yeah. Kinda," I replied.

At dinnertime, Abby still hadn't returned. I kept glancing to the driveway every minute, hoping to see her car pull up.

For our last meal together, I made the kids' favorite—macaroni and cheese out of a box. Did they know I was leaving? I had no idea if Abby had told them, so I didn't say a word about it.

Jackson had called from his car. He was on his way. I was nearly packed. I just needed Abby to return so I could make my getaway.

After dinner, I stuck Heather and Brandon in front of the TV, turned on Nickelodeon for them, and then went to my room to finish packing.

As the sun lowered, a heavy fog floated off the ocean, blanketing the backyard. Gazing out the bedroom window at the waves of fog floating past the house, I suddenly felt as if I were on an airplane, staring out the window, seeing nothing but thick, gray clouds.

I could barely see the guest house at the top of the dune. The fog carried a damp chill into the room. And I started to shut the window.

But I stopped when I saw a figure out on the dune, moving slowly through the fog, almost as if swimming through it. Squinting hard, I struggled to make out who was out there.

Jackson?

Why didn't he come to the front? What on earth was he doing back by the guest house?

"Hey!" I called down to him. I waved both arms.

But he continued his slow walk down the gray dune.

And as he came closer, I saw a dark figure running toward him from the house. A man. In a dark leather jacket. I could see the jacket clearly. Was it the jacket Chip had been showing off to me?

Yes. It had to be. Chip in his leather jacket. Running with his right arm extended.

I gripped the windowsill with both hands and

watched Chip come running at Jackson, as if in a dream, as if in a cloudy nightmare. Chip shot toward Jackson, arm outstretched. And I saw a gleam of soft light from Chip's hand.

A low moan escaped my throat as I saw the gleam of the knife and Chip running, running so fast, and he didn't stop, and the arm stretched out straight, and Jackson fell back, tilted back as the knife cut into his chest.

He toppled backward and sat on the ground. His hands flew up as he tried to protect himself. They flew up and fluttered above his head like two white birds lost in the fog.

Leaning out of the window, I let out a scream. *"Stop! Stop it!"*

But I saw Chip shove the knife in again. Again.

I pushed myself away from the window and took off. I had to get there in time—to stop Chip, to save Jackson. I flew down the stairs two at a time, lurched outside. I burst out onto the deck, startled by the chill of the night air. I stumbled down the steps, fighting off my dizziness, my horror, and began to run through the swirls of fog at my ankles.

"I'm coming, Jackson. I'm coming. Stay alive. Please stay alive!" I screamed as I pulled myself up the wet, grassy dune.

No sign of Chip. He had vanished into the fog.

My side ached. My chest felt ready to burst. Slipping on the soft, wet ground, I forced myself up the dune, to the dark line of trees in front of the guest house.

I dropped down beside Jackson. Sprawled on his back, arms at his sides. So still and lifeless. Streams of blood soaking his shirt, his khaki shorts. So much blood.

I dropped down beside him, gasping for breath. Leaned over him.

And I uttered a hoarse cry of shock. "Oh, my god!"

It wasn't Jackson.

47

Clay?"

His name caught in my throat. I couldn't breathe. Couldn't move.

"Clay?"

With his eyes open so wide, so glassy, he really did look like a teddy bear. A teddy bear that had been cut and ripped open.

I touched his face. I don't know why. I couldn't think. It was all I could do to keep from shrieking. How could I let all the horror out?

"Clay?"

He didn't go away. He had come back to say good-bye in person.

"Good-bye, Clay." His cheek was still warm. Trembling, I climbed to my feet. Blood soaked the ground all around him. A swarm of flies buzzed around the blood.

Why would Chip kill Clay? Chip didn't even know Clay.

He was out of control. And where was he hiding? Was he watching me now?

Trembling, I turned to the house. The police. I had to call them for the second time today.

Only this time, I wouldn't show them animal bones.

This time I had a human corpse to show them, a human who had been stabbed again and again by a sick, twisted bastard.

Slipping on the wet sand, I took two steps toward the house. I stopped at the sound of a voice—a man's voice behind me, calling my name.

Startled, I cried out and turned back to the guest house.

An orange light flickered in the window. Firelight. Someone had a fire going in the little house. Why hadn't I noticed it before?

Fog settled around me. Again I felt as if I were floating, floating in a dreamworld.

Someone called my name. A soft whisper carried on the fog.

"Who's there? Chip? Is that you?"

My muscles tensed. I prepared to run.

Yes. Of course it was Chip. Waiting at the side of the guest house with his knife. Waiting to stab me, too. Waiting to cut me and cut me and cut me.

Isn't that what he's wanted all along? Isn't that why he's been torturing me?

Abby's words ran through my mind: *He promised me he'd take his medication.*

Far down the beach, the low drone of a foghorn cut through the air. The sound woke up seagulls all around and sent them flapping and squawking from the trees.

And then the voice again. More insistent. "Ellie? Come here."

The guest house door swung open. Flickering orange light washed over the gray, sandy ground. Someone stepped into the pool of light.

I raised my eyes and stared into the face of a ghost.

48

I recognized Will from the way he stood leaning against the door—one leg crossed casually over the other, his shoulders stooped. The orange light from the fire inside formed a ring around him, like an aura, but his face was hidden in shadow.

Of *course* I recognized him immediately. I'd been seeing him, chasing after him, for seven years.

Staring at him now, it was as if the fog had lifted, and I felt only the tiniest tingle of surprise, not the shock I'd imagined I'd feel at seeing a dream come true—and not the horror of seeing a dead person come to life.

"It's you," I said, keeping my distance, staring at the dark figure inside the halo of orange light. "You're alive."

"No thanks to you," he said coldly, his voice deeper than I remembered.

He moved quickly. He eased forward, three or four quick steps, then grabbed my hand, and pulled me roughly into the guest house.

The fire crackled in the wide fireplace. A beer can rested on the mantel. The glass eyes in the deer head glowed in the light. Glancing to the back, I saw that the bed was unmade. Clothes had been tossed on the floor.

Will let go of me, shoving my hand away. He turned his face to the fire, blond hair long and unbrushed. He wore a faded denim shirt, torn at the elbows, over straight-legged, black pants.

"Somehow I knew," I said. "I had the strongest feeling that you didn't die . . . back then."

Silence for a long moment. And then he turned to me slowly. "I wish I did die," he whispered. "Here. I'll show you why, Ellie. Take a look at what you did to me."

He turned to me, grabbed my hand again, and tugged me close. I let out a whispered cry as his face came into the light.

His face was red and raw and scarred. Faded red stitch marks crossed both cheeks. A deep purple scar dug into his chin. And his nose . . . His nostrils didn't match—one gaping open, the other half-closed. I saw stitch marks down the front of both ears. His left eye kept blinking. He had no eyebrows.

He held me close, forcing me to study his face—a monster's face.

I gasped and took a step back. "I—I don't understand," I said, lowering my eyes. "Why are you here? Why did they tell me you were dead?"

He crossed the room and closed the guest house door. Then he turned, remaining in the shadows.

"Do you really want to know? Do you really care? Well . . . after the crash, my parents rushed me away. To a hospital in San Diego. My uncle is a surgeon there. He specializes in plastic surgery, Ellie. And I needed a lot of that, *years* of that. Surgery and rehab therapy."

He took a deep breath and continued, the words pouring out as if he couldn't hold them back. "My parents blamed you, and so did I. They never wanted us to see each other again. So my mother told your mother that I died. I wanted her to. I wanted you to feel bad, as bad as I did. Because you ruined my life. I've had seven lost years, Ellie. Seven. And in all that time . . . In all that time, Abby is the only one to care about me."

I gasped. "Abby? You and Abby?"

He nodded. "She's why I'm here."

I suddenly felt weak. I pressed my back against the wall. Too many shocks to take in all at once. Will alive? Abby and Will?

"What about Chip?" I asked.

He snickered. "He's a tool. I've been here in the guest house for months, and he's totally clueless. Abby just stays with him because he's rich, and she and I really need the money she gets from him. She's going to leave him. She doesn't love him. Never has."

I realized I was shivering. I moved closer to the fire, my mind spinning. Seven years I'd dreamed of this moment. But it wasn't anything like what I'd imagined.

"I . . . never stopped thinking of you, Will," I blurted out, my voice breaking. "I never stopped—"

"*Shut up!*" he screamed, slamming his fist against the door. "Shut the fuck up, Ellie. I don't want to hear it. I couldn't believe it when I saw you walking into their house. Seeing you was like a nightmare, my worst nightmare."

"You—hate me that much?"

He nodded. The fire danced, and the red scars and stitches on his face appeared to glow, like a monstrous Halloween mask. "I just never wanted to see you again, Ellie. I thought I was safe here. I thought you were probably still in Madison."

My throat closed up. A wave of panic swept over me

as I suddenly realized I was alone here, alone with the person who hated me most in the world.

Clay had been murdered. Clay lay a few yards outside the door. And now here I was, alone.

"You hate me so much, you've been torturing me since I arrived," I whispered.

His eyes widened. "Huh? What the hell are you talking about?" The scarred mask twisted into a scowl. "Torture you? You're not worth my time. I just want to forget about you."

"Then why did you murder my cat?" I cried. "Why did you take Chip's car and try to smash us off the road? Why did you cut off that old woman's hand and—and—"

I stopped as the guest house door swung open.

I heard laughter. Then a soft voice. "Will doesn't know anything about that, Ellie. You'll have to blame *me* for your troubles."

Her face cold and hard even in the warm firelight, Abby stepped into the room.

49

Abby moved past Will and strode to the center of the room, her hands balled into tight fists. She wore Chip's brown leather jacket over jeans. Her face glistened with sweat.

"How are you two lovebirds getting along?" she asked. "Isn't this a sweet reunion? I may puke."

"You!" I cried. "Abby, *you* killed Clay?"

Behind her, Will gasped. "What? What did you say?"

Abby nodded. "Is that who that was? I saw him prowling around back here. I couldn't let him ruin our happy reunion, could I?"

"Whoa, wait, Abby." Will crossed the room and grabbed her arm. "What did you just say? You *killed* someone?"

"Shut up, Will," she snapped. She pushed him away and stormed up to me. "No one is going to ruin this for me."

I made a move to the door. But she grabbed me by both shoulders and dragged me in front of the fire. "Why don't you remember me, Ellie?"

My mouth dropped open. The flames danced high, leaped out at me. "Remember you?"

"You stood in that shop in town, and looked into my

face, and you didn't remember me," Abby said through gritted teeth, squeezing my shoulders. "How could you not remember me? How?"

"I—"

Her eyes grew wide with anger, with fury. Her jaw clenched tightly. "Try to remember. Try real hard, Ellie. I want you to remember!"

I stared at her. I didn't say a word. Did I know her? Did I? I had no memory.

"I was in the class ahead of you. *Now* do you remember? Will and I went together for three years. And then you stole him away from me. How could you forget that, Ellie? How could you forget me?"

She shook me by the shoulders, eyes blazing. "Was it because I was nothing to you? Was it because I was invisible? I was a bug you could crush under your shoes? Will was the only one in the world I cared about. The only one, Ellie. I loved him so much. And you stole him from me *without even looking at me. Without even remembering me!*"

"Abby, please—!" I cried. "You're *hurting* me!" Her hands dug into my shoulders.

She was right. I didn't remember her. I knew Will had been with somebody. But I didn't remember who.

"Look what you did to him," Abby said, ignoring my cry. "Look at him. Look at his face, Ellie. You *ruined* him. You *ruined* him!"

A sob escaped her throat, but she didn't loosen her grip. "So now do you understand? When I saw you in that shop, I knew it was for a reason. I knew you were sent to me so I could finally pay you back."

"You—you hired me so you could torture me? You

did all those things to me?" I said, still unable to believe it all.

"What's going on here?" Will demanded. "Abby, what the hell are you talking about? What did you do to her?"

She ignored him, keeping her eyes on me. "I planned to kill you the night of the storm. I sneaked back from the party in a friend's car. I wanted to terrify you first, then murder you. But your damned friends showed up and ruined it."

"Abby, listen. I'm so sorry," I whispered.

She grabbed my head and twisted it. "Don't look away from Will, Ellie. Keep looking at him, at the face you made. Don't look away—because this is what *your* face is going to look like now. *You're going to look just like him!*"

"Abby—let go of her," Will shouted. He lurched toward her. "I mean it. You're not doing anything to her. I won't let you."

Abby gave me a hard shove that sent me stumbling into the wall. She picked up the wrought-iron fireplace shovel and, with a furious groan, swung it at Will's head. It made a sick, cracking sound as it hit the left side of his face.

Will uttered a startled grunt. His eyes rolled up in his head, he dropped to his knees, and then he collapsed in a heap on the floor.

Stunned, I started to scramble away. But Abby grabbed me again, grabbed me with such fury and slammed my head hard against the stone fireplace.

I let out a scream, a high, shrill wail, as she shoved me, shoved me down, shoved my head into the flames.

50

I shut my eyes against the bright orange glare. Hot flames licked at my face. I smelled my hair starting to singe and felt the flames on my cheeks, on my forehead, like knife stabs . . . like hot, stabbing knife blades.

I can't breathe.

I twisted my head, struggled to duck away, to wrench out of her grip. But Abby was stronger than me. She held firm, pushing me down, holding my head on the fire.

Flames wrapped around my face, swept over me, hot pain, stabbing like a hundred knife blades at once.

I opened my mouth to scream and choked on the smoke. I couldn't see. Couldn't breathe. My lungs ached. My chest felt ready to explode.

With a final burst of energy, I dropped my head hard, swung my body around, and drove my elbow into Abby's stomach.

She groaned. Backed up a step. Loosened her grip.

Dizzy from the burning pain, I edged my head out of the flames—and saw Brandon enter the room.

Brandon moved quickly. He appeared to float across the floor, to the harpoon leaning against the back wall. How did he know it was there?

As I wrestled with Abby, my head roaring as if the flames were inside me, I saw Brandon lift the harpoon in one hand above his head. He lifted it high and prepared to toss it.

How can a little boy raise such a heavy harpoon?

How is it possible?

And then, I realized *it wasn't Brandon*!

I was staring at another boy, a red-haired boy in knee breeches. A red-haired boy with glowing green eyes sunk deep in his pale, white face.

He stared at me with those eyes. He stared for a long, terrifying moment.

"Nanny die!" he called in a hoarse, raspy voice. *"Nanny, die now!"*

Oh, my God. Mrs. Bricker's story is going to come true.

It's about to happen again.

I'm the nanny.

Jeremiah is going to kill the nanny.

I gave Abby a hard shove with my shoulder, sending her sliding against the wall. But I couldn't move away in time.

I screamed as he heaved the harpoon at me.

I shut my eyes and waited for the pain to course through my body. Waited . . . waited for the crushing pain . . .

"Aaaaiiiiiiii!"

Behind me—a howl, a high, shrill animal howl.

My eyes shot open. I turned to see Abby crumple to the floor, the harpoon stuck through the brown leather jacket, through her shoulder, clear through her body, the rusted tip poking out of her back.

Abby twisted onto her side, her head thrown back, screaming in agony, thrashing her legs, slapping the floor with her free hand. Blood bubbled from under the jacket, puddling beside her as she thrashed and shrieked.

Will raised his head from the floor. "Huh?" he groaned. "Huh?" Blinking his eyes, opening and closing his mouth.

Dazed, my face still burning, the hot flames dancing in my eyes, I turned and saw Jackson at the doorway, his mouth open in shock. "What the hell is going on?" he cried. "I saw a body out there. And—and—"

"Jackson. Call 911," I said.

"Hunnnh," Will groaned. His arms and legs twitched. He couldn't seem to form words. "Hunnnh. Hunnnnh."

Jackson had his cell to his ear, calling for the police and an ambulance. I turned to the boy.

Brandon?

Brandon sat on a chair against the wall, shaking his head.

The red-haired boy had vanished.

Was it Jeremiah Halley? Did he try for his revenge—and fail again? Did he try to murder me, the nanny, and hit Abby instead? Did that mean the curse of the guest house would continue for another generation?

I ran to Brandon and bent to wrap my arms around him. "Are you okay? Let's get you out of here."

"Where am I?" he asked, blinking at the fire. "Was I asleep? Is Daddy here? Where's my daddy?"

He's talking, I realized. In a little boy's voice, a voice I hadn't heard before.

I pulled him from the chair and lifted him onto my shoulder. He felt so light and frail. His little body was trembling.

"Where's my daddy? Where is he?"

"He'll be home soon," I said softly. "Hear those

sirens? Help is on the way. Help for your mommy. Your mommy is hurt, see? But she's going to be okay."

Abby uttered a loud groan.

Brandon peered over my shoulder at her. "No," he said in a tiny, high voice. "That's not Mommy. That's Abby. That's my nanny."

51

I still held Brandon in my arms when Chip arrived. He came trotting up the dune, wearing city clothes, jacket and tie, his face twisted in confusion as he saw the grim activity.

Two EMS workers were sliding Clay into a long, black body bag. Another white-uniformed crew had somehow managed to saw away most of the harpoon handle, leaving only the tip embedded in Abby's shoulder. They had piled her onto a wheeled stretcher, attached a blood drip, and were starting to roll her down the dune.

At the guest house door, two police officers were standing over Will. He had managed to sit up, but kept groaning, "Hunnnh . . . hunnnh . . ." over and over, his mouth hanging open, blinking and shaking his head.

"What the hell?" Chip shouted, running toward us. "What the hell happened here?" When he realized it was Abby on the stretcher, he began running faster. "Abby? Are you okay? Tell me. Are you okay?"

"Tip-top," she muttered, eyes closed.

"Are you Chip Harper?" A young, blond-haired police officer moved to block Chip's path. "I'm Lieutenant

Harris. We need to talk to you, sir. There's been a lot of trouble here, including a fatality."

Chip grabbed Abby's hand. But when he saw the stub of the harpoon through her shoulder, he jerked back. "Oh, shit. Oh, shit. What is *that*?"

He turned to the EMS workers. "Is she going to be okay? How did this happen? Who did this?"

"I'm sorry, Chip," Abby whispered. "You're a nice guy. You didn't deserve—" Her head slumped to one side.

The EMS worker signaled to his partner. "Let's roll." They started to push the stretcher cart down the hill. "She's lost a lot of blood," he called back to Chip. "We've got to get her to the hospital fast."

Chip uttered a cry of frustration. "But what the hell is going on?" He glanced up at Will at the guest house door, still on the ground, still shaking his head. "Who is he? Who the hell are these people?"

And then Chip noticed me for the first time, saw that I was holding Brandon. He hurried over and reached for Brandon. But the boy pulled away and clung tighter to me.

"Ellie, can you tell me what's happening here?" Chip demanded.

Before I could answer, Brandon chimed in. "She's not mommy, Daddy. Tell them. She's Abby, right? She's not mommy."

Chip raised a finger to his lips. "Brandon, not now," he said softly. And then he realized: "Oh, my God— you're talking! Brandon, you're talking again. That's so wonderful! But let's not talk about Mommy, okay?"

He reached for his son again, but Brandon slid to the ground and started to run clumsily toward the guest house. "Mommy!" he cried. "Mommy!"

"Brandon, where are you going?" Chip cried. He took off after the boy. "Brandon, what's wrong, baby? Why are you running away from me?"

Brandon darted around to the back of the guest house. He dropped down on the ground where he had dug earlier. The two officers abandoned Will and followed Chip to the spot where Brandon had started to dig again, digging furiously with both hands.

"Brandon? Why are you doing this?" Chip asked. "I know you're upset. Let me pick you up. Let me hold you." Chip turned to me. "We have to do something. The poor kid must be in shock."

"Mommy!" Brandon cried, leaning over the hole, tossing up the sand. "Mommy."

I knelt beside him. "No, Brandon. Stop," I said. "It's only a dog skeleton, remember? It's just a dog."

"Brandon, please. Come to me," Chip said softly. "You'll be okay. I promise, sweetie." He moved to grab Brandon, but an officer held him back.

"Remember? It's just a dog?" I repeated.

Brandon looked up from the hole in the sand. "Over . . . under," he said. "Over . . . under . . . Over . . . under."

"Brandon? That's from *Sesame Street* on TV," I said. "Why are you saying that now?"

"Under," he said, and continued pawing up the sand. "Under . . . under . . ."

Chip grabbed Brandon and hoisted him up and away. "It's okay. It's okay," he whispered. "There's nothing there. It's okay."

"Under . . . under . . ."

"Mr. Harper," Lieutenant Harris said firmly. "Put the

boy down. And please step away from the hole. I want to see what's beneath these dog bones."

Chip stepped back. But he held on to Brandon, pressing him against his chest.

Flashlights swept over the hole. Two of the officers found shovels in the garage. As the fog thickened around us, they began to dig.

Now there was silence, except for the wash of waves on the ocean shore over the dune and the steady scrape of the two shovels.

Shovels clinked when they found the dog skeleton we had unearthed earlier. Groaning, the two men lifted it out and set it aside. Then they returned to their digging.

"Under . . . under . . . ," Brandon repeated softly, still in Chip's arms.

And a few minutes later, I gasped as the shovels clinked again. Another skeleton poked up from the hole. No. Not a skeleton. A woman. A decomposing woman.

The head came into view first in the white circles of light from the flashlights. A woman's head, chunks of skin clinging to her skull, eyes sunk deep into their sockets, fat worms crawling through her dirt-caked hair.

"Oh, my God. It's Jenny," Chip said, beside me, his voice breaking. "My wife. Jenny. Jenny. How—how is this possible?"

Lieutenant Harris had been watching from the other side of the sand hole. Now he moved quickly beside Chip and grabbed his arm. "We need to talk, sir."

Chip didn't respond. He lowered Brandon to the ground, turned, and stared wide-eyed as more of the flesh-eaten body came into view. "Abby told me . . . Abby said Jenny packed her bags and left."

"When was this, Mr. Harper?" the lieutenant asked.

Chip's eyes were glazed, rolling in his head. His voice came out in a harsh whisper. "When was it? When was it? Last March. Just before I hired Mrs. Bricker."

"Mr. Harper, I think we need to get you away from here," Harris said, tugging gently at Chip's arm.

But Chip pulled free. He took a few stumbling steps toward the corpse. He went down on his knees in the sand. "Jenny caught me. She caught Abby and me together," he said, talking to himself now. "She was too angry and hurt to face me. So Jenny packed up and left. That's what Abby told me. That's what Abby said, and I believed her. I believed her. Why? Why—?" Sobbing, he choked on his words.

He reached out an arm and smoothed his hand over the corpse's worm-infested hair. Tears ran down his cheeks. "I never saw Jenny again. I thought she went home to her family. But Brandon must have seen. Is that why he went silent? Yes. He must have seen Abby bury her here. Poor guy. Poor little guy."

Still on his knees, he turned and motioned for Brandon to come to him. Brandon ran into his open arms. Chip hugged his son and wept, pressing his face into Brandon's chest.

Is that really why Brandon had been silent? Is that why he had done all those violent things?

Or had he been possessed by the ghost of Jeremiah Halley?

I knew I'd never know the answer.

"Sir," Lieutenant Harris said, putting a hand on Chip's shoulder. "I need to talk to you about this further. But perhaps you should take the boy away from here."

He helped Chip to his feet. Then he started to guide Chip down the dune toward the house. They passed another stretcher cart on its way up the hill, coming for Will.

Jackson slid his arm around my shoulders. "You're shaking," he said.

I shut my eyes and pressed my face against his chest. So solid. So warm and solid.

"Jeremiah had his revenge," I murmured. I couldn't stop thinking about it. "He hit the nanny, after all. Abby was the nanny, hiding with her lover in the guest house. Jeremiah had his revenge. It's over now. For everyone."

"I don't know what you're talking about," Jackson said softly. "But, let's just get far away from here. Far away from all of this. Just you and me."

"Yes," I said. I forced a smile. "I'm already packed."

My cell phone rang. It startled me. I'd forgotten I'd tucked it into my jeans pocket.

I picked it up and raised it to my ear. "Hello?"

"Hi, Ellie, it's Mom. Just wondering what's up with you. How's the nanny job going? Any better?"

For a preview of R. L. Stine's
next thrilling novel,

EYE CANDY,

please turn the page . . .

Available at bookstores everywhere.
Published by Ballantine Books.

Is this going to be the most boring date I've ever been on?

Would a cold sore be more fun?

Brain liposuction?

I had a lot of time to think about these questions as I struggled to stay awake. I must have fidgeted a lot because at the intermission Jack said, "Lindy, do you want to leave the theater?"

And of course I wasn't brave enough to say what I really want to do is set my hair on fire and run up the aisle singing "I Enjoy Being a Girl" just to get over my boredom.

So, I said, "No, I'm enjoying it. It's really . . . interesting." I covered my yawn. I don't think he saw it. "Great idea for a musical," I added.

O, America! It was sort of the U.S. Constitution set to music.

"How did you ever get such good seats?" I asked. The theater was half empty. I was trying to be a good sport here. I really was.

"I got 'em for free," Jack said. "At my dad's company where I work. We do marketing for the production company."

After that, I didn't know what to say. So I pretended to read my program. I don't think anyone has ever read a *playbill* so thoroughly. I could even tell you which Italian restaurant Bernadette Peters recommends.

"I'm working on a really nifty marketing project," Jack said, when I raised my head from the program for air. "I'll tell you all about it at dinner."

Oh, right. Dinner.

Why did I pick this guy? I should have guessed he might be a tad boring from his name. I mean, Jack Smith?

When he picked me up at my apartment lobby, I made a joke. I asked, "What's your *real* name?"

He narrowed his eyes at me. I could see he was surprised by the question, as if no one had ever asked that before.

"That *is* my name, Lindy. Well, actually, I'm Jack Smith the Third, but I don't use that."

Three Jack Smiths in his family?

"What's your middle name?"

"I don't have one."

Figures.

I guess I picked him because he had a nice smile in his photo. Jack isn't a bad-looking guy, actually. He has crinkly blue eyes (I'm a sucker for eyes that crinkle up at the sides), short, brown hair spiked up a bit just in front, and that winning, reassuring smile. Plus he turned out to be almost as tall as I am.

I'm five-eleven, so believe me, size matters. I just feel

so awkward when I can reach down and pat my date on the head.

Well, I made it through the second act of O, America!, hoping I didn't snore too loudly. When it ended, Jack jumped to his feet, applauding wildly, shaking his head in awe. . . . I guess. Everyone else stood up to put their jackets on and leave. The reaction wasn't terribly enthusiastic, but Jack didn't seem to notice.

We stepped out into a chilly night. The wind blew pages of a newspaper down the sidewalk. I was wearing a red linen vest jacket, open over a sleeveless white T-shirt, and matching red linen pants, and I wished I'd picked out something warmer.

We were halfway through May and, so far, the city hadn't any spring at all. Depressing weather, especially when you don't have a guy you really care about to snuggle up to.

I took Jack's arm, mainly for warmth. He led me past a group of people, middle-aged and older, huddled at the stage door. The door swung open, and a shaggy-looking bear of a man in a gray sweatshirt and black overalls stepped out. Was he Ben Franklin or Cotton Mather? I didn't recognize him. But the small crowd of fans cheered and surged forward to greet him.

"I love New York!" I gushed.

"It's too crowded," was Jack's reply.

Leaning into the wind, we walked up Eighth Avenue, past small groups of people, all desperately trying to wave down taxis.

"Where are we going for dinner?" I asked.

"My dad's company does some work for this great Italian place on Forty-sixth. I think you'll like it."

Another freebie.

I'm not exactly the Material Girl. But you'd think Jack might have spent at least a dollar or two on our first date.

But hey, the restaurant turned out to be the very one that Bernadette Peters recommended!

Momma Mangia's was long and narrow, the red walls covered with framed paintings of Italian villages. Two rows of tables, each with a red-and-white checkered tablecloth, stretched to the back wall. At a front table, people were toasting one another loudly, clinking glasses and laughing uproariously.

The hostess had trouble finding Jack's reservation. Finally, she led us to a table next to the kitchen door. Two men stopped talking to their wives and watched me as I lowered myself into my seat.

I'm used to it. When you're tall and blond, you notice men watching you. You can feel their eyes on you without even looking. I guess I'm lucky. I mean, would I like it better if they didn't look? I doubt it.

As soon as we sat down, a white-aproned waiter leaned over the table and, in a very heavy Italian accent, asked if we'd like a drink. A totally phony accent. He had to be an out-of-work actor. I ordered a glass of red wine, to warm up, and Jack ordered a Diet Coke.

Jack clasped his hands on the tabletop and leaned closer. He grinned at me. "That play got me all psyched. I mean, I'm not the most patriotic guy. But those songs . . . they really made me feel something."

Was he for real?

"Tell me about your exciting project," I said. Clever change of subject?

He unclasped his hands, then clasped them again. He had very smooth, large hands, I noticed. Very well-groomed. "It's the biggest assignment I've had since I joined Dad's firm."

"How old are you anyway, Jack?" I interrupted.

"I'll be twenty-six in July."

"So I'm out with an older man. That could be dangerous," I teased, squeezing his hand.

He didn't pick up on it at all. "Why? How old are you, Lindy?"

"Twenty-three."

And going on 110 tonight!

He nodded. "My sister is twenty-three."

So what?

"It's for Cat Chow," he said.

I had lost the thread for a moment. "What is?"

"My marketing project."

My hair fell over my face. I swept it back with a shake of my head. I glanced to the next table and saw the two men still staring at me. They looked away when I stared back.

"It's the biggest Cat Chow promotion we've ever done, see. And Dad tossed it in my lap."

I pictured Dad tossing a cat into his lap. My face started to itch. I'm allergic to cats.

"And here's my great idea," Jack said, his eyes going bright, his whole face suddenly alive. "I thought of it while I was watching cartoons. You know. Sylvester the Cat and his little cat son."

"You watch cartoons, Jack?"

He nodded excitedly. Eager to tell me his big Cat Chow idea. "I call it The Whisker Walk."

He raised two fingers on each hand to the sides of his face, like little cat whiskers, and he began moving the "whiskers" up and down in a little dance while he meowed a little song.

That's when I faded out. Or rather, that's when Jack faded out.

I didn't hear another word he said. I just kept picturing him meowing and doing his little Whisker Walk with his fingers. Would I ever be able to forget it? Where is a rewind button when you need it?

O, America! O, America! I had no idea the play would be the best part of the evening.

How did I get into this? Why am I going out with guys I meet on the Internet? After all, Jack isn't the first. Last week was Brad. And next week will be Colin. And here's what I *don't* know as I sit here pretending to listen to Jack . . . here's a little detail I haven't learned yet . . .

One of the three guys is a murderer. One of them plans to murder *me*.

I'll find this out really soon. And then, here's the punch line: The only way I'll stay alive is to keep going out with all three of them.

A nightmare? Yes, and it's only beginning. How did I get myself into this mess? I'll tell you. I guess it started the night Ben was killed.